ELIZABETH ELIOT
MRS. MARTELL

Lady Germaine Elizabeth Olive Eliot was born in London on 13 April 1911, the daughter of Montague Charles Eliot, the 8th Earl of St Germans, and Helen Agnes Post.

She twice married—first to Major Thomas James in 1932, then to Captain Hon. Kenneth George Kinnaird, the 12th Baron Kinnaird, in 1950. Both marriages ended in divorce. She apparently applied for American citizenship in 1971. She published five novels, the first of which, *Alice* (1949), was a Book Society Choice. Her non-fiction *Heiresses and Coronets* (1960, aka *They All Married Well*), about prominent marriages between wealthy Americans and titled Europeans in the late Victorian and Edwardian period, was a success on both sides of the Atlantic.

Elizabeth Eliot died in New York in 1991.

GW00660203

WORKS BY ELIZABETH ELIOT

Fiction

Alice (1949)*
Henry (1950)*
Mrs Martell (1953)*
Starter's Orders (1955)
Cecil (1962)*

Non-fiction

Portrait of a Sport: A History of Steeplechasing (1957)
Heiresses and Coronets (1960, aka *They All Married Well*)

*available from Furrowed Middlebrow/Dean Street Press

ELIZABETH ELIOT

MRS. MARTELL

With an introduction by
Elizabeth Crawford

DEAN STREET PRESS

A Furrowed Middlebrow Book

FM28

Published by Dean Street Press 2019

Copyright © 1953 Elizabeth Eliot

Introduction © 2019 Elizabeth Crawford

All Rights Reserved

Published by licence, issued under the UK Orphan Works Licensing Scheme.

First published in 1953 by Cassell & Co.

Cover by DSP

ISBN 978 1 912574 63 6

www.deanstreetpress.co.uk

To

THE TRESAWNAS

OF

LAMELLYN

'. . . *beloved of many friends.*'

INTRODUCTION

REVIEWING Elizabeth Eliot's debut novel, *Alice*, for the *Sunday Times*, C.P. Snow noted in the author 'an astringent sympathy, a knowledge from bitter experience that life is not easy' while the *Times Literary Supplement* review of her second novel, *Henry*, mentioned her 'light-heartedness, delicious wit and humanity lurking beneath the surface'. Comparisons were drawn with the work of Nancy Mitford and Elizabeth von Arnim, although Snow observed that 'Alice was set in the world of the high aristocracy, loftier, though less smart, than the world of Miss Mitford's "Hons"'. This 'high aristocracy' was, indeed, the world into which, on 13 April 1911, Germaine Elizabeth Olive Eliot was born, her birth registered only as 'Female Eliot'. Time was obviously required to select her full complement of names, but by the time she was christened decisions had been made. 'Germaine' does not appear to have been a family name, although it echoes that of the earldom – St Germans – of which, at that time, her great uncle, Henry Cornwallis Eliot, the 5th earl, was the holder. 'Elizabeth' was the name of her maternal grandmother, Elizabeth Wadsworth, whose grandfather, General James Wadsworth, had been military governor of Washington during the American Civil War. Transatlantic connections were to prove important to this 'Female Eliot'. No hint of an 'Olive' appears in either her paternal or maternal line, so that may have been a mere parental indulgence. Of these three forenames 'Elizabeth' was the one by which the future author was known.

At the time of Elizabeth's birth her parents were living in Marylebone, London, the census, taken just ten days previously, giving us a glimpse into the household. At its head was her 40-year-old father, Montague Charles Eliot, who, with a script replete with flourishes, completed the form, listing also her 26-year-old American mother, Helen Agnes; a butler; a lady's maid; a cook; two housemaids; and a hall boy. Doubtless a few days later a nursemaid would have taken up her position in the nursery. Montague (1870-1960) and Helen (c.1885-1962) had married the previous June. Helen (or 'Nellie' as she was known), although American-born and of American parentage, had, in fact, spent most of her life in the United Kingdom. Her father had died when she was four-years-old and her mother had then married Arthur Smith-Barry, later Baron Barrymore of Fota House, near Cork, Ireland. As Elizabeth Eliot's novels reveal a knowledge of Irish estates and relations, she probably had on occasion visited Fota.

In the newspaper reports of his marriage no mention was made of Montague Eliot's connection to the St Germans earldom, so far was he at that time from inheriting. However, tragedy has long hovered around the St Germans family and in 1922 the death in a riding accident of the 6th Earl meant the title and estate passed to Montague Eliot's elder, unmarried and childless brother. On his death in 1942 Montague Eliot became the 8th Earl of St Germans and his daughter Elizabeth acquired the title of 'Lady'. Montague Eliot had joined King Edward VII's household in 1901 and at the time of Elizabeth's birth was Gentleman Usher to George V, later becoming Groom of the Robes. He held the latter unpaid position until 1936 and from 1952 until his death was Extra Groom-in-Waiting to Elizabeth II.

The 8th Earl's heir was Elizabeth's brother, Nicholas (1914-88) and the family was completed after a long interval with the birth of another son, Montague Robert Vere Eliot (1923-94). Around this time Elizabeth and her family moved to 111 Gloucester Place, a tall house, one of a long terrace on a canyon of a road that runs north-south through Marylebone.

While it is on record that her brothers were sent to Eton, we know nothing of Elizabeth's education. Was she taught at home by a governess; or did she attend a London day school, or an establishment such as 'Groom Place', where we first meet the two young women in *Alice*, or 'Mrs Martell's 'inexpensive but good school on the south coast of England'? Elizabeth's mother, certainly, had had a governess, 70-year-old Miss Dinah Thoreau, who took rat poison in December 1934 and killed herself in her room in Paddington. Lack of money was not a problem for the Eliots, unlike the Pallisers, whose daughter, Anne, narrator of *Henry*, remarks that her family had been 'too poor for my sister or me to be properly educated (although Henry, of course, had been sent to Harrow)'. Naturally boys had to go to school in order 'to have a good answer when people asked where they had been at school. That was why Henry had been sent to Harrow.' The fact that the young women in her novels invariably received an education inferior to their brothers may indicate that Elizabeth did indeed feel that she had not been 'properly educated'. Whatever the reality, a review of the US edition of *Alice* revealed that Elizabeth 'Like many authors, has been writing since she was 10'.

Nor do we know anything of Elizabeth's relationship with her parents. What is one to make of the fact she dedicated *Cecil*, the story of a loathsome, manipulative mother, to her own mother? What is one to make of the tantalising information contained in the publisher's blurb for *Cecil* that the book is 'based on fact'? Which strand of *Cecil*'s plot might have been developed from a factual base? For the novel, quite apart from placing a 'veritable ogress' of a mother centre stage, also deals with drug-taking, murder, and impotency. *Cecil* was published in November 1962, a couple of months after Nellie Eliot, Dowager Countess of St Germans, committed suicide in a hotel room in Gibraltar, having arrived the day before from Tangier where she had been visiting her son Vere. Whatever their real-life relationship it is fair to say that in Elizabeth Eliot's novels mothers tend to be seen in a somewhat negative light, while fathers are noticeable by their absence.

In 1922 the elevation to the earldom of St Germans of her unmarried uncle brought significant changes to Elizabeth Eliot and her family, with visits to Port Eliot becoming more frequent. In 1926 Elizabeth had the honour of opening the St Germans parish fête, held in the grounds of Port Eliot, and made, according to the *Western Morning News*, 'an effective and amusing speech'. Port Eliot, an ancient house, shaped and reshaped over the centuries, is so extensive that, its guidebook confesses, not once in living memory has the roof been completely watertight. If not so ancient, similarly large houses, often in the west-country and sometimes decaying, certainly play their part in Elizabeth Eliot's novels. When Margaret, the narrator of *Alice*, visits 'Platon', Alice's Devonshire family home, she sat in 'one of the drawing rooms. There was no fire, it was bitterly cold, and everything in the room, including the chairs and sofa on which we sat, was covered with dust sheets.' 'Trelynt', the west-country home of Anne Palliser is, post-Second World War, similarly large, damp, and servantless.

Naturally Elizabeth Eliot's position in society meant that in due course she 'did the Season' as a debutante, her presence recorded at hunt and charity balls and even in a photograph on the front of *Tatler*. In *Alice*, Margaret admits that 'The basic idea was rational enough. When a girl reached marriageable age, she was introduced by her parents into adult society, where it was hoped she would meet her future husband. There are many examples of such practices in *The Golden Bough*. Only somehow by the nineteen-thirties it had all got rather silly.' Margaret is presented at court, her Uncle Henry, like Montague Eliot, being a member of the royal household, and observes that this connection 'meant that we had seats in the Throne Room, which was fun, as there was always the chance that someone would fall down. Not that one would wish it for them, but should it happen, it would be nice to see it.'

Elizabeth's 'Season' produced the desired result and in January 1932 her engagement to Thomas James (1906-76) was announced in the press on both sides of the Atlantic. The wedding took place barely two months later in St George's Hanover Square. Thomas James' father, a former MP for Bromley, was dead and his mother too ill to attend. The bishop of Norwich gave a particularly didactic address, much reproduced in press reports, stressing the seriousness of marriage. Were the words of the cleric tailored specifically for this flighty young couple?

After a honeymoon in Rio and Madeira in early 1933, delayed perhaps until after the death of Thomas James' mother, the young couple settled down to married life. Tended by five servants, they occupied the whole of 4 Montague Square, a five-storey house, five minutes' walk from the Eliot family home. In the years after the Second World War Thomas James was employed by BP, but it is not clear what his occupation was during the years he was married to Elizabeth. On the ship's manifest for their 1933 trip he is described as a 'Representative'. Was fiction imitating life when, in *Alice*, Alice and her new husband Cassius sailed to Rio where he was 'to represent a firm of motor-car engineers'? Despite both Elizabeth and dashing, Eton-educated Thomas James having family money, rumour has it that during their marriage they ran up considerable gambling debts, a contributory factor to their divorce in 1940.

On the outbreak of war in 1939 Lady Elizabeth James, now living alone in a flat in St John's Wood, was registered as an ambulance driver with the London County Council. However, nothing is known of her life during and immediately after the war until the publication of *Alice* in 1949. A few months later, in March 1950, she married the Hon. George Kinnaird at Brighton registry office. When asked by the *Daily Mail* why they had married 'in strict secrecy', Kinnaird replied 'We are both too engrossed in our work'. The *Daily Mail* then explained that 'Lady Elizabeth is authoress of Book Society choice *Alice*. Mr Kinnaird is a literary adviser.' Kinnaird was at this time attached in some capacity to the publishing firm of John Murray. This marriage ended in divorce in 1962.

For some years in the 1950s Elizabeth Eliot lived in Lambourn in Berkshire, a town renowned for its association with horse racing. This was clearly a sport close to her heart for during this period, apart from *Henry* (1950) and *Mrs. Martell* (1953), she produced two books devoted to horse racing, one, *Starter's Orders*, fiction, and the other, *Portrait of a Sport*, non-fiction. In *Henry* the narrator's much-loved but feckless brother, the eponymous Henry, is a haunter of the race track. As he observes, 'I can always reckon to make quite a bit racing, and then there's backgammon. Backgammon can be terribly paying if you go the right way about it.' Of Elizabeth's brother, thrice-married Nicholas, *The Times*'s obituarist wrote, with some circumspection, that he was 'a supporter of the Turf in his day, as owner, trainer and bookmaker'. On inheriting the title and estate on the death of his father in 1960, Nicholas Eliot, 9th Earl of St Germans, made the estate over to his young son and went into tax exile.

After her second divorce Elizabeth seems to have spent a good deal of time in New York, mingling in literary circles, and in June 1971, while living in Greenwich Village, at 290 Sixth Avenue, applied for US citizenship. Thereafter she disappears from sight until *The Times* carried a notice of her death in New York on 3 November 1991. For whatever reason, detailed facts of Elizabeth Eliot's life have become so obfuscated that even members of her own extended family have been unable to supply information. Fortunately for us, her mordant wit and powers of social observation survive, amply revealed in the four novels now reissued by Dean Street Press.

Elizabeth Crawford

MRS MARTELL lived at the top of a house in Baker Street, London, and she was much interested in a murder which had lately been committed in the antique shop on the ground floor.

There were evenings when Mrs Martell decked out in snoods and golden earrings appeared to be around thirty, and there were other evenings when she hadn't tried at all and then she looked thirty-five. Her actual age was thirty-eight. So all the times when Mrs Martell had lain on her bed after luncheon, and all the hours she had spent patting this and that into her face, had after all been well spent.

Mrs Martell lay on the sofa in her ugly but pretentious sitting-room. It wasn't after luncheon, it was nine o'clock in the evening, but one must make the most of every opportunity one got of taking the weight off the feet; for was that not one of the best ways of resting the face?

Mrs Martell had had her supper—slip sole and cabbage, at seven o'clock and now, the servant having gone out, she was left alone to listen to the wireless and think about herself. She was wearing a pair of blue stockinette trousers and a red jersey; but she had taken the trouble to pin a brooch into the jersey; it was the sort of brooch that gets sold quite a lot in the shops of Swiss resorts. She looked thirty-five.

Mrs Martell was thinking about herself, and also about her cousin Laura's husband Edward West. It was rather wonderful about Edward, but how would it ever end? Laura, of course, must never guess, never be told.

But was there really so much to tell? Cathie Martell could wish that there were more, but, so far, Edward had insisted upon being faithful to his wife.

Mrs Martell sighed deeply and her mind strayed to the brocade housecoats she would wear if she were ever married to Edward; and on other evenings there would be wonderful semi-transparent tea-gowns—only not too transparent because of the butler.

How unfortunate that she had not met Edward until he was married to Laura. She forgot that if Edward had *not* married Laura it was unlikely that she herself would ever have met him at all.

For, most fortunately for herself, Cathie Martell was Laura's cousin, second cousin if you wanted to be accurate about it, which Cathie did not, and she had appeared rather suddenly in Laura's life quite soon after Laura had married Edward.

Before that Laura had been of little account and Cathie had only been vaguely aware of her existence. But Laura married to Edward West of Abbotsmere in the county of Shropshire, was a cousin whom it was well worth while to take up, and Cathie had lost no time in taking up Laura.

It was terribly unfair, terribly wrong really that Laura should be married to Edward. On the few occasions when she left them alone Mrs Martell hated to think of them at Abbotsmere together.

But tonight Laura was in London, Edward had told Cathie so when she had rung him up this afternoon. And Cathie had been annoyed that Laura should spend a night in London without letting her know, it was unaccountable and she didn't somehow believe that Laura had only come up to see her doctor.

The wireless made a horrible screeching sound. Mrs Martell frowned as she got up to retune it. Edward in Shropshire and she in Baker Street were supposed to be listening to this concert 'together'. Thus united by the B.B.C. they would float away together on the Beauty that is Brahms. When she spoke to Edward on the telephone Mrs Martell had arranged with him that they should do just that. She had got the basic idea of such a spiritual getting together many years ago out of a book called *Countess Kate*, or rather her subconscious mind had got it out of that, for Mrs Martell didn't personally remember anything about the book.

Having returned to the Beauty that is Brahms, she lay down on the sofa again, crossed her ankles—she had neat ankles and beautiful legs—and closed her eyes. She started to float, but not with Edward and not towards a land of butlers and expensive restaurants in the South of France, instead she returned over some twenty years to a classroom of an inexpensive but good school on the south coast of England.

'Cathie,' Miss Longman said, and then more peremptorily, 'Cathie!'

'I'm so sorry, Miss Longman, I didn't hear you,' and Cathie Hartley-James looked up with the frank open smile that she kept for members of the staff. She got up from the long table at which she had been working. That was one of the privileges of the sixth, they had a table covered with a green cloth, whereas the other forms had desks. Their pictures were more sophisticated too, the Belle Dame Sans Merci belonging to the fourth form, and the engraving of Titus Livy which hung in the fifth having given way to 'Sun Flowers' and 'Dancers dressing for the Ballet' (not in colours). And it was in this room that the school library, or what there was of it, was housed in a tall glass-fronted bookcase which ran the length of one wall.

'I'm glad I've found you alone,' Miss Longman said, 'it's about the Drama League,' and she consulted a sheaf of papers which she held in her hand.

Cathie smiled encouragingly. She was the secretary of the league which met on Thursdays after school hours. Its purpose was the reading aloud of plays, and Cathie liked to think of it as the Evelyn Bernard School equivalent of the societies which she understood existed at Eton and Harrow.

'Macbeth,' Miss Longman said, consulting her papers again. 'I thought we might just run through the parts for tomorrow's reading, if it's not decided beforehand, so much time is wasted in preliminary discussion.' She spoke in the bright hopeful manner which she had acquired during Debating Society meetings at her Training College.

Cathie sat down again, leant back in her chair and scowled. Macbeth had not been of her choosing, Macbeth was going to be an awful bind and a waste of time. Anyone could do Macbeth, they had in fact done it when she was in 3b, which proved how childish it was. Whereas a league should be occupying itself with something more advanced, more definitely worthwhile, such as *Ghosts* or *The Doll's House* or *The Importance of being Earnest*.

Unfortunately, at the last meeting of the league none of these suggestions had met with general approval, and, having turned down each of them in turn, the league, encouraged by Miss Longman, had voted almost solidly for *Macbeth*, which, as everyone agreed, was a good solid play which it was useful to know.

Rather patronisingly, but still holding on to the frank smile, Cathie looked over Miss Longman's list. *First Witch, Second Witch*, none of it was very important. When she came to: *Macbeth—Cathie Hartley-James*, she drew a pencil through her own name and substituted that of Monica Floyd.

'Oh!' and Miss Longman, peering over Cathie's shoulder, sounded quite disappointed.

'It wouldn't do, would it,' Cathie said, 'if I was Macbeth every week?'

Regretfully, Miss Longman agreed and said that anyhow it would be practice for Monica.

Practice for what, Cathie wondered, and thought what a silly little thing Miss Longman was. Silly and unsure of herself. She had only arrived at the beginning of this term, of course, so it was still possible that she might improve. If she didn't there really wasn't any point going on with the league unless they could get another president.—but then the English mistress always *had* been president. It was very awkward, because undoubtedly something would have to be done about it.

The four o'clock gong rang. That meant that everyone who was not engaged in extra games, extra gymnasium, extra Latin, French, or art, was now free to go home. They would collect their attaché-cases, change from black indoor to black outdoor shoes, put on their panama hats with the school hatbands and return to the suburban houses and flats from which they came. They would queue for buses and spread out over the red-brick pavements and there would be much earnest discussion of what Margaret had said to Miss Longman, and what had been said to Hermione when she had been sent for in the middle of the afternoon. Some of the little ones would have been invited to play in each other's gardens, some of the older ones would have been invited out to tea.

Cathie got up, and smiled dismissingly at Miss Longman, waiting for her to leave the room. Two or three other members of the sixth came into the room to collect their books. Angela was on cloakroom duty, wasn't she, but it seemed that she wasn't yet back from the swimming baths. Cathie offered to do the duty instead of her and hurried downstairs before she could be forestalled by anyone else. Miss Longman, ignored by them all, faded away into the corridor.

'Girls!' Cathie stood at the door of the crowded cloak-room and shouted into the uproar. There was a slight, a very slight, abeyance in the noise.

'Silence!' Cathie thundered again, and seized an unfortunate child of about nine years old by the arm.

'Camilla, have you been given permission to speak in the cloakroom?'

The child remained silent and Cathie told it to take an order mark. It looked at her with blank beseeching eyes.

By now the room was reduced to an approximation of silence. Cathie strode into it. Behind the second row of lockers there was a fight going on between two small girls who lay scuffling on the floor. Watched by the owners of the adjoining lockers, who made a great show of changing their shoes, Cathie stood over them menacingly.

'Rosalie and Diana!'—there was no answer from either of the children.

'Get up immediately.'

Rosalie, who had been distinctly winning, was the first to obey. She appeared to be ashamed of herself and stood, shuffling her feet and not looking at Cathie. Diana remained where she was.

'Diana!'

Diana still didn't move, presently she said that she had a broken back. There was a suppressed giggle of encouragement from the onlookers. Diana said that nobody would walk about with a broken back—not even a horse. Cathie told her to stop making an exhibition of herself.

'You and Rosalie can remain behind, I wish to speak to you after the others have gone.' Then Cathie stalked back to the door where she remained. There was no more talking. Those children who had not incurred her direct displeasure finished changing as quickly as possible and hurried away to freedom.

'Please,' Camilla said, 'please need I take the order mark.'

'I'm afraid you must.'

Camilla's mouth drooped. 'Lots of people were talking besides me.'

'Then they shouldn't have been, and you must hurry up now, or you'll be late.'

'But . . .' Camilla began and then thought better of it. Cathie watched her leave the room and then went over to Rosalie and Diana; they were sitting side by side on the long bench but got up as she approached them.

'Really,' Cathie said, 'I don't know what to say to you.'

Rosalie murmured that she was sorry, but Diana stared rebelliously at Cathie, waiting for her to think of something to say.

'You will have to go to Miss Kennedy'—Miss Kennedy was the head mistress.

'Couldn't we take an order mark instead?' Diana asked.

'Fighting!' Cathie said, 'rolling about on the floor, at your ages it's disgraceful. You will go to Miss Kennedy tomorrow morning before prayers, and I can only imagine that she will be as shocked as I am.'

'I can imagine that she will be extremely cross,' Diana said.

Cathie told her that if that was all she could think of to say she had better put on her hat and go home. If Diana and Rosalie couldn't see the impropriety of their behaviour for themselves it was of no use anyone trying to explain it to them. Diana and Rosalie had behaved in an utterly disgusting and degraded manner; evidently neither of them had any feelings of self-respect.

She went on for a long time, speaking always more to Rosalie than to Diana. For Rosalie, as Cathie very well knew, was amongst the number of her worshippers, whereas Diana was not. At the end of it Rosalie was in tears but had enjoyed the lecture tremendously. Diana was still rebellious.

'And now you may go.' Cathie turned on her heel and left them.

As they reached the street, Diana told Rosalie that it was all very well to go on like that, but that there were a great many women wrestlers in the world, in fact there were international championships for them; her father and mother had seen one when they were in Paris.

'I don't believe it'—Rosalie was scandalised—'and why do you always go on about your father and mother going to Paris?'

'I don't,' Diana said, 'and we're going to Brittany for the summer holidays. Where are you going?'

'Birmingham,' Rosalie said, and kicked a non-existent stone off the red-brick pavement.

Despite her triumph Diana was not to be deterred from her main topic. She said that it was all very well to talk about people being common, but what about Cathie herself.

'What about her?'

'Well,' and Diana paused to draw a deep breath, and then she told Rosalie all about how Mummy believed that Cathie's father was in prison and how Mummy wasn't at all pleased about Cathie being at the same school as Diana, and how you only had to look at that awful poky little flat that Cathie and her mother lived in, and that Diana's mother didn't believe for a moment that Cathie was paying full fees.

Rosalie said that she didn't expect it was true and she expected that Diana's mother was just jealous because Cathie was so much prettier than Diana.

Diana said that anyone who had got a crush on Cathie must be mad.

'Then you must think that practically the whole school's mad.'

Diana said that she did and they continued to quarrel until they reached the gate of Diana's house where they parted on very bad terms.

Cathie Hartley-James arrived home just as her mother was about to start tea.

'Is that you, dear?' Mrs Hartley-James called as Cathie opened the door of the flat.

'Yes, Mother,' and Cathie crossed the dark little hall, which was also the dining-room, and came into the lounge.

Mrs Hartley-James bent down and switched on the electric kettle which stood in the fireplace. The tea-tray was already arranged in front of the sofa, there were paper doilies under the little cakes and a silver-plated tea-strainer, and there were folded organdie napkins which had been bought in Madeira.

'I thought Aunt Violet was coming.'

'Well yes, dear, she is.'

'Then we ought to wait for her,' and Cathie left the lounge, edged her way round the table which stood in the hall and went into her bedroom.

Obediently, but regretfully, Mrs Hartley-James bent down again and switched off the kettle.

In her bedroom Cathie put down her case and then, having first washed her hands and face in cold water, sat down in front of her dressing-table. Looking at herself in the glass she started to comb her hair, but was so struck by the simple fact of her own beauty that she was obliged to stop in order to contemplate it. 'Lovely,' Cathie murmured to herself, 'quite lovely—and un-spoilt.'

She opened a drawer and took out a pale pink lipstick. She at least knew what was suitable to her age, not like some of the girls at school with their rouge and powder spread thickly over their spotty skins, making perfect guys of themselves. But could one really expect them to know any better? She smiled tenderly at her own image, gloating over her own superiority.

The doorbell rang, that would be Aunt Violet, mother's sister. Cathie half rose from her stool and then sank back; mother could be left to deal with the door. It would be time enough for Cathie to be attentive and chivalrous when Aunt Violet with her dangling earrings and her fox furs should be installed on the sofa in the lounge.

Aunt Violet, Cathie realised, was one of the problems of her life. If Aunt Violet had not had money, Cathie would have forbidden her mother to see her and that would have been that; but it isn't possible to put an absolute ban on one's only rich relation, particularly when that relation pays one's reduced school bills.

There was the sound of Aunt Violet's high-pitched cheerful voice, the sound of her high-heeled shoes crossing the hall, and, in her imagination, Cathie could see her aunt's patent-leather shoes, and her aunt's fat little feet bulging out of them.

'Size three and a half,' Aunt Violet would say, and consider them with evident approval and then glance pityingly at Cathie's long, narrow, distinguished-looking feet which she had inherited from her father. 'Never mind,' Aunt Violet had said good-naturedly, and more than once; 'when you've finished growing the instep will probably draw up and you'll be able to take a whole size smaller.'—But it would never be size three and a half!

'Have they managed to change your room yet?' Mrs Hartley-James asked her sister as they waited for the kettle to boil.

'Oh yes,' and Violet Clavering nodded her head vigorously and her earrings dangled against her cheeks. 'They' were the hotel on the front where she was staying, where she had already been for a week and where she would remain for another two months during the duration of her annual visit to her 'poor sister'.

'A much nicer room,' Mrs Clavering said, 'with the sitting-room leading directly out of it and quite away from those dreadful children.'

'I'm so glad,' Mrs Hartley-James said, and, 'it's too bad that they didn't put you there in the first place, I mean it isn't as if they didn't know you.'

'Well, it's all over now,' Mrs Clavering said bravely, and then asked if Cathie was going to be in to tea.

'She's just washing her hands. I don't expect she'll be more than a minute.'

'Because to tell you the truth I want to talk very seriously to you about her future.'

'Oh,' and Mrs Hartley-James bent nervously down to the kettle; she took off its lid to make sure that the water wasn't secretly boiling.

'To be quite frank with you, Mabel, I'm not happy about her.'

Mrs Hartley-James with her face turned away from her sister continued to minister to the kettle and didn't answer.

'It's my belief,' Mrs Clavering said, 'that she's getting above herself. You see I'm being perfectly frank.'

'Good afternoon, Aunt Violet.' Cathie, having shut the door of the lounge behind her, crossed the room in a few easy strides and bent to kiss her aunt on the cheek.

'Good afternoon, Cathie; we were just talking about you.'

Cathie smiled and waited to hear, if they wished to tell her, what they had been saying.

Mrs Clavering considered her niece from the top of her head to the toes of her elegant feet; finally she said that she supposed it was all right for Cathie to wear such a very short gymnasium tunic.

'Oh yes, Aunt Violet,' and Cathie sat down, taking great care to display a very great length of her long and beautiful leg.

'Won't you have a sandwich, Aunt Violet?' Cathie leant forward, took a plate off the tray and offered it to her aunt. The plate contained a pile of narrow cucumber sandwiches made with brown bread cut very thin. It was Cathie who had taught her mother to make sandwiches having that appearance; left to herself Mrs Hartley-James would have used thick white bread and cut the sandwiches cross-wise, perhaps not even bothering to remove the crusts.

'There are a great many things that will have to be discussed while I am here,' Mrs Clavering said, 'but first I hope that there isn't going to be any more nonsense about being confirmed.'

Mrs Hartley-James, who had at last succeeded in making the tea, looked up alarmed, and asked if it was really necessary to go into all that again, just now. 'After all, dear, I don't think they have them at this time of year.'

'That's not the point, Mabel.'

'Even so it could wait,' and poor Mrs Hartley-James nervously poured too much milk into all the cups and hoped that Violet wouldn't notice.

Cathie, who was quite pleased by the introduction of this particular subject, on which she had thought a great deal and taken a very strong line during Lent, said that she had already explained to Miss Kennedy *and* to the vicar exactly how she felt about confirmation and the taking of communion.

'Without belief, Aunt Violet, you know it would be a mere travesty.'

Mrs Clavering said, as she had said before, that all that was rubbish, and that all Cathie was trying to do was to draw attention to herself.

'But as an atheist, Aunt Violet . . .'

'Now look here, Cathie,' Mrs Clavering interrupted, and at the same time helped herself to another sandwich, 'you may bully your mother and you may think you're impressing them all at that school of yours; but you know perfectly well that I'm paying for you to be educated and for you to be clothed, so you've got to listen to me and do what I tell you.'

Cathie blushed to the roots of her hair. The vulgarity of her aunt's words (or so she told herself) seared themselves into her very soul. How dared Aunt Violet speak to her like that? She jumped to her feet and stood looking down disdainfully at the little woman who sat on the sofa munching sandwiches.

'As far as I am concerned, Aunt Violet, I don't want another penny of your money. I can go out and earn my bread,' and she saw a distinct picture of herself working her fingers to the bone and being seduced by goodness knows whom.

Mrs Clavering told Cathie not to shout at her and said that of course Cathie would have to earn her own living, there had never been any question as to that. 'The point is, what are you doing to do?'

'Miss Kennedy wants her to try for Oxford,' Mrs Hartley-James put in anxiously, 'but of course that's out of the question?'

'Quite, I should think.' Mrs Clavering didn't bother to add that she knew perfectly well that Miss Kennedy had never said anything of the kind.

'Don't be silly, Mother.' Cathie had had time in which to recover her temper and remember that there was nothing to be gained by quarrelling with Aunt Violet.

'I used to think that you'd want to go on the stage, but lately I don't think you're so keen on it?' Mrs Hartley-James smiled at Cathie, hoping that she had said the right thing.

'I could try it if you wanted me to.'

'Have you no ideas of your own, Cathie?' Mrs Clavering was becoming impatient.

'Not really, Aunt Violet. Of course I could do modelling, or go to Elizabeth Arden's or somewhere.'

'But think of the waste,' Mrs Hartley-James said, 'when she has so *much* talent.'

Mrs Clavering, who had once been a hospital nurse, said that there was no nobler profession than that of a hospital nurse and she thought that Cathie ought to think very seriously about that before making up her mind.

'I have thought about it, Aunt Violet, but I know I'd never be strong enough, so there's no use considering it.'

'As far as I know you've always been perfectly strong.'

'Not what you'd *call* strong, Violet.' Mrs Hartley-James had seen the look on Cathie's face and realised that the idea of hospital nursing had displeased her.

'I hope you're not going to let her start getting ideas about her health.'

Cathie, who for the last few minutes had been wandering about the room, now came and stood beside her aunt's chair; she smiled charmingly and said that she didn't think it was really so very important *what* she did.

'Of course it's important, and we've got to try and work things out so that in a year or two you will be earning a living wage. You can't go on being a charge on other people *all* your life.'

Cathie smiled again and now, with Mrs Hartley-James completely ignored, she spoke to her aunt as one adult to another, 'But I imagine that I shall marry.'

Aunt Violet conceded that that was possible but said that it didn't do to count on it.

Cathie said nothing, she felt that she could count on it. The only important thing was to get to London and meet people—and a hospital nurse might quite easily receive her training in the provinces and so never meet anyone at all.

'I don't know,' Mrs Hartley-James said, 'that I altogether *like* beauty culture.'

'Why not?' Cathie asked.

Mrs Clavering said that if Cathie was really seriously considering going in for it, it would be necessary to find out what were the prospects of a living wage.

'I think they're quite good.' Cathie was moving towards the door. 'Will you excuse me if I go and start my homework?'

'You haven't forgotten the concert?'

Cathie said that she hadn't and that she would be ready at a quarter past seven, which would allow heaps of time even if they were unlucky with the bus.

Mrs Hartley-James was anxious to know which dress Cathie was going to wear, but Cathie didn't seem to have heard the question and the door shut behind her. The two sisters were left alone.

Back in her room Cathie took a folder containing snap-shots out of her dressing-table drawer and then lay down on her bed. She was smiling as she went over her plans for her future. She would stay at school for another year—ladies did not finish their education until they were seventeen. Then, somehow, she would contrive to go abroad—-it didn't matter for how short a time, the point was to have *been* there. After that she would be ready to take a job. The job must be the kind of job which ladies took for their entertainment, to fill in the time which might elapse between being presented at court and being married. Flower shops and interior decorators came quite definitely under that heading; mannequins and assistants in beauty parlours were better paid. And only the other day she had read in the gossip columns of a popular women's magazine about an Honourable Rosemary and a Lady Daphne who'd entered a beauty establishment; both of them had wonderful skins: both of them were having a wonderful time; they were hoping to go a long way in their chosen profession: Cathie knew that what each of them was really hoping for was a rich and romantic marriage.

She smiled, the smile that she was beginning to think of as mysterious, and picking up the folder began to look through her photographs. She always kept snapshots for several weeks before sticking them into her album. She liked to turn them over to consider them and to gloat over her triumphs. Now she began by looking at a portrait study of Reggie. In spite of portrait attachment which had lately been fitted to her camera, the picture hadn't turned out a great success—he didn't look nearly handsome enough. She would get him to have a real photograph taken, one which she could keep on her dressing-table and which would impress her friends when they came to tea. And she would get him to write 'with love from Reggie' across the corner of it, or perhaps 'with fondest love', that might be better still. Reggie worked in one of the local house agents, he wasn't much, Cathie knew that, but there was no doubt that he was handsome and had a good square chin and always had a white handkerchief peeping out of the breast-pocket of his suit, and gold cuff-links, all of which things would look well in a photograph taken by a professional.

The next snapshot she picked up was of herself with Monica Floyd and Angela Guggenheim. She studied it very carefully; the three of them were lined up in a row, arm-in-arm with Cathie in the middle. The great, the only interesting, thing about this picture was the legs, Monica's fat and shapeless, Angela's crooked, and her own, their beauty considerably pointed up by contrast with their surroundings, long and perfect. Cathie had already anticipated all this when arranging for the photograph to be taken; the result was excellent.

There were several other snapshots in the same genre, the one where Monica hideously licked an ice-cream cornet while

Cathie sat beside her and looked beautiful (her own cornet held out of the camera's range) was a good example.

She supposed she must make a start with her homework and then change for the concert at the Pavilion. She would wear her crisp pink cotton dress—so suitable to her age, so much smarter really than the artificial silks in which Monica Floyd and Angela and the others tried, and failed, to attain even a provincial sophistication.

At 7.27, Cathie and her mother and aunt, having been lucky with the bus, were taking their seats in the concert hall which formed part of the huge modern Pavilion. It was in fact so 'modern' in its architecture that only a few of the inhabitants of the town were able to appreciate it; Cathie, of course, was amongst the few. Nearly everyone else, including Mrs Hartley-James, preferred the smiling Edwardianism of their own houses and flats.

While the orchestra was taking its place Cathie looked round the hall with satisfaction. Because Aunt Violet had paid for the seats they were good ones, and she was hoping that amongst the audience there were at least one or two people from the school.

'I was telling your mother just now that I think I shall go down and see Miss Kennedy tomorrow afternoon.' Aunt Violet leant across Mrs Hartley-James to make this announcement to Cathie.

'That *is* kind of you, Aunt Violet.'—Now she had definitely decided what she was going to do in the next few years, there was no point in not being gracious to her aunt. Aunt Violet was after all the person who in the end must pay for Cathie to spend those few months abroad. She was also the person who in the end must leave Cathie money in her will. Mrs Clavering had always stated clearly (in order that there should be no mistake) that she would not do this and that her money was to go to her late husband's nephews and niece. Cathie, because it would be so pleasant to inherit her aunt's money, chose to ignore the clarity of this statement. There was heaps of time, not so very many nephews, only one niece and after all anything might happen.

The conductor made his appearance, and as the clapping died down Mrs Clavering said that she thought three-thirty would be a good time for her to see Miss Kennedy.

Cathie nodded and smiled and then the concert began.

Cathie allowed herself to relax, at first attempting to follow and 'understand' the music and then allowing it to roll over her. Her own thoughts, her own life, became more important than any music in the world.

The telephone rang in the ugly but pretentious flat in Baker Street. Mrs Martell frowned as she got up to turn off the wireless.—How inconsiderate people were in their use of the telephone! Or could this possibly be Edward who had rung her up so that they might talk intimately together as they listened to the music? But although it would have been pleasant she somehow didn't think that that was likely.

Having switched off the Beauty that is Brahms—Edward was now left to float by himself—she lay down on the sofa again, crossed her neat ankles and beautiful legs and reached for the telephone.

'Hulloa'—the word as she pronounced it had three syllables, and she gave to each of them a full and equal value.

2

'AM I speaking to Mrs Martell?'

He was, and the reporter on the other end of the line went on urgently. He was the *Sunday World Post*; it was about this murder, they were going to do a feature on it, and he would appreciate it very much if Mrs Martell would grant him an interview. He could come along right away in a taxi, if that would be convenient.

'I'm afraid,' Mrs Martell said, 'that I have no comment to make.'—That was the correct way to speak to the press, it was the phrase Mrs Martell's mother had used over and over again, when Mrs Martell's father had behaved so wrongly in the early nineteen-twenties. As it so happened Mrs Martell had had nothing to do with the murder which had occurred in the antique shop downstairs, that is to say, she had not committed it herself and had not been an accessory of the young criminal who had. All the same, nice people do not like to have their names in the papers, except in the obituary columns.

The reporter was quite used to this attitude, which was the one which had always been taken by his own mother towards the newspapers. He told Mrs Martell that he had every sympathy with her and rang off.

Mrs Martell replaced her receiver; and was vaguely disappointed. Now there was nothing to do but return to the Bliss that is Brahms. She wished that she hadn't been quite so adamant with the *Sunday World Post*. She turned on the wireless again; but as far as she was concerned, Brahms had had it; and for a few terrifying moments, Mrs Martell ceased to be a creature of her own imagination but was herself lying on the sofa, and her back ached. Her back ached and so did her ribs under her left breast; perhaps she had cancer, or perhaps she had T.B., perhaps her beautiful body had started to decay and would have to be hacked at with knives and carted away to Switzerland. It was monstrous, unthinkable; she closed her eyes, and it was as though she could see her dark curling lashes lying on the ivory skin—the colour of ivory, the colour of ripe apricots—Mrs Martell was quoting from a succession of her lovers, and she didn't pause to consider that if her skin had been the colour of apricots which were *not* ripe, it would be green.

This was strange, because one way and another Mrs Martell had had quite an experience of skins.—Hadn't she worked long ago in Madame Sondheim's beauty salon in Dover Street?—It hadn't been Elizabeth Arden's after all, because when, at the age of nineteen, she came back from that expedition to France which had been known ever afterwards as 'being finished in Paris', there had been this wonderful opening with Madame Sondheim.

Just why it had been so wonderful, Mrs Hartley-James had never really understood. And she continued to find it a matter for regret that Cathie had not decided to become an architect, or to go on the stage, or anyhow to get into Oxford. Oxford, of course, had been Violet's fault—even if Cathie (with all her talents) hadn't exactly won a scholarship, Violet ought to have paid for her to go there.

Meanwhile Cathie, with a small allowance from her mother (which her aunt didn't know about) and an even smaller one from her aunt (which her mother did know about), was very contented with her life in London and with Madame Sondheim's. Madame Sondheim's, or so Cathie told Mrs Hartley-James, was not *like* other beauty parlours. First of all Madame Sondheim's methods were far more 'scientific' than those of her rivals, but that is a peculiarity which is common to every beauty parlour in the world. Secondly, Madame Sondheim believed in employing 'ladies'.

The ladies, including Madame herself, all wore smart raspberry pink uniforms made out of hygienic linen, and (in order to stress their connection with science) white ruffled nurses' armbands. The salons, of which there were three floors, were done up throughout in raspberry pink and for the patients there were raspberry pink dressing-gowns. The whole place smelt strongly of almond oil with an undercurrent of lanoline.

The four years or so which Cathie spent in this establishment were by no means wasted. She learnt quite a bit about the skin and what to do with it. She learnt a very great deal about women, and that was useful, for to be fore-warned is, as she told herself, to be fore-armed.—Other women, of course, were to be her natural enemies, it was in the nature of things, in the very structure of society that that should be so. Not that that prevented her, especially at the beginning of her London life, from sharing various sordid temporary little flats with various temporary girl friends. These flats all smelt exactly the same, of sweet almonds, lanoline and frying-pan cooking—and they were all, as far as Cathie was concerned, meticulously neat. If the current friend turned out to be untidy, Cathie would immediately quarrel with her and the association would be dissolved.

Her friendships with men were also inclined not to last, and on the whole, they followed a routine pattern. Stage one: the man was completely bowled over by her beauty and sensibility, 'you are quite lovely, but it's your mind I like' (any man who was not completely bowled over was never considered at all). Stage two: the man took Cathie to endless dinners, theatres and drives into the country, love play was intermingled with long interesting talks about literature and things of the spirit. Stage three: the man got sick of it.

Then, at last, when she was twenty-four, Cathie met Maurice Martell. She met him first, as she met most of her friends, at a cocktail party. He had straight mouse-coloured hair. He was young and serious. His father was the head master of a respectable public school, which gave him a certain cachet in Cathie's eyes; he himself was a schoolmaster—but only for the time being, later on he meant to be a writer. Stage one was reached within half an hour of her first speaking to him—he was, or anyhow seemed to be, quite bowled over by her beauty. That was good, especially as rather a longer time than usual had gone by since the sudden and unwelcome ending of her last adventure. She had begun to be afraid that perhaps she was losing her flair. When they had known each other for three-quarters of an hour she had already recited to him most of 'Kubla Khan'—'his flashing eyes his floating hair', which description, of course, could clearly be applied to herself; Mr Martell with his straight mouse-coloured hair was not at all that kind of character.

The cocktail party was coming to an end, now he must ask her to have dinner with him. She waited, but nothing happened; in the end she had to resort to asking him back to dinner at her flat, her friend Vivian, with whom she shared it, would be so interested to meet him. Vivian, she explained, had many connections with the literary world. Mr Martell accepted the invitation, and Cathie asked him to excuse her for a tiny moment while she went to fetch her coat. She went into her hostess's bedroom and shut the door behind her, she telephoned Vivian and told her that on no account was she to be in when Cathie returned. Vivian, quite a new friend, and an adoring slave, said that there was nothing she would like better than to go at once to the pictures all by herself.

'How sweet of you, and, darling, you won't be back too terribly early, will you?'

Vivian said not to worry, after the pictures she would probably pop round and see Eunice; anyhow Cathie was not to worry.

When, fifteen minutes later, Cathie and Mr Martell got to the flat it was, of course, empty.

After that evening Cathie had no more trouble with Maurice Martell, not, that is to say, until very much later. From that evening forwards he was never slow with his invitations; they poured in, they were pressing, they were continuous.—'Shall I compare thee to a summer's day?' and 'you shall live more bright in these contents.' She was wonderful; she was unique; she was more beautiful, more witty, more—how should he put it—*alive* than anyone he had ever known.

After only a few weeks they were engaged to be married and Cathie was wearing a beautiful diamond and sapphire ring which had belonged to Mr Martell's grandmother.

They spent a week-end with Mr Martell's parents. They went down to Redbourne and visited Cathie's mother. This was perhaps the more successful of the two visits. Mrs Hartley-James had lately moved to a new flat on the seafront. It was nice, Cathie told Maurice, and convenient, but, of course, she would never feel the same about it as she did about the home where she had lived as a child.

Back in London, she took him to call on Aunt Violet, an aunt vaguely supposed to be by marriage, and from whom she had expectations.

The wedding itself might have been difficult, there was no old grey church or family veil immediately to hand. A registry office was probably a good solution; hygienic and sensible and in accord with Cathie's beliefs; but then there would be no wedding presents. The problem was solved by Maurice's family, the school chapel—what could be more suitable, and an old family veil was borrowed from one of the girls at Madame Sondheim's.

Cathie made a very beautiful bride—radiant and triumphant and attended by three beautiful bridesmaids, all of whom worked for Madame Sondheim. The fourth bridesmaid was Maurice's sister.

The honeymoon, spent in Madeira, was more expensive than Maurice could afford. They returned from it to a flat in South Kensington. The flat was on the fourth floor of a house built in nineteen-hundred. Cathie, with the help of a lot of books of art photographs, and a young man from Peter Jones, did her best to give it the appearance of a house built in Sweden in nineteen-thirty. One way and another she used rather too much brown, but the final result was less pretentious than the one she was to achieve later in Baker Street.

Every day during term time Mr Martell travelled by underground to the public school where he was employed as a master. Cathie was left at home to organise the work of the daily woman. She found, rather to her surprise, that she had very few friends. But, not even to Maurice, was she prepared to admit this. She complained to him only that they had very few 'amusing' friends, in saying which she somehow managed to imply a reproach to him.

With time on her hands in which to read, she read a great many volumes of reminiscences, which had on her a very unsettling effect. The people in the books knew T.S. Eliot and Virginia Woolf. Cathie did not, but she felt that Maurice, with his advantages, might have done so if only he had concentrated more on what he was doing.

When she was not reading she wrote poetry which didn't mean anything very much. The clear bright images, the breath-taking turns of phrase were missing. She bought lots of little jars of poster paint and took to painting strange wild pictures which didn't mean anything either.

She decided that she was sexually cold, a snow maiden, a child forced too young to take up the responsibilities of married life. She would look at Maurice with large frightened eyes. Later she discovered that she was warm, loving and sensual and that Maurice, being an Englishman, was unable to satisfy her.

They were invited through one of the other masters at the school to a literary party.

Maurice looked at her doubtfully as they were starting. 'I say, do you think that's really the right sort of dress?'

Cathie experienced a moment of misgiving. Although her dress was dark there was certainly a good deal about it that glittered and caught the eye, and gold entered into the composition of her red velvet hat. Her make-up, somewhat heavier than usual, emphasised all that was most eastern in her appearance.

She asked Maurice what he expected her to wear, and, apparently without warning, they were involved in a most bitter quarrel. It swayed between them, lurching from one subject to another, but always and inevitably coming back to the bitterness of money. They shouted at one another and their voices were harsh and ugly. Then they went out and found a taxi and had themselves driven to the party.

Cathie had a wonderful time. She met two novelists and a famous critic. The critic, dazzled by her beauty, asked her to have lunch with him the following day. She had a long conversation with a young poet. They sat together on a sofa, one sensitive elective spirit reaching towards another. Unfortunately, Cathie was not familiar with his poetry. She promised that the very next morning she would go to Foyles and buy a copy of his one published volume. In a burst of unreflecting generosity the poet said that he would send her one. Then it was arranged that he should come to tea with her and bring it with him.

In nineteen-thirty-nine Maurice Martell, who, despite Cathie's disapproval, was in the Territorial Army, was called up. Cathie started her war by wavering between various ambulance stations, the Red Cross and the M.T.C. Finally she settled herself into a Ministry settled somewhere in England. The flat in South Kensington was given up. The few unhappy years of her marriage were now at an end. Eventually the position was regularised by a divorce.

The war came to an end and Cathie returned to London. Her financial prospects were now very much improved. One of Aunt Violet's nephews by marriage had been killed in the Middle East and the niece had died in an air raid. The other nephew had been spared, but was unwise enough to get himself married to a German girl and Aunt Violet held very strong views about Germans. Our soldiers had not fought and suffered in order that a German might enjoy Aunt Violet's money. It was all very worrying and Mrs Clavering allowed herself to worry about it a good deed. The money, which had been made by her late husband, *ought* to go to some member of his family, but somehow there didn't seem to be any of them left, and the only one who was not physically dead was so morally.

After a great deal of hesitation, Mrs Clavering made a will leaving practically everything to Cathie; she was never quite happy about the will but before she had time to alter it she caught pneumonia and died.

Cathie did a great deal of house-hunting and eventually she found the flat in Baker Street. She started to take up the threads of her old life.—One's friends had been so scattered by the war, one had lost touch with so many people. It was better to see no one than to see people who were not amusing. She started to write poetry again. She bought a lot more poster paints. She had several lovers in quick succession. She moved a little way into artistic and intellectual circles. She was still very beautiful. But somehow it wasn't enough. She deserved something better than this, and optimistically, almost as an idealist, she continued to seek for it; for some deep experience which should be all-satisfying. She had visions, which she managed to see through scudding clouds, of power and fame and of a great love.

She started a novel beginning of course with a sentimental account of childhood—the little girl who dared to dream.

Her week-ends she mostly passed alone in London, or, very occasionally, she would go and visit her mother.

It was during one of these visits and while they were sitting together in the Pavilion gardens that Mrs Hartley-James read aloud to Cathie a paragraph from the *Daily Telegraph*. It announced Laura's engagement.

'Laura?' Cathie frowned, trying to remember.

'One of your father's relations'—and then grudgingly: 'She seems to be doing quite well for herself.'

'Of course I remember now; she came down here when we were both children, and you had to find rooms for her and her governess at one of the boarding houses.'

'She was quite a little thing,' Mrs Hartley-James said, 'and so frail.'

Cathie wondered if Mrs Hartley-James was intentionally reminding her that Laura was younger than herself.

'I could never understand it,' Mrs Hartley-James went on; 'a mother giving her child away to be brought up by a stranger.'

For Laura, the fifth daughter of impoverished parents, had been adopted from the moment of her birth by a friend of her mother's. This had (amongst its other effects) that of making Cathie's relationship to Laura somehow more distant and confused than it was in any case. But Cathie remembered only that Laura's mother had indisputably been *some* kind of a cousin of Mr Hartley-James.

She determined then and there that she would send Laura a wedding present.

'I remember being so sorry for her,' Mrs Hartley-James continued to complain, 'always alone with that governess, and I believe she was never even sent to school.'

'Oh well,' Cathie said, 'I don't expect it did her any harm.'

'And I always thought it was so funny the guardian writing to me about the rooms when we had never even met.'

'But Laura was our cousin.'

'Your father's cousin,' Mrs Hartley-James corrected; 'they were no relations of mine.'

Cathie sent her present and attended the wedding. She thoroughly approved of her cousin Laura and she approved of Edward.

As soon as they returned from their honeymoon she started to make herself useful to them. She told Edward how sad it was that Laura, partly due to her rather secluded upbringing and partly due to the war, should have so few friends. She took the trouble to produce a few minor (and even one major) celebrities.—It was so important that Laura, in her position, should have nice friends.

But really there was no service that she was not willing to perform for Laura. She advised her about her clothes and about soft-furnishings. She trailed all over London in order to match up materials. She sent Laura to Madame Sondheim's for a complete course of treatments. And, taking one thing with another, it wasn't long before she had succeeded in making herself indispensable. And although it wouldn't have been fair to say that Cathie exactly lived with Edward and Laura, it was nevertheless true that they were seldom at Abbotsmere without her.

Even from Laura's point of view the arrangement was quite satisfactory. Laura liked Cathie, who was so good at keeping Edward in a good temper, and then Cathie was so useful when they had parties; so good at arranging the flowers beforehand and making sure that there should be enough food. In fact it was all very pleasant and convenient. Only unfortunately Cathie had fallen in love with Edward.—Not that Laura knew anything about that. Cathie wouldn't have had her know for the world. Tragedy was very near to them all, but somehow and by some heroic act of renunciation she would avert it. She would wrestle with destiny and overcome it. But how? Sometimes in moments of deep discouragement she would wonder if Edward were really hers to renounce. If that particular destiny was there to be wrestled with. She would lie on her bed, or as now, on the sofa in the sitting-room, and be afraid that Edward wouldn't in the end 'come up to scratch'. What a horrible phrase! She reconsidered it, 'That he wouldn't in the end marry the woman he truly loved'—that was better. Of course she was sorry for Laura who was so inadequate as a wife, and here, without her being aware of it, Mrs Martell's face was lit with a smile of triumph.

She moved restlessly, she was bored now and Brahms was becoming increasingly noisy. Anything that tried to float on that would go straight to the bottom; and then wonderful only half-expected relief, there was the sound of the doorbell. Mrs Martell got up and glanced at herself in the ornate looking-glass which hung over the sofa. What a nuisance that Ruth had gone out; now she herself would have to toil down all those flights of stairs to open the door to whoever it was who had rung the bell—but she had very little doubt but that it was the reporter. She drew aside the curtain and looked down into the street; a taxi was driving away from the door. Mrs Martell started down the stairs.

3

RICHARD HARDY stood in the doorway and thought about the article he would write as a result of his interview with Mrs Martell. He stared curiously in at the window of the antique shop. Not a good place for a murder one would have thought—too much china about; nevertheless, three days before a murder had been committed and a head had been battered in right in that very shop, 'those elegant Dresden figures had looked on while their owner had been done to death, that exquisite little cupid, that deplorable figurine of Britannia'—oh lord, that wasn't the stuff he wanted. But now he could hear footsteps on the stairs, and he turned towards the door which led into the private part of the house.

'Good evening.' Mr Hardy smiled at the woman who had opened the door; he felt reasonably sure that he would get his interview.

Mrs Martell looked at him inquiringly, reprovingly and seductively, all at the same time. She managed this by raising her eyebrows, opening her eyes very wide and by throwing her head just a fraction backwards, and on her beautiful mouth—partly opened to show her beautiful teeth—there was a suggestion of a smile.

A few moments later Mr Hardy was following her up the flights of stairs, and had the advantage of studying her light tread and her youthful movement. When they arrived at the top Mr Hardy was breathing rather heavily. Mrs Martell helped him off with his overcoat, and then led the way into the sitting-room.

Unfortunately Brahms had turned into a poetry reading, and Mrs Martell switched the wireless off impatiently.

'Won't you sit down?' and she indicated a hard chair in the French style.

Mr Hardy sat down heavily, his knees slightly apart, wondered if he was going to be offered a drink, and murmured words of thanks for her goodness in seeing him.

Mrs Martell, who was back on the sofa, smiled graciously; one hand was behind her head, the other trailed towards the floor, her ankles were crossed and her feet in their heelless slippers jutted out from the edge of the sofa. She repeated that she had no statement to make, and knew nothing whatever about the murder, except what she had read in the papers.

Mr Hardy said, no, and of course, and that that was all right; he just wanted, or rather the Feature Editor just wanted to get a human angle on the story; and that it must all have been very upsetting for her.

'Oh, it was,' and Mrs Martell shuddered and momentarily closed her eyes.

Mr Hardy lowered his head, and they remained for almost a minute in complete silence, which probably denoted respect for the dead. Mr Hardy wondered if he might smoke, and looking round for an ashtray, couldn't see one.

'Dreadful case,' Mr Hardy said. 'They got the man though; arrested him this evening in Manchester, they'll be charging him tonight. Just another crime of violence. Don't suppose he was even known to his victim?'

'I suppose not.'

'Never seen anyone of his description hanging round the place?'

'Certainly not.'

'Oh well,' Mr Hardy said, 'what we really want is the human slant.—By the way, I suppose you haven't any idea where we could get hold of the sister?'

'Mrs Keble?'

'That's right, she's managed to hide herself pretty success-fully. None of us can get a line on her. You wouldn't know where she was, I suppose?'

Mrs Martell said rather fretfully that she *didn't* know, and that it was very inconvenient, as there had been trouble about the dustbins.

'The two of them used to live on the first floor, didn't they?' and Mr Hardy wondered if there was any chance of Mrs Keble having been involved in her sister's murder; but, disappointing-ly for Mr Hardy, Mrs Keble, who had been at the pictures at the time, had *not* murdered her sister; and Mrs Martell, also disappointingly for Mr Hardy, had had nothing whatsoever to do with the murder. Miss Codrington, who was the owner of the house, as well as of the shop, had been her landlady.—They had met when Mrs Martell had paid her rent, and at other times over such things as dripping taps (Mrs Martell), complaints about hammering (Mrs Martell) and announcements that the water would be turned off for two hours because of the plumber (Miss Codrington). Mr. Hardy didn't see where he was going to get his story.—'Beautiful Woman Befriends Lonely Recluse', or 'An-tique Dealer Foretells her own End', and at once there was a picture of Miss Codrington, old and wrinkled, and Mrs Martell, beautiful, leaning over a table on which the cards had been laid out for fortune-telling, and all the time Miss Codrington was pursued by the Ace of Spades, was unable to get away from the Ace of Spades; but apparently, Miss Codrington and Mrs Mar-tell had not been on those terms of intimacy.

'It must be so interesting,' Mrs Martell said, 'to work on a newspaper.'

Mr Hardy looked up sharply from his note-book. In a second or two she would tell him that all her life she had wanted to write. He considered her as a proposition. Mrs Martell shifted on the sofa, arching her back and drawing in her stomach. She looked lovingly at the large unframed photograph of Edward which stood propped against a china vase on one of the little tables; then she asked Mr Hardy if he wouldn't like a drink.

Mr Hardy said, well, that would be very nice, and Mrs Martell went to a corner cupboard and started delving about at the bottom of it. The top part of the cupboard consisted of open shelves on which were displayed a selection of dinner plates; there were as well one or two little china and enamel objects of an indeterminate character.

The drink which Mrs Martell eventually offered was disappointing. It consisted of a bottle of gin, rather less than a quarter full, a bottle of lime-juice, the clear sticky kind which ought really to be labelled 'poison', and two very small glasses. The glasses appeared to be dusty, or at any rate, not quite clean. Mrs Martell put all these on a table and then, having poured the lime and the gin into the little glasses, sat on the sofa, leaving room for Mr Hardy to sit beside her if he should wish to do so.

Mr Hardy had been wrong when he had thought that she would tell him about how she had always wanted to be a writer. Instead, she smiled enchantingly and asked him about himself; and Mr Hardy, like everyone else, always enjoyed talking about himself.

'But how wonderful,' and 'how interesting,' Cathie Martell kept saying at intervals, 'and what a fascinating life,' and 'do you really know *him*?' when Mr Hardy mentioned the name of a not very famous artist. Mr Hardy smiled deprecatingly and only just resisted the temptation of reeling off the names of even more celebrated people he had met in the course of his work. Instead, he told her about the Feature Editor, and how the Feature Editor had said to him, 'Dick,' the Feature Editor had said, and here Mrs Martell had interrupted to say 'Richard' in a low clear voice, and she put her head on one side and listened to herself saying 'Richard 'as though she was considering all the implications of this most beautiful and unusual name.

And then, quite maddeningly, the telephone had started to ring.

'Yes,' Mrs Martell said into the receiver, and then again, 'yes,' and of course it was Edward speaking from Shropshire. Usually Mrs Martell liked Edward to ring her up, insisted in fact that Edward should ring her up, whenever it was possible, at least once a day when they were apart.

So now Edward was only doing that which he thought would please her.

'That you?' Edward said, and 'how are you?' and 'had a good day?' and 'it's been raining here.'

'Yes, darling,' and 'yes, darling,' and 'how extraordinary, it's been quite fine in London.'

And then Edward remembered that he ought to have been listening to the concert on the Third Programme, and said how much he had enjoyed the concert. And because Cathie did not seem to be as responsive as she usually was, he said, 'Are you all right?'

'Yes, quite all right, only I've got somebody here.'

So Mr Hardy got up and said should he go, and Edward said, oh dear, and that he would ring back later.

And Mrs Martell said, 'Oh please don't,' to Mr Hardy, and 'Oh please do,' to Edward.

And Edward said, very well he would then, and was it anybody he knew?

And Mrs Martell said, no, it was a reporter as a matter of fact.

'Good lord.' Edward sounded alarmed.

'It's all right, he only wants a human slant on Miss Codrington.'

Edward said that really the papers were impossible and that she ought to send the fellow packing. And Mrs Martell said, yes, and that that was what she was doing; and then she put her hand over the receiver and told Mr Hardy to sit down again and help himself to a drink because she would only be a moment. So Mr Hardy sat down again and helped himself to gin and skipped the lime.

'Very well, darling,' Mrs Martell said, 'I'll ring you later.'— But she wouldn't, of course, she would wait until Edward rang her, for trunk calls were expensive.

Mr Hardy said that really he wouldn't keep her more than a few minutes, and, without appearing to notice what he was doing, he poured some more gin into his glass—the bottle was practically empty now.

Mrs Martell said that there was no need to hurry, and composed her face into its most becoming lines; and Mr Hardy, rather to his surprise, found that he very much disliked whoever it was she had been speaking to and whoever it was whom she had called 'darling'. He supposed that it was that pompous-looking ass whose photograph was propped up against the china vase.

Mrs Martell saw that he was looking at Edward's picture, and she smiled a secret self-satisfied smile; and then was rather alarmed in case Mr Hardy should recognise the photograph; usually when anyone came to the flat she put it away in a drawer. But she needn't have worried, because Richard Hardy was not that kind of journalist; his own paper did not run a society column, and he only became concerned with people like Edward after they had committed crimes, been sued for breach of promise, or filed their petitions in bankruptcy.

'Well now,' and Mrs Martell smiled invitingly at Mr Hardy, 'where had we got to?'

Mr Hardy smiled back and thought that as far as Miss Codrington's murder was concerned, they hadn't got anywhere at all.

'Actually,' Mr Hardy said, 'we were talking about salmon fishing.'

Strangely enough they had been, and Mrs Martell remembered that when the telephone rang she had been going to show Mr Hardy the photograph album which had two very good pictures of salmon in it and at least five of herself fishing for them. Mrs Martell still 'went in' for photograph albums, and they were always ready to hand; now she reached for a large green one and began flipping through the pages, looking for the salmon. At some of the pages she paused and smiled indulgently. Almost without knowing what she was doing she patted the sofa beside her. Mr Hardy would be able to see the pictures so much better if he were sitting on the sofa.

* * * * *

'Oh damn and blast!' Edward West leant back in his armchair and scowled at the portrait of his great-grandfather which hung over the mantelpiece. He was thinking about Laura and he was thinking of her with irritation.—She was inconsiderate, she was feckless and she could be quite maddening. Take today, for instance. Just after breakfast she had said that she was going up to London and would probably not be back until tomorrow. She ought to have let him know earlier. She must have known that she had this appointment with the doctor.

'But I didn't, truly I didn't,' Laura had said, 'I just looked in my engagement diary and there it was, "Mr Gideon three o'clock."'

And that was so typical of Laura. She was muddled and untidy. If he had known that she was going to be away he would have made some plans of his own. Perhaps have gone up to London with her, or asked somebody over to dinner, or invited Cathie to come down. But you couldn't do any of those things at the last moment. So he had spent a long dull evening by himself. Even the Beauty that is Brahms had been missing, for he had forgotten to turn on the radio.

Edward poured himself a drink and went and stood by the fireplace, staring into the fire, his foot on the fender. He had been very patient with Laura, endlessly patient. But things couldn't go on like this for ever, and here Edward kicked the fender and scowled furiously at his great-grandfather who looked down at him with the pouting crimped smile of the 1830's.

Laura was maddening and inconsiderate and yet he couldn't finally make up his mind to leave her.

On the other side of the room was a much smaller picture of Edward's great-grandmother.—A determined, not very agreeable expression, ringlets and puffed velvet sleeves. 'Lady Ophelia West', it was written in gold letters on her black skirt, and she had lived on and on until she was nearly a hundred years old. There was even a tradition that she had held Edward in her arms when he was a baby.—somehow he had never been able to bring himself to believe it. Charles, Edward's younger brother, younger by rather less than a year, had also, so it was

said, been held in her arms, and Charles, who had a great sense
of the past, believed it implicitly; the old mad woman and the
little new baby—bone of my bone, flesh of my flesh, and with
their traditions stretching back and back into history, it was a
romantic, and to Charles, a very satisfactory picture which took
no account of the fact that Lady Ophelia, far from being mad,
had never, even in extreme old age, so much as lost her memory.
And the past, such as it was, existed only on Lady Ophelia's side
of the family. For her husband, whom she had very sensibly
married when he was already middle-aged and extremely rich,
had almost certainly been born in a Lancashire slum.

Looking at this grandmother, Edward felt no sympathy towards her. She had known what she was doing all right and he
knew, or thought that he knew, that no one had ever made use
of her. She was not beautiful and that might well have been a
misfortune. For women ought always to be beautiful. And now,
almost without knowing that he did so, he was thinking of Laura.

He was thinking of Laura and not of Cathie.

Lady Ophelia had had many children and, on the whole, she
had been successful in arranging their lives for them. From the
very day the first of them was born she had been grimly determined that they should not be made to suffer for their father's
lack of rank. She had felt very deeply on that subject and she
was also equally determined that Mr West himself, her dearest
Cosmo, should be received into Society.

Her reasons were never purely snobbish for it was absolutely necessary to be where there was power. And power lay,
not in the House of Commons of which Mr West was already a
member, but in the great houses round Grosvenor Square.

Power was dispensed, or could be withheld, by women; by a
very few women.

Lady Ophelia fought for her family in the drawing-rooms of
ladies who in the beginning were not particularly well-disposed
towards her. She fought and she triumphed. Probably her dearest Cosmo never fully understood the extent of her triumph. But
it was very well understood and appreciated by her eldest son,

her dearest Augustus, who inherited all his mother's ambition. He was not a lovable man.

Laura was heartbreakingly beautiful and yet she could be quite maddening. It seemed to Edward that she made no effort at all to please him. She was pathologically inconsiderate and there were times when she looked quite ugly.

He remembered the first time he had ever seen her. It had been in the drawing-room of her guardian's house in Yorkshire. He had been staying in a house a few miles away and his hostess, at a loss as to what to do with her guests, had taken them over to luncheon with Mrs Pemberthy.—'I thought that perhaps we might come over on Saturday, there will be just the twelve of us.'—Before the war hostesses had been able to say things like that to each other. So there had been a crowd of people in Mrs Pemberthy's drawing-room and Laura, not yet quite grown up, had come into the room.

He remembered the turn of her head and the quality of her voice. And yet at the time he had not known that he was particularly interested in her?

He tried to think back across the years.

He had been placed next to her in the dining-room, but luncheon was half over before he turned away from his other neighbour and condescended to speak to her.

What had they talked about? About politics?—for in those days he was determined that when he was finished with the army he would go into the House of Commons.

In those days he had still been ambitious. It had seemed possible that there would be some kind of continuity. The Federated States of Europe. It might not be possible to avoid war; but after the war the world would go on. He had faith in the world and in his country. The situation might be complicated; but all problems were in the end capable of being solved by wise statesmanship.

Charles still believed that.—Get rid of the Socialists, get rid of Russia—don't think about America. The war had passed over Charles and left his faith intact. He still believed in the past and in the future. He had no doubts either about Lady Ophelia or about his own son (when he should at last be born).—Inevitably, and rightly, they would both be where there was power.

Edward turned in his chair and spoke to Laura and he found her enchanting. What had they talked about? It was so many years ago that he couldn't remember. It was so many years ago that he didn't remember that it was he who had talked while Laura listened.

And all the time he was acutely aware of her beauty and of the intensity of the spirit that lay behind her remoteness.

They didn't meet again until the war was over and very soon after their second meeting they were married. Edward poured himself another drink; he had been very patient with Laura, endlessly patient, but things couldn't go on like this for ever.

Mrs Martell leant across Mr Hardy and switched off the light.

Mr Hardy had been very interested in the photographs of salmon being caught by Mrs Martell. In turning over the pages of the album their hands had met and had not parted again. In examining a photograph—'it's rather blurred, I'm afraid, but you *can* just see his tail if you look carefully'—their heads had come together, and from then on Mr Hardy had been in no doubt as to the outcome of their friendship. It was only a question of timing. For the moment Miss Codrington went into abeyance, and so did the Feature Editor.—But there would be tomorrow and there would have to be a story. As he kissed Mrs Martell Mr Hardy thought of, and discarded, various possibilities, he had forgotten to ask if there had been any domestic animals.—'Canary flutters to its mistress's defence'—'Canary sings on in cage unaware of mistress's fate.' He wondered if he could ask Mrs Martell if there had in actual fact been a canary, or a dog? Dogs were pretty corny but they were useful in an emergency.—'Dog gives the alarm. Baby carried to safety through flames.' But whatever else she had had Miss Codrington certainly had not had a baby. He was beginning to doubt whether there was a story here, and yet, there must be one somewhere if only he could find it.

At this point Mrs Martell interrupted his thoughts by saying that this was really terribly naughty of them, wasn't it?

'But very pleasant.' Mr Hardy's reply was practically automatic.

'We mustn't,' Mrs Martell said decisively, and withdrew very suddenly to the far end of the sofa.

Mr Hardy was left feeling aggrieved; after all it was not *he* who had switched off the light.

An alteration in the tension of the sofa springs told him that she was standing up, now she was stumbling across his feet, and the next moment she had turned on the light.

Mrs Martell smoothed her hair and laughed, the gay laugh of someone who has had their own way.

'But, darling,' Mrs Martell said, 'we must be sensible,' and Mr Hardy was furious.—And then, unexpectedly, Mrs Martell was being nice. Could his story wait until tomorrow morning, as she had an idea, but he must understand that it was only an idea, that Miss Codrington's sister would be coming to the house sometime before twelve o'clock. An interview with Miss Codrington's sister would be a scoop for the *Sunday World Post*.

Mr Hardy, although he was still annoyed, had to admit that that was true.

'And, if you'll give me your number, I'll telephone you the moment she arrives.'

'That's extremely kind of you.'

Mrs Martell looked a little doubtful and added the rider that he must promise not to tell Mrs Keble anything about the arrangement. Because now that Miss Codrington was dead, the house probably belonged to Mrs Keble and she was very touchy, not to say difficult, and already there had been trouble about the dustbins.

Mr Hardy promised faithfully that he would be discreet.

'It's very naughty of me really,' Mrs Martell said, 'because I happen to know that she particularly *doesn't* want to meet the press.'

Mr Hardy said, 'ah well,' and 'there it was'. He got up preparing to leave.

'And she *is* very difficult.' Idly, Mrs Martell had picked up the album which had fallen to the floor. It was open at a photograph of herself sitting on a gate with the wind blowing through her hair.

'I shan't be at the office tomorrow morning, but you can get me at this number.' Mr Hardy put a slip of paper down on the table beside the empty bottle of gin.

'Of course,' Mrs Martell was saying, 'there mayn't be any truth in it, but Ruth, that's my maid, heard from their charwoman that Mrs Keble's husband blew his brains out in India because *she* was having an affair with another man.'

'Husband commits suicide: Now sister is murdered.'

Mr Hardy was really excited; there *was* a story here after all.

Mrs Martell turned over several pages at once, and saw a photograph of herself and Edward in the garden at Abbotsmere. They were standing on either side of a sundial. Her legs were looking particularly good in that photograph, and her hips were turned at just the right angle; but then, in all the photographs her hips were turned at just the right angle.—How distinguished Edward looked, and how suitable. Especially suitable, of course, as a husband.

'Well then,' Mr Hardy said, 'I'll be getting along. Don't bother to come down. I can find my own way out.'

Mrs Martell looked up, vaguely surprised. She had almost forgotten Mr Hardy.

4

THE NEXT MORNING began for Mrs Martell as all other mornings: that is, with a glass of hot water.

Sipped slowly, this was good for the complexion, wonderful for the figure and good for the intestines. It was certainly disgusting.

Ruth, who had brought in the glass of hot water, drew the curtains and said that it was a lovely day. Mrs Martell moved her head unhappily on the pillows and closed her eyes. She couldn't remember how often she had told Ruth *not* to speak to her in the mornings before she had had her breakfast: weak china tea and thin toast. This would be brought to her in exactly half an hour after she had had her bath, put on a slightly grubby dressing-gown and returned to her bed. Then she would read the *Daily Mirror*; look at the social page of the *Daily Telegraph* (*The Times* was too expensive) and discuss with Ruth what shopping had to be done for the day.—Another cabbage perhaps if Ruth had finished the whole of the last one for her supper. And, surely, this was one of the days when the kitchen floor had to be scrubbed—as against a day when it had merely to be wiped over. Of course Ruth had not forgotten? And here, Mrs Martell would give Ruth a bright encouraging smile, and Ruth would smile gaily back at her and say 'yes, madam'. They had taught her to say 'madam' when she was in the Forces, so it didn't come so strangely to her as it might have done otherwise. She had been with Mrs Martell for over a year now. She didn't like her particularly, but Mrs Martell was away such a lot that she found the place convenient. When Mrs Martell was away, Ruth was able to entertain her young man. Once Miss Codrington had met him when he was leaving the flat at eight o'clock in the morning; that had rather shaken Ruth, but Miss Codrington was a good sort and she hadn't 'let on'.

'But surely,' Mrs Martell was saying reprovingly, 'we can't have run out of biscuits *again*?'

Ruth agreed that she didn't see how they could have.

'But I went into the kitchen last night and the tin was empty.'

'Well fancy!' And Ruth looked expectantly at Mrs Martell as if waiting for her to propound some interesting theory about the biscuits.

But Mrs Martell only said resignedly that she would have to get another packet and, 'that would be all' and of course Ruth wouldn't forget about boiling the dish-cloths? Not in the brown enamel basin, which was chipped, but in the white one.

Ruth rather thought that the white one was chipped as well, but she didn't mention it.

Mrs Martell picked up the *Daily Telegraph* again. Ruth withdrew to the kitchen. Mrs Martell lit a cigarette. She knew it was rather naughty of her; cigarette smoke, especially in the morning, was death to the complexion; all the same, she would smoke just one cigarette, and then she would do her exercises.

Her exercises, for most of which she lay on the bed, were rather complicated and a spectator might have found them slightly indecent. She practised them on the whole for the sake of the intestines, and in order to keep the stomach in its proper place.

One, *two* and hold it; one, *two* and hold it. Mrs Martell, rolling briskly from side to side, was annoyed when she heard the doorbell. It couldn't be the fishmonger or the greengrocer, because all her shopping was done by hand. It couldn't be the postman either because he had already been.

One, *two* and hold it; one, *two* and hold it. She heard Ruth open the door of the flat and start down the stairs. It might just conceivably be the window-cleaner, but she didn't think so. She passed on to the next set of exercises; one, two, three and *heave*. She heard Ruth coming back up the stairs, and there was somebody with her, and then Ruth was tapping on the bedroom door.

Mrs Martell gave a final and very energetic 'heave' and asked what was the matter.

Ruth, from outside the door, told her that Laura was here and had been put in the sitting-room.

Mrs Martell registered this fact and registered, with annoyance, that the sitting-room had not yet been 'done'. She looked round the bedroom; the breakfast tray; her underclothes hanging over the back of a chair; the dressing-table, not quite tidy; the room did not have an attractive appearance.

'Ask her to wait a few minutes,' Mrs Martell said through the door; and then she raised her voice and called to Laura that she had nearly finished dressing.

Laura sat in the ugly and pretentious sitting-room and waited for Cathie.

She was too unhappy to notice whether the room was tidy or untidy, whether or not there was cigarette ash on the carpet. She ought not to have come, Cathie didn't want her at this hour of the morning—and she looked at her wristwatch and saw that it was a quarter to ten. And why had she come anyhow, to get reassurance, in order not to be alone. For to be alone was terrifying. One's thoughts turning, reshaping themselves, things which were better forgotten remembered with a terrible clearness. Memories, half-memories which were more tangible than anything which had actually happened.—Soon Cathie would come into the room and she would not be alone any longer; that was why she had come, in order not to be alone.

'I wish I were dead.' Laura went and stood by the window.—'It will be a life with a great many assets'—that had been Aunt Anne when Laura had told her that she was going to marry Edward.

'I shall probably have to see your husband,' that had been Mr Gideon in his consulting-room yesterday afternoon.

And then the dinner party last night. A dinner party which had not been planned in advance, but which had just happened.—Only Edward would think that it had been planned. What fun it had been at the time.—But she had talked too much and too loudly, the things she had said had been very silly, probably this morning the Chapmans were angry with her, and Mr Langham? Mr Langham had seemed to like her, had dropped her home and suggested that they should meet again; but he hadn't meant it, really he hadn't liked her at all.

She looked down at the traffic in Baker Street and wished that she were dead.—'You can't have anything without paying for it'—'happiness is always followed by remorse'—'however happy you are now, one day you will be unhappy.'

Self-pity, you make your own unhappiness, and you will not *let* yourself be helped.—They were right, of course, they must be right, or they wouldn't all say the same things; but what was the use of that? Laura pressed her forehead against the window-pane.

Mrs Martell, fastening a suspender, glanced at her reflection in the long glass: really, she had a wonderful figure, and although there was no one but herself to look in the glass her hips were turned at just the right angle.—Surely, no one would guess that she was a day over thirty, perhaps not even as much? How annoying it was of Laura to come to the flat without first ringing up, and even if she had rung up it would still be inconvenient. There was the housework to be done, to say nothing of Mrs Martell's remedial exercises, and surely, even Laura must know that housework was done in the mornings! But then Laura never thought of anyone but herself! Laura was utterly, utterly selfish and egotistical. Even if she had not been in love with him Mrs Martell would have been sorry for Edward. She felt disinterested and charitable. She was not taking, or trying to take, Edward away from Laura. Sooner or later Laura, who was so terribly selfish, would lose him anyhow. It couldn't be otherwise. Even if (although such a thing was difficult to imagine) there had been no such person as Cathie Martell, Laura would have lost Edward. And, added to everything else, there was the fact, or what Mrs Martell was very nearly certain was the fact, that Laura was not able to have children. And by children Mrs Martell of course, meant a son. Children were noisy, boring and tiresome; but a son to inherit Abbotsmere was something entirely different.

And a son should be for ever and for always fourteen, just old enough to be visited at Eton on the fourth of June.—'Mrs West and her young son seen together at the match', and of course Mrs West's hips were turned at just the right angle, and, of course, the photograph was in the *Tatler*.

There was a prolonged knocking on the door of the flat. Mrs Martell had been aware of the same sound a few seconds earlier, and had been rather surprised, for she had not heard the street bell. However, all those kinds of noises were Ruth's affair, it wasn't necessary to do anything about them, or to listen to them very carefully.

The knocking was repeated, and where was Ruth anyhow? Departed on a squalid errand to the dustbins, or just down at the grocers buying a bar of soap? Mrs Martell was annoyed, she liked to do the shopping herself, and she bought soap only when she thought it proper for the last bar to have been finished.—But Ruth was extravagant. She used soap and floor-polish with regal lavishness, and then upset the whole of the household routine by 'popping out' at inconvenient times in order to get further supplies. In the meantime there was the door to be answered.

With a very bad grace, Mrs Martell put on her dressing-gown and went into the passage. As her hand reached for the door-handle she was scowling, and she had very nearly opened the door before she remembered to arrange her mouth in a becoming smile.

The little woman who stood facing Mrs Martell was fashionably dressed. She had overdone the rouge and something had gone very wrong with her hair, otherwise she would have been elegant.

'Mrs Keble!' Mrs Martell was not very pleased, she did not like being caught like this in her dressing-gown.

'I hope I am not disturbing you,' but Mrs Keble was already inside the flat and advancing towards the sitting-room.

Ordinarily, Mrs Martell would have been able to thwart her; but there was the disadvantage of the dressing-gown; there were the prerogatives of recent and violent bereavement.

As Mrs Keble and Cathie came into the room Laura swung round from the window. She had been wishing she were dead; she smiled guiltily and apologetically, it was as though they had caught her in something disgraceful.

'Mrs Keble, my cousin Mrs West. Laura, Mrs Keble is my landlady.'—Cathie hoped that she had warned Laura not to say anything about the murder.

But, so far, Laura had not said anything.

Mrs Keble opened her bag and searched for a handkerchief, but when she found it she did not use it, only held it clasped tightly in her hand in case of emergency.

Mrs Martell hoped that she wasn't going to start crying again about her sister.

Mrs Keble said that she was sorry and that she hadn't known that Mrs Martell was busy.—'I only wanted one little word with you.' She had lowered her voice to a whisper.

'Yes?' Mrs Martell did not lower her voice at all and she did not invite Mrs Keble to sit down.

'As a matter of fact, dear, it's about the rent.'

Mrs Martell did not like being asked for the rent in front of Laura, and she very much resented being called 'dear'. She told Mrs Keble that all that would be seen to. The phrase implied that she would probably get in touch with her Estate Agent.

'I was wondering, dear, if it would be convenient for you to pay it right away,' and, without being invited to do so, Mrs Keble sat down on the sofa.—'You see, dear, I would like to have the cash, because the lawyer says I can't write any cheques until after the will has been proved, or something. It's very awkward, isn't it, and it isn't as if I could take anything out of the till, because there isn't anything *in* the till.'

Mrs Martell considered that in all the circumstances the reference to the till was in extremely bad taste.

'That dreadful man,' Mrs Keble said, and 'poor Gladys,' then she returned to the money. It was all so awkward and there were so many things that had to be paid for. The milkman for instance had been quite rude to her on the doorstep just now; those people hadn't got any feelings.

Mrs Martell said that Mrs Keble mustn't allow herself to dwell on it; and now, if Mrs Keble would forgive her, she really must go and finish dressing.

'And the money?'—Mrs Keble, it seemed, had no intention of going away until she had the rent, and the rent, under an income-tax-evading arrangement made between Miss Codrington and Mrs Martell, had to be paid in pound notes.

Mrs Martell said that as soon as she was dressed she would go to the bank, but that it wasn't convenient, she had a great many things to do this morning.

'Oh dear, I promised the milkman that if he would call back in half an hour . . .'

The telephone started to ring. Mrs Martell picked up the receiver. It would have been wiser if she had taken the call in her bedroom, for it was Mr Hardy.

Mr Hardy was very amiable, slightly apologetic, slightly flirtatious, but insistent.—Had the old girl shown up yet?

'Yes, yes, well, as a matter of fact, yes.' Mrs Martell hoped that what Mr Hardy was saying could not be heard by Mrs Keble, but she was sitting very near the telephone.

Mr Hardy said that that was splendid and that he'd be round right away, in the meantime Mrs Keble was not to be allowed to escape. If necessary Mrs Martell had better hit her over the head with a blunt instrument.

Mrs Martell thought the last remark was unnecessary. And Mr Hardy certainly was not going to be allowed to interview Mrs Keble in this room. Downstairs in her own flat if he liked, or in the shop, but not *here*. Unfortunately, just as she was putting down the receiver, Ruth came into the room carrying a tray on which was the kitchen teapot and three kitchen cups. Mrs Martell was furious with her.—Not here when she was wanted to answer the door, and then coming in to produce officious cups of tea at inappropriate moments—to say nothing of wasting the rations. Ruth should have known better!

'Really, Ruth, I don't think that we require that.'

But Ruth was setting the tray down in front of Mrs Keble.

'How very, very kind, but I oughtn't to stay?' Mrs Keble looked at Mrs Martell.

'Now, you drink it up; it will do you good,' Ruth was solicitous and she at least knew the proper treatment of the bereaved.

'It's what she needs, isn't it?' Ruth appealed to Laura, who still stood by the window.

'I expect so,' Laura said, and then, because that didn't seem sufficiently sympathetic, 'Let me pour it out for you.'

Mrs Keble sighed deeply and relaxed against the cushions.

Mrs Martell shrugged her shoulders; tea-drinking was extremely bad for the complexion—not that Mrs Keble *had* a complexion anyhow; but if she was going to continue to ruin it, she might at least do so downstairs. And what business had Laura to treat the house *and* the teapot as if they belonged to her. And any minute now Mr Hardy would arrive and start battering his way in.

Mr Hardy! and she was still wearing her dressing-gown and it was the grubby faded dressing-gown kept exclusively for home wear. She turned and followed Ruth out of the room, banging the door behind her.

'Oh dear, I do hope that she isn't annoyed,' Mrs Keble said anxiously.

'Why should she be?' Laura put another lump of sugar into Mrs Keble's cup. 'I do think it's so dreadful for you about your sister.'

Mrs Keble said not to speak of it and that of course it had been terrible and that sympathy was a wonderful thing.

She had been staying down at Woking with a very dear friend, but that wasn't the same as one's own people, was it? When trouble came one needed one's own people.

Laura agreed that one did and wondered if there were any among her own many relations who could be thought of as her own people 'in that particular sense.'

'My sister who lives in Bombay is flying home to be with me.' Mrs Keble stirred her tea.

'That will be nice for you.'

There was a kind of bleakness in the tone of Laura's voice which caused Mrs Keble to look at her sharply. Mrs Keble wasn't always so sensitive about other people, but Gladys's death, the shock, the subsequent misery and sleepless nights, had sharpened her sensibilities. She looked at Laura and realised that here was someone who was almost, if not quite, as unhappy as herself.

'On the other hand,' Mrs Keble said, 'sometimes I think it's better to be with strangers; with strangers one has to make an effort, but with relatives one can let oneself go and that isn't always a good thing.'

Again, Laura tried to imagine a sister who would fly from Bombay in order to comfort one, or a brother who would arrive from Essex and be kind and sympathetic. A schoolroom table covered with a red cloth and an old nurse to sympathise and fuss over one and end by telling one that things were not as bad as one thought. But Laura had not had that kind of nurse and owing to her adoption her sisters were lost to her.

—'I will be brave, I will be brave, and no one shall ever know that I'm unhappy'—'with strangers one had to make an effort,' and Laura smiled at Mrs Keble who surprisingly, and for no reason that she could understand, seemed for a moment to be less of a stranger than anyone else in the whole world.

They were interrupted by Ruth bursting into the room.

'Please, madam, there's a gentleman to see you and he won't take no for an answer. He says he's got an appointment with you, though I told him that he couldn't possibly have because nobody knew you were coming, and anyhow you wanted to be quiet, and he isn't a policeman either because they always say that they are.'

—During the last few days Ruth had had much experience of the ways of police and detectives.

'No one has an appointment with me and I can't see anyone.' Mrs Keble shrank into the corner of the sofa. 'I won't see anyone,' she repeated; but she might as well have saved herself the trouble for Mr Hardy had pushed his way past Ruth and was already in the room.

It can be said in Mr Hardy's favour that he conducted his interview with Mrs Keble with as much dispatch as possible. He caused her a good deal of pain, but plainly that could not be helped; the Feature Editor had insisted on a scoop and this was Mr Hardy getting it for him. Before the interview finished Mrs Martell came in. She was wearing a black dress, partly out of respect for Mrs Keble's mourning and partly because she thought it was very becoming.

At last, completely shattered, humbled and upset, Mrs Keble was allowed to retire to her own part of the house. It was only when she was on the stairs that she remembered that she still had not got the rent which was due from Mrs Martell; and the milkman was certain to come back; there was in fact no chance that the milkman would *not* come back. Mrs Keble hesitated, but rather *ten* unpaid milkmen than one Mr Hardy.

Mrs Martell, Laura and Mr Hardy were left in the pretentious sitting-room. The sun had come out, and this made the fact that the room had not yet been 'done' more apparent. More apparent that is to Mrs Martell, Laura and Mr Hardy didn't notice it. Mr. Hardy was so delighted with the interview that the memory of it would be pleasant to him, Laura was distressed for the stricken Mrs Keble. Only Mrs Martell saw the dust on the table-tops, last night's *Evening Standard* lying on the floor, the unwashed ashtrays.

'Well,' Mr Hardy said, 'I must get down to the office and get this stuff written up.'

'Oh dear.' Mrs Martell had hoped that he would ask her out to luncheon. If there was no luncheon to get Ruth would have that much more time in which 'to get on' and 'to catch up'. Also she didn't want to be left alone with Laura.

'I think there's quite a lot in the Indian business,' Mr Hardy said.—'Husband commits suicide: Now sister is murdered,' and a faint suggestiveness in the first paragraph about the reason for the late Mr Keble's suicide, 'Beautiful wife's Indian friend—Calcutta Society.'

He would have to look it up in the files, but it was obvious that there was something there.

'Why don't we go and get a drink,' Mr Hardy said—he had hoped that Mrs Martell would offer him one. He did not take into account that he had finished her gin the evening before.

Mrs Martell said austerely that it was far too early, and that she had to go out and do the shopping, she was late as it was.— Perhaps that would get rid of Laura.

Mr Hardy immediately offered her a lift, and although Mrs Martell's original intention had been to go only as far as the corner greengrocers, she accepted.

'The bank,' Laura said suddenly; 'you won't forget the bank, will you?'

Mrs Martell was not pleased to be reminded. 'If I have time,' she said vaguely, and 'Can we drop you anywhere, Laura?'—For now, Mr Hardy's taxi was her private car and she could use it in order to get rid of Laura.

'I wanted,' Laura said, 'to talk to you,' and then more urgently as Mrs Martell seemed to be making preparations to leave the flat, 'Can you come down to Abbotsmere with me this afternoon?'

Mrs Martell paused in her progress.

'It's terribly important,' Laura said, 'but I'd have to explain.'

'I don't see how I possibly can.' Mrs Martell frowned slightly. Both Mr Hardy and Laura must be given to understand that her days were extremely busy, filled with important and interesting engagements.—'Official dinner at the Savoy, sentimental dinner at the Caprice,' and never, of course, blank evenings broken only by—'old school chum to supper.'

'I don't see how I possibly can,' and Mrs Martell frowned.

'It's terribly important,' Laura repeated and wished that Mr Hardy would go away.

'I'll have to see,' Mrs Martell said and then, just in case she had not made herself clear. 'I don't see how I can possibly get out of this evening; and luncheon tomorrow, and I have two appointments in the afternoon.'

—It was true about the appointments, one of them was with her manicurist and the other with a fortune-teller who lived in a Wimbledon basement.

'You will be catching the three-thirty, I suppose?'—for of course and when it came to it Mrs Martell would go to Abbotsmere.

'Yes,' Laura said. 'I'll get your ticket and I'll try and get there first and keep a seat for you.'

Mrs Martell nodded an abstracted consent. Naturally when there were seats to be kept Laura would get to the station first; and of course Laura would buy her ticket for her. For somehow and quite naturally Mrs Martell, from the first time of her going to Abbotsmere, had managed to have it understood that if she was not driven down in the car her ticket must be paid for by Laura or Edward. And this was not because she was mean, parsimonious, or grasping, it was simply that she was not rich. In addition Laura and Edward were compelled to exercise great delicacy over the transaction in order that Mrs Martell's feelings should not be hurt, and in order that she should not be made to feel herself a poor relation.

Mrs Martell, closely attended by Mr Hardy, had already started down the stairs; there was nothing for Laura to do but follow them.

As she reached the front door Mrs Martell thought that she might as well keep her promise to Mrs Keble and go to the bank, for her bank was in Fleet Street and that would give her a nice long drive with Mr Hardy. Besides, she had to go to the bank some time.

Mr Hardy said good-bye to Laura and hoped that they would meet again.

'I hope so,' and 'see you at the station,' Laura called after Cathie; and was left on the pavement wondering what she would do with the four hours which must elapse before she went to catch the train.

Mrs Martell had not thought it worth while to repeat her offer to drop Laura somewhere in Mr Hardy's taxi.

'While I stand on the roadway or on the pavement grey', but Laura heard nothing but the noises of the traffic and the voice of the man who sold papers on the corner, and in her heart there was only the terrified longing not to be alone.

'The unhappiness which comes only once or twice in a lifetime.' Laura started to walk down Baker Street. She wondered what she should do until it was time to go to the train. She still had her suitcase to pack and there was some shopping that she ought to do—none of it very interesting.—'While I stand on the roadway—I oughtn't to be so unhappy, my life has a great many assets.'

She had reached Oxford Street, standing on the curb; she was suddenly afraid that she would never be able to get through all that traffic and cross the street.

5

AT ABBOTSMERE Nelly Brewster sat at the end of the kitchen table; she was smoking a cigarette and listening to the wireless; she had just finished her second cup of strong tea.

The kitchen was very untidy and most of its open spaces were covered with sheets of newspaper, as this was popularly supposed to save work. Unopened groceries stood on the dresser. Nelly's mackintosh, several old sweaters, belonging variously to herself, her husband and her son, were draped over the chairs. At several points on the floor there were saucers which had been put down for the cat and never taken up again. The sink was piled with 'washing up' which had not been done and there were basins in which articles of clothing had been left to soak, presumably, for all eternity.

The kitchen faced north, where there were two rows of windows one above the other. In one of the southern corners there was a mortar which had been installed about the year eighteen-hundred, the handle of the pestle was held in place by an iron ring fixed in the wall about ten feet above the stone floor.

Nelly, lighting one cigarette from the butt of the preceding one, saw nothing amiss in the muddle by which she was surrounded and she had no plans for eventually clearing it up.

On the high mantel, under which the cooker now cowered, and from which the spit had once been suspended, there were three, partly used, packets of cereal, a carton soap powder, a framed snap of Nelly's husband as he had appeared when in 1944 he had been a driver in the Royal Tank Corps, and a picture postcard of Blackpool which had been sent to Nelly several months ago by some one called Joan who was having a wonderful time there. Nelly had been friends with several Joans when she worked in the factory; and it might be any of them who had sent the postcard.

The hands of the kitchen clock (it had been placed against the wall in about 1870) came to eleven-fifteen; regretfully Nelly got up. It was the end of her lunch-time and Nelly was surprisingly methodical about time. Also she was an extremely good cook—a fact which never ceased to irritate Mrs Martell, who never skipped any opportunity she got of persuading Laura to get rid of her; but Laura, so suggestible about everything else, was stubborn about Nelly.

'Old bitch,' Nelly thought, as, *en route* for the sink, she stepped carefully over the saucers; and then again 'old bitch,' for if Mrs Martell did not like Nelly, Nelly simply hated Mrs Martell.—Always smarming round and thinking she could do just as she liked; and that sickly namby-pamby voice, and that namby-pamby smile.—'Oh, Nelly, I wonder if you would mind if I just took a tiny biscuit?' and the raised eyebrows because the kitchen didn't look like one of those canteen dumps that everyone had got so sick of when there was a war on.

'Nasty,' Nelly thought, 'that's what she is, nasty; and underhand; running after a married man; leading him on; and all the time pretending to be so friendly with his wife; and if she thinks it isn't noticed she's wrong, because it is.'

At this point in Nelly's thoughts the dance music changed to a talk and she wiped her hands on her flowered cotton apron before switching over to the other programme. Back at the sink her mind insisted upon turning in two directions at once.—Ten of them to dinner and would the farm remember to send up the extra chickens in time—they should have a piece of her mind if they didn't—and should she take it on herself to warn Laura about what was going on under her very nose if only she wasn't too blind to see it. This question had occupied Nelly for some time now and it was a ticklish one, for she wasn't one to make trouble—always running from one to the other with some story or other; and there was always the chance that the whole thing would blow over. On the other hand, it was probably only right that someone should drop a hint to Laura; but then again, and here she was at the crux of the matter, Laura, seemingly so friendly, so unstuck-up, was, when it came to anything serious, so curiously difficult to approach. It was odd, Nelly thought, you couldn't put your finger on it and yet it was there.

She wished there was someone to whom she might go for advice; but the asking of advice from any of the women about the place would only lead to gossip and further talk, and talk never did anyone any good; talk only made things worse. There was her husband, of course, but Nelly would never have dreamt of asking Arthur about anything like that, there was a disloyalty, albeit only dimly apprehended, about bringing men into a thing like that. Men made enough trouble as it was without bringing them into things.—But she would tell Laura, she would tell her tomorrow morning when they were supposed to be discussing the menus. Nelly drew in her breath sharply, marking her decision.

She wouldn't have to say very much, a hint would be enough.—'And will Mrs Martell be staying over the weekend?' a perfectly proper question for a cook to ask; and then, 'I expect she'd like to stay here always,' and then—and then what? 'Everybody's saying that she's in love with Mr West'—'Everybody's saying that Mr West is in love with her.' Even with the safe anonymity of the 'everybody' she wouldn't be able to get it out, not to Laura, and although she was alone, although she had not even said the words aloud, Nelly felt a blush mounting to her cheek. But she would do it, somehow she *would* do it, see if she didn't. It wasn't right that Mrs Martell should have things all her own way, nasty thing!

But if she ever *does* come into this house, permanently that is, or if she ever does get Mrs West turned out of it, I shall go out too, the very self-same day, Nelly promised herself, and then remembered that most likely she wouldn't be able to do that for the house was her home. The four rooms which had been the laundry were furnished with Arthur's and her own furniture, and what hadn't been theirs when they arrived had been given to them by Mrs West, and it made a nice little home, self-contained and with a bathroom, and near Arthur's work and less than half a mile from young Jimmy's school—and not a single road for him to have to cross either.

But if that woman came, and here Nelly repeated her promise, only she knew that if Mrs Martell ever did 'come in' she and Arthur and Jimmy would be out on their ears.

'Bitch,' Nelly said again, and hated Mrs Martell as much as if in fact she had just been dismissed by her. 'There ought to be a law against women like her, and there ought to be a law about people who stole other people's husbands; and about people who turned other people out of their houses.'

There *were* laws about that kind of thing, of course; but somehow, they never seemed to do one any good. In particular there was a law called 'enticement', a nice thing if Mrs Martell could be had up for that; and have her picture all over the Sunday press; that would show her up; that would show people what she was like. It might even take that silly smile off her face. But what was the use? It wouldn't ever happen, and she and Jimmy and Arthur would have to look for somewhere else to live; and just after Arthur had distempered the living-room, and she had been going to ask him to paper their bedroom. Roses would have been nice and wallpapers were coming in again now; and she could have had a pink quilt to tone in with it.

So hard had she been thinking that, without noticing it, Nelly had finished the washing up; she was quite taken by surprise. She glanced at the clock, getting on for twelve, she might as well start the potatoes; and there was Mr West's lunch to think about; but the rest of the cold beef and a salad would do for that with an omelette to begin with; and the beef would do for young Jimmy as well. As for herself, it would probably be bread and butter and another pot of strong tea.

'Call yourself a fool'—Nelly went into the scullery, where there was another sink, and on into the larder—'it's being alone so much that does it, you run away with yourself—I'm not saying that he hasn't 'looked at her'—more fool him; but he'd think twice before he'd break up his home for her.'

She returned to the kitchen carrying a willow-pattern dish on which was the cold beef—more fat on it than she remembered, but trimmed up and cut into thin slices it would be all right.

Time that girl was here—'that girl', the daughter of one of the local masons, was the part-time kitchenmaid; she was tied to her home by the fact that a year ago she had been delivered of an illegitimate baby which her mother refused to look after unaided.

A grey-haired, respectable-looking man put his head round the door and asked Nelly whether she knew that ten were expected to dinner this evening.—'I thought I'd mention it in case Madam had forgotten.'

'That's all right, I did know, I had her on the phone this morning when you'd gone up to your breakfast.'

'Young Norah not turned up yet?' and Mr Hackett clicked his tongue sympathetically. He didn't altogether approve of Nelly, who, as he often remarked to Mrs Hackett, wasn't used to things and couldn't therefore be expected to 'know', but he knew a worker when he saw one; and Nelly, despite the deplorable state in which she habitually kept the kitchen, was certainly a worker. Also, she was a very pretty woman which of course had quite a lot to do with his amiable feelings towards her.

'Cup of tea, Mr Hackett, or is it too near your dinner time?' Nelly, for her part, didn't whole-heartedly approve of Mr Hackett—too narrow, and too set in his ways; but then what could you expect of someone who had been a butler all his life?—Most exciting time *he'd* ever had was in the 1914 war when they'd sent him to France.

Mr Hackett said that if Nelly didn't mind, it *was* rather near his dinner-time and he offered Nelly a cigarette.

'Any idea what the menu's going to be?' This was not idle curiosity, Mr Hackett had to know the menu in order that he might get out his silver and lay his table.

'Cold consommé, boiled salmon, chicken and a sweet, think that will do?'

Mr Hackett thought that it would, unless Nelly would like to put in asparagus, and did she want him to send up his boy to meet the fish off the train?—'You know what they are about sending it down.'

Nelly said that that would be very kind and that the station were getting a bit much of a good thing.

'You see,' Mr Hackett said, triumphantly pursuing an ancient argument, 'you've got to come to it, it's nationalisation.'

'Nationalisation hasn't got anything to do with it, it's just bone laziness—that, and being allowed to do just as they liked in the army.'

Mr Hackett said, now, now, he hadn't meant to upset her and that everyone was entitled to their own opinions.

'All I meant was it's silly to go and vote Conservative, and it's not fair to keep blaming Labour for everything that happens.'

Mr Hackett said that people ought to vote according to what they felt; and that it was no good being swayed first by one side and then by the other.

'Have it your own way,' Nelly said pacifically, 'but I still think it's silly.' She searched for a less controversial subject.—'I hope this isn't going to be one of young Norah's days for not turning up at all. Arthur will give me a hand when he comes in of course, but he'll probably be late.'

'I could send Robert down on his bicycle to see what's happened,' Mr Hackett offered.

'It isn't really worth while; if she hasn't turned up it's because she's ill or something. She was saying yesterday that the kid wasn't looking too good.'

'There's her mother to look after it, isn't there?' Mr Hackett was disapproving.

But here, conversation was brought to an end by the scuffling return from school of Nelly's son Jimmy. Mr Hackett retired hastily to the sanctity of his pantry.

Mrs Martell devoted the first part of her taxi drive with Mr Hardy to getting him to invite her out to luncheon. They had just about reached the Haymarket when she succeeded.

'But that's sweet of you,' Mrs Martell said, 'only it will have to be a very very quick luncheon because of going down to Shropshire with poor Laura.'

'What was the matter with her, anyhow?' Mr Hardy said; 'I didn't get it.'

'Poor Laura,' and Mrs Martell sighed. 'Well, you know how emotioned some people are; she's my cousin, of course, and of course I'd do anything for her; but she can be very demanding.'

'Bit much, wasn't it, expecting you to rush off to Shropshire like that at a moment's notice?'

Mrs Martell allowed that it was not convenient, suggested that Laura was inclined not to think of others, and gave it as her opinion that there was probably no valid or sensible reason why

Laura should demand her presence at Abbotsmere that very afternoon.

To all of which Mr Hardy replied that Laura was extremely lucky to have Cathie.

'Oh, I don't know about that,' and Mrs Martell cast down her eyes, the lashes fluttered on her cheeks. 'One does what one can, and I'm terribly sorry for Laura. Of course, it's all terribly trying for her husband.'—Without actually saying it she had managed to hint that Laura was not quite responsible for her actions, or, at best, that she was suffering from a nervous breakdown.

'She's very pretty,' Mr Hardy said.

'Yes, isn't she?' Mrs Martell looked up sharply, this was not the way she had planned the conversation to continue.

Mr Hardy left Mrs Martell at her bank, they would meet again in about two hours' time.—Bus journeys to and fro across London and packing to be done into the bargain. Despite the pleasure of going to Abbotsmere Mrs Martell felt resentful towards Laura. If she had only let her know last night, there would have been time for the washing and drying of underclothes and her best nightgown—now Ruth would have to post them on to her. Laura was completely thoughtless.

Luncheon with Mr Hardy was a success. The Feature Editor had been pleased with the story; Mr Hardy was more than grateful to Mrs Martell.

'When will you be coming back to town?'

Mrs Martell wasn't sure, not anyhow until after the weekend.

'There's a first night on Wednesday that might be rather fun.'

Mr Hardy had chosen well, Mrs Martell was immediately interested.—'If I can possibly leave poor Laura.'

Mr Hardy said, oh good heavens! and that he would call for her at about a quarter to seven. Now he would have to get hold of the *Sunday World Post* tickets, but there shouldn't be much difficulty about that. The *Sunday World Post* hardly ever gave more than three lines to its theatre criticisms, and there was seldom much competition for the tickets it received for first nights.

Mrs Martell and Mr Hardy dawdled over their coffee and mutually considered each other.

Mrs Martell was in very little doubt but that Mr Hardy was definitely an asset. A personable young man who was in a position to take her to first nights.—He needed smartening up, of course, but that shouldn't be difficult. Cathie was quite good at smartening people up, and last night had been an indication that he would probably make a satisfactory lover. Mrs Martell, leaning forward to have her cigarette lit for her, smiled an experienced smile at Mr Hardy.

Mr Hardy, smiling back at her, merely considered that he had got hold of a very pretty woman. Also, and without his being exactly aware of it, he had been impressed by the description of Abbotsmere which Cathie had taken care to give him while they were eating.

Mrs Martell arrived at the station with only a few minutes in which to catch the train; but it didn't matter, Laura would be waiting for her at the barrier, and Laura would have kept a seat for her. Mrs Martell, walking a few steps in advance of her porter, was a commanding figure, her head was held high, her smile was gracious, and her hat and suit were perfect for travelling; had in fact been chosen for travelling and for being met by other people's chauffeurs at country stations. But by rights it should have been her own chauffeur who met her, her own stately front door at which she descended; and soon, very soon, it *would* be. Mrs Martell, smiling a recognition at a hatless Laura, was determined about that. Edward should be *made* to come up to scratch; in the bustle of the crowded platform she had no time to arrange the thought in a more suitable form of words.

They reached their compartment, which Mrs Martell saw they were to share with a Bishop (who was being seen off by a curate wearing a cassock); an elderly lady and a prosperous-looking man in a blue suit—Mrs Martell suspected him of being in business in Birmingham. On the floor between her own seat and Laura's there was a brown carton tied around with string and partly open at the top.

'Look,' Laura said immediately, 'aren't they perfectly sweet.'

Mrs Martell, peering into the carton, saw two small wriggling bodies.

'What on earth?' Mrs Martell was disapproving.

They were pekinese puppies.

The train started and Mrs Martell, glancing at the Bishop, suggested that the puppies would be happier in the corridor.

Laura didn't agree with her. 'I know,' Laura said, 'that one shouldn't *ever* buy them from a dog shop, but they looked so sweet in the window, or at least one of them did, and I got the other to be a companion to it.'

'They must have been very expensive.'

And, because they had been, Laura didn't answer.

—'They looked so sweet in the window'—'I was so terribly unhappy and I was going to be alone for four hours and I couldn't bear it,' The second explanation was nearest to the truth; but Laura was hardly aware of it.—An unhappiness which comes only once or twice in a lifetime; a melancholy which is so complete that against it there is no help, no, not even in a psychiatrist's consulting-room.

Mrs Martell peered again at the dogs; was relieved to see that as they no longer wriggled they could be presumed to be asleep and turned to Laura.

'Now then, what's all the excitement about?' Her voice was calm, sympathetic and astringent; thus might a private nurse, of the more sycophantic variety, have spoken to her patient.

'There's no excitement really,' and Laura glanced fearfully at her fellow passengers; the Bishop was immersed in a newspaper, the business man had closed his eyes, only the elderly lady, seated beside Laura, stared straight in front of her, a potential listener to other people's conversations.

'If I'd thought it would be inconvenient,' Laura said, 'I wouldn't have asked you, only I thought you liked coming to Abbotsmere for the week-end.'

Mrs Martell let the remark pass in silence. Laura must not be encouraged to think that coming to Abbotsmere was a convenience to herself. Mrs Martell came to Abbotsmere *solely* to please her cousins.

'Of course we always love having you'—Laura had been brought up by her guardian to be polite; and Mrs Pemberthy's favourite bible story was that of Sarah and Abraham taking off their shoes and waiting personally on their guests as they dined. *There*, Mrs Pemberthy said, was true hospitality and a beautiful example of the spirit in which an English lady should receive her guests.

'I don't know what we should have done without you,' Laura said, and then, as Mrs Martell still remained silent, 'you've been simply wonderful to us.'

'Nonsense,' Mrs Martell said, and then, 'one does what one can.'

'It isn't anything very particular,' Laura said, 'only I've got these doctors coming, and after it was all arranged I thought that Edward might be cross about it.'

'Doctors!' Mrs Martell frowned. 'Not staying in the house, are they?' She put her head on one side, considering such a fantastic possibility.

'They're very nice,' Laura said; 'anyhow Mr Gideon is, I don't really know Sir George.'

Mrs Martell pursed her lips.

'You don't think I was wrong, do you?' Laura said anxiously.

'Have you told Edward?'

'Well no, that's the point, I haven't, and they're arriving this evening, they're taking the next train after us.'

'Really, Laura!' Mrs Martell's voice was no longer sympathetic; the private nurse had reached the end of her patience, very soon she would announce that she must throw up the case. Then she smiled. Laura was quite exasperating, quite irresponsible; but wasn't that a good thing? The more exasperating, the more irresponsible Laura was, the less could any man be expected to go on living with her.

'They're not coming exactly as guests,' Laura said. 'I mean they will be guests; but they'll be doctors as well, if you see what I mean.'

'Mr Gideon's a gynaecologist, isn't he?' Mrs Martell's smile had become very knowing; she was the progressive mother explaining frankly and without embarrassment the facts of life to a backward child.

'Yes,' Laura whispered.

The elderly lady waited, the Bishop turned over a page of his paper, the business man slept on, the puppies started to whimper.

'We'll talk about it in the car, shall we?' and Mrs Martell directed a glance of disapproval at the elderly lady.

The journey continued uneventfully. The Bishop got out at Rugby; through the window Laura could see that he was being met by a clergyman wearing a cassock. The elderly lady moved into the vacated corner seat. The puppies whimpered and the elderly lady, who said that she was used to dogs, told Laura that they would be difficult to rear.

'You can never be sure of a peke until it is six months old.'

'They said in the shop that two were easier than one; if you only have one they get lonely and need hot-water bottles.'

The elderly lady said that in her experience it was a mistake to buy dogs out of shops. Distemper! and now there was hard-pad.

'But they'll be in the country,' Laura pleaded; 'there won't really be anyone for them to catch it from.'

The elderly lady told several stories of 'dogs she had known' who had died of the disease. One of the puppies started to bark on a high uncertain note. The business man woke and told it that it was a sporting little fellow. Mrs Martell read her book; she would not be involved in this fraternisation with uninteresting fellow travellers.

They arrived, and were met at the station by a hired car. The days when there had been an Abbotsmere chauffeur were over, the last one had disappeared into the war and had returned from it only to work in a garage. Mrs Martell wondered if it would ever be possible to employ another and decided that 'later on' she would do something about it. Her dream chauffeur was dark and good-looking and touched his cap on every opportunity.

The driver of the hired car was very interested in the puppies, wanted to know their names, said that he was very fond of dogs, and warned Laura about hard-pad.

Laura said that they hadn't really got names yet, she had thought of 'Constantia' and 'Augustus'.

'Bit of a mouthful, wouldn't it be?'

'I expect they'd get shortened in the end, but they would do as a beginning. Oh dear, I do hope Edward's going to like them.'

'So you haven't told Edward about the dogs either,' Mrs Martell said.

'Well, there wasn't time, I only got them just before we left. I suppose I could have telephoned to him, but it would have been so awful if he had said, no, not to bring them.'

The partition which should have divided the driver from Laura and Mrs Martell was down. Mrs Martell, after several attempts to do so herself, asked him to put it up.

The driver said that he couldn't, because it didn't work any longer; all the teeth were torn off the ratchet.

Mrs Martell shrugged her shoulders, as who should say really these people are impossible; but the implied rebuke was lost on the driver, who was looking straight ahead of him. Mrs Martell lowered her voice.

'Laura, what on earth induced you to ask Mr Gideon to come to Abbotsmere?'

'It was his idea,' Laura said, 'and he's got to see Edward somewhere, so it might as well be here.'

'But surely the place to see a doctor is in his consulting-rooms, and anyhow'—for Mrs Martell was consumed by curiosity—'why does he have to see Edward?'

'To make sure that it isn't him who can't have a baby.'

'Really, Laura!' For a variety of reasons Mrs Martell was very shocked.

'But it's best to be sure, isn't it?' Laura asked. Her voice trailed off, she wasn't certain any more that it *was* best. A plan which had seemed sensible and wise when she had discussed it with Mr Gideon yesterday afternoon now seemed to be silly and imprudent; and she hadn't told Mr Gideon that she would not tell Edward that he was coming. Would not tell him, that is, until it was too late to do anything about it, for Mr Gideon was already on his train.

'You must be mad,' Mrs Martell said; her voice was loud and the driver moved uneasily in his seat.

Laura didn't say anything; she sat unhappily in her corner holding the carton which contained Constantia and Augustus on her lap.

'If they have a room to themselves with newspapers on the floor, I don't see how Edward can really mind about them; he needn't even meet them if he doesn't want to.'

Mrs Martell said nothing; she hoped that the dogs would be one more nail in the coffin of Laura's doom. But, whatever else happened, Laura must not have a baby, must not have a son.

They reached the lodge gates, which stood open. Mrs Martell would have preferred for them to have been shut and for a curtseying lodge-keeper to have come out and opened them in answer to a summons from the horn. But there was no lodge-keeper and the lodge was occupied by a family who had first come here as evacuees and never returned to their original slum.

Edward, in the library, heard the car drive up to the front door. He heard the peal of the front-door bell by which Laura announced their arrival. He heard their voices in the hall, and the slow footsteps of Hackett as he came up the stairs which led to his pantry. Edward heard all these things, but he did not go out to greet Laura and Cathie. He remained where he was, sitting in a chair by the fireplace, a glass on the table at his side.

'Darling, where are you?' It was Laura.

'Mr West is in the library, madam.'

'Oh thank you, and, Hackett, I've got some dogs. Nelly will have to find them something to eat; I'll come down and see her later.'—'Darling!' and Laura opened the library door; followed by Cathie, she came into the room. Edward got up.

The next quarter of an hour was not very pleasant. Laura, whose courage had failed her at the last moment, had to be prompted by Cathie to tell Edward about the imminent arrival of the doctors. And Edward was perfectly furious.

'But, darling, it will be very interesting and I had planned it as a surprise.'

Edward, standing with his foot on the fender, turned and told her that she must be crazy.

'I thought it was rather a sensible idea.'

'You must be crazy,' Edward said, 'the place to see a doctor is in his consulting-rooms.'

'You see,' and Cathie looked accusingly at Laura.

'Now look here . . .' Edward began.

Laura begged him not to be cross.

'I'm not in the least cross, only I *forbid* you to fill the house with doctors, do you understand?'

'But it's too late, they're already on the train; and I've ordered a car to meet them, so there isn't anything we can do about it.'

'I shall give orders for them to be driven away again the moment they arrive at the front door.'

'You can't do that, it would be too rude, and anyhow, I don't expect they'd go.'

'You had no right to invite them here against my wishes and without telling me.'

'I'm sorry,' Laura said.

'Had you forgotten you'd asked a lot of people to dinner this evening; that's going to make it rather awkward for you, isn't it?'

'I didn't put them off on purpose. I thought it would some-how make it better.'

'So you have people to dinner in order that they may meet your doctor and hear all about your private life?'

'Doctors don't talk about that sort of thing at dinner.'

Mrs Martell had pulled off her hat and sat, leaning back a little, in an upright chair; her arm was thrown carelessly over the arm of the chair, her beautiful ankles were crossed, a little sympathetic smile played round her lips. She was enjoying herself very much. Now Edward, ignoring Laura, looked across at her.

'Who was coming to dinner this evening, do you know?'

'Only the Templetons with their daughter, and Robert and Diana.'

'Oh, damn!'

'Edward,' Laura said, 'promise you'll be nice to Mr Gideon.'

Hackett came into the room. 'Shall I let the little dogs out, madam?'

And then of course there was another row centred round Constantia and Augustus. Edward was so irritated that he refused even to look at them. They must live out their lives in the disused conservatory, or they must be returned to the shop from whence they came, for preference they must be returned to the shop; but whatever happened they were *not* to come into the house.

'But we can't possibly keep them in the conservatory, it's too draughty.'

'You should have thought of that before you bought them.'

'But I didn't buy them to keep in the conservatory.'

Edward turned his back on Laura while he explained to Cathie that he would not have objected to a dog, he was not after all unreasonable, but puppies! All over the carpets, and it would be months before they were broken to the house.

'But they're practically trained already,' Laura said.

The wrangle over the doctors was superseded by the wrangle over Constantia and Augustus. The greater evil was forgotten in the less. Laura said that the puppies could live in the small room next the kitchen.

'Anyhow Nelly will be nice to them.'

Constantia and Augustus were removed from the hall, replaced in their carton and carried downstairs by Laura. Hackett had already tactfully disappeared; Edward and Cathie were left alone.

'She's impossible,' Edward said.

'I did my best'—Mrs Martell's voice was smooth, insinuating—'but she's so headstrong. Half the time I don't think she knows what she is doing.'

Edward sighed deeply, he wanted to be reassured; he felt that his anger about the dogs had been slightly ridiculous; only it was not about the dogs that he had been angry.

'Robert and Diana are going to think that it's the most extraordinary party.'—Mrs Martell was impressed by Robert and

Diana. Colonel and Mrs Templeton were of no account anyhow, so it didn't matter what they thought.

'It says in the book that everything they eat must be very finely chopped.' Laura leant against the kitchen table and talked to Nelly. The puppies, happy for the first time since they left their shop, played about on the floor. They were very interested in all the saucers which had been put down for the cat, they found a cabbage leaf and they thoroughly explored the recess under the sink. Nelly was delighted with them, and indignant that they had been banned from the rest of the house.

'Did you ever hear anything like it!'

'Oh well,' Laura said, and then, 'is it all right about dinner?' which of course it was, 'and you told the refugees about getting the rooms ready for Mr Gideon and Sir Henry Moorhouse?'

And of course Nelly had, and the refugees had seemed to understand.

'That girl', who had after all turned up, came in from the scullery with a pile of dishes.

'I suppose I ought to go and change,' Laura said, but she didn't immediately move away, for, like the puppies, she was happy when she was in the kitchen; and this evening, after the disagreements with Edward, it was especially pleasant. Moreover, sweet added to sweet, Nelly's odious little boy was not here; probably he was somewhere in the park, tearing branches off the trees in the company of the evacuees from the lodge.

The dinner party when it took place was quite, quite terrible. The only people who enjoyed it at all were Robert and Diana, they were provided with a splendid story which they could tell against the Wests, so the party, from their point of view, was successful. The Templetons and their daughter, who were kind, were embarrassed for themselves and distressed for Laura.

Edward was simply furious.

Mr Gideon and Sir Henry were embarrassed and displeased. Laura was miserable. And Mrs Martell, who ordinarily would have enjoyed any situation in which Laura showed to disadvantage, had her pleasure ruined by dark thoughts of what Robert and Diana would say about the whole affair.

Things had begun to go badly from the moment when Mr Gideon and Sir Henry had arrived. They were greeted in a very unfriendly manner by Edward, his attitude was that since they were here they might as well stay the night, but that they had really been very foolish to come. He did *not* say that he suspected them of fee-chasing, or 'making a job' but the thought was there integrated in his manner, in the tone of voice in which he offered them a drink and showed them to their rooms.

Laura did not appear in the drawing-room until just before dinner. Her manner was nervous, her eyes rather too bright. She found Edward and Cathie exchanging stilted conversation with the guests—who weren't only guests but doctors who were here in their professional capacity. It was a relief when the Templetons arrived; the Templetons could be counted upon to be co-operative. Robert and Diana were late. They went into dinner; already the atmosphere was strained and things got worse as the meal proceeded. The food was excellent, Hackett's waiting (he was helped by the boy, whom he kept as far as possible in the background) was adequate. Only the guests were not satisfactory, at no point did the party come together, or get into its stride.

Laura became more and more nervous; looking down the table at Edward she was in no doubt but that he was very angry. He spoke not at all to Mrs Templeton and very little to Diana. When they were all gone he would be really angry with her. But Mr Gideon and Sir Henry would not go, they would remain until tomorrow. They would remain, and between them they held her fate. If they gave it as their opinion that she was incapable of having a child but that Edward was not, then . . . then what? 'It would be nicer if we neither of us could,' Laura thought, and answered Robert at random. Robert looked at her rather strangely and did not try any further remarks.

'And it isn't even as if I liked babies,' Laura thought—'Edward didn't like babies either, but he ought to have a son; a clean quiet little boy in a sailor suit; who would come into the dining-room after luncheon and then be whisked away again by a nurse. A little boy who would be the great-great-grandson of

Lady Cornelia.'—But did little boys still wear sailor suits, she didn't think so. The little boy in a sailor suit belonged to a period long long ago; she had met him at the children's parties to which she had been taken by Mrs Pemberthy.

Laura's son was much younger than Mrs Martell's. Too young as yet to dance attendance upon his mother, or accompany her to cricket matches. His features were indistinct, but once, long ago, she might have met him at a children's party.—And then, from the other end of the table, she heard a voice, cool and insolent. And Laura experienced a moment of intense hatred. It took her completely by surprise; usually, if she wanted to hate somebody, she had to work herself up to it, but this hatred came without being called on.—The unhappiness that comes only once or twice in a lifetime—and from out of her misery she heard her own words clear and light. She heard her own voice telling them all exactly why Mr Gideon and Sir Henry were here, and she was telling them in a voice which she did not recognise.

6

MRS HARTLEY-JAMES, sitting on her balcony, looked out with some dissatisfaction at the garden in front of her flat. The garden, then the broad motor road, then the grass lawn and concrete path of the parade; and below them, and of far less interest the beach and the sea. There was nothing that could properly be complained of about the beach, no authority who could be written to about the sea, at this point on the south coast it did not corrode the land, it very seldom even splashed over the parade. But everything else, beginning with the garden, was a constant source of her complaints. The garden belonged to 'downstairs' and 'downstairs' was a retired colonel and his wife. They planted marigolds in the flower border, marigolds of all things; they rolled the grass with a creaking roller; and were constantly to be observed sitting in the garden in striped canvas chairs and chattering to each other. They were a disturbance, an annoyance, and a nuisance, and they never even went away for a holiday; but remained in stubborn constant occupation of their flat.

The Colonel was there now, using the roller; his wife sat in one of the striped chairs and talked to him—would they never cease saying things to each other? Mrs Hartley-James coughed, a stern admonitory cough, and went indoors shutting the glass door after her. She was in her bedroom—it was one of the inconveniences of the flat that the way on to the balcony lay through her bedroom and not through the sitting-room.

Mrs. Hartley-James' bedroom was not only the place where she slept, it was a temple of memories. On the walls there were framed, and usually tinted, photographs of herself when she had been younger and prettier than she was now; there were views of the prettier parts of Switzerland; and there were photographs of her parents; there were photographs of the handsome man who had been her husband, and who had behaved so very wrongly in the 1920's and who was now presumed to be dead, and, of course, there were the photographs of Cathie. Cathie as a little simpering girl in white muslin, Cathie in various stages of growth and adolescence, Cathie as a bride, Cathie against a background of palm trees, and finally, Cathie with her hips turned at just the right angle to the camera, on the lawn at Abbotsmere.

From the number of these photographs the casual observer (not of course that there were, apart from constantly changing charwomen, many casual observers in Mrs Hartley-James' bedroom) might have thought that Mrs Hartley-James was extremely fond of her daughter; she was, but, as the years had gone on, she had become jealous of her.

It was all very well for Cathie, things had gone well for her—and here, Mrs Hartley-James magnificently ignored quite a lot of Cathie's life, including the marriage to Mr Martell—whereas Cathie's mother had never been anything but unfortunate. Unfortunate in Mr Hartley-James, unfortunate in her sister Violet who had chosen, when the time came for her to die, to leave her money to Cathie instead of to her sister. Mrs Hartley-James could never understand it. At least Violet had not followed her original unnatural intention of leaving her money to the niece and nephews of her late husband, that would have been dastardly; but nothing could excuse her cutting her own sister entirely out of her will. Mrs Hartley-James could never quite bring herself to believe that Violet had meant her to have nothing at all. She must have been thinking of death duties; with the money left directly to Cathie there would only be one set of death duties, that was what Violet must have been thinking about when she made the will. But she had never meant Mrs Hartley-James *not* to have the money, or anyhow some of it, during her lifetime. Violet had meant Cathie to make her mother an allowance; but as she had left no letter, memorandum or instructions to this effect Cathie was free not to do so. But it wasn't what Violet would have wished—especially as Cathie was getting all that money from her ex-husband! The money from the ex-husband was, on the whole, a figment of Mrs Hartley-James' imagination, but by taking refuge in 'not understanding these things' it somehow gave her an extra grievance against Cathie.

Mrs Hartley-James glanced at the pale blue enamel travelling clock which stood on the table beside her bed. Nearly a quarter past three; if Cathie had caught the train due to arrive at three-ten she should be here in a few minutes.

It was Friday, exactly a week had passed since the unfortunate dinner party at Abbotsmere. Not that Mrs Hartley-James knew anything about the dinner party. Although naturally she knew that Cathie had spent the week-end at Abbotsmere. Abbotsmere, of course, was another of Mrs Hartley-James' grievances, as was the cousinship with Laura which, if it existed at all, and there were times when Mrs Hartley-James allowed herself to doubt even that, was through the best-forgotten Mr Hartley-James. It was letting oneself down, Mrs Hartley-James said, to 'run after people' and claim relationships with them.

She went into the spare bedroom which was next to her own. It was looking very nice, with a bunch of flowers on the dressing-table, and the new rayon bedspread with the interwoven border which went so nicely with the quilt—not that one needed a quilt in this weather, but its presence made the room look more attractive. Mrs Hartley-James straightened one of the oak-framed water-colour sketches which hung on the wall—a view of Dartmoor to include a bubbling brook and rushes—and looked approvingly at a Chinese print framed in black passe-partout, which long ago had been given her as a wedding present.

There was a ring at the front door; that would be Cathie. She must have come on the three-ten after all. Mrs Hartley-James had somehow not expected her until the four. Her hands went up to straighten her hair, she glanced quickly in the mirror, then she was hurrying down the hall—the passage was just wide enough to be called a hall. As usual, the door caught on the mat, the well was not deep enough; really she must have something done about it, it was too aggravating.

'Darling!' Mrs Hartley-James opened her arms to receive her daughter.

Mrs Martell, who was paying off her taxi, turned and kissed her mother on the cheek.

'How are you?' Mrs Hartley-James said, and 'you're looking thinner.' She stooped to pick up the lighter of Mrs Martell's two suitcases and preceded her down the hall and into the spare room.

Mrs Martell said that she was all right really, and sighed deeply. She told her mother that she was looking well. They really had very little to say to each other; but actually confronted with her daughter, after a separation which had lasted several weeks, Mrs Hartley-James ceased, for the time being, to be jealous of her and was filled with admiration.—She was really extraordinarily handsome and how beautifully she wore her clothes—that suit, for instance.

'I was sitting on the balcony,' Mrs Hartley-James said.

'All right, I'll just do some unpacking and I'll come and join you.' Mrs Martell went over to the dressing-table and took off her hat. She didn't say anything about the sweet-peas in their cut-glass vase and Mrs Hartley-James was disappointed.

'You've got everything you want, dear?' But the question was only formal and Mrs Hartley-James returned to the balcony.

Mrs Martell, sitting in front of the dressing-table, combed her hair and redid her mouth. She composed the mouth into a smile, turning the head a little on one side, then she tilted her chin forward, resting it in her hand. She fluttered her lashes on her cheeks. Seen like this through half-closed eyes, she looked almost pathetically young. She suppressed a sigh, because in her heart she knew that she was beginning to be old.—Death and decay and it was possible that such things should happen to her.—Anyhow, I shall never go in for pink shaded lights; but she had forgotten that the lampshades in her bedroom in Baker Street were pink. Pink shaded lights, or lampshades which happened to be coloured pink; in her mind they were not the same thing. But beauty and youthfulness were to be judged by results, and at this very moment there were two men who were in love with her. And one of them at least might be described as being desperately in love; but that was not the one she was determined to marry, although Edward *would* marry her in the end, she was determined about that; and without her having noticed it her lips had drawn themselves into a thin line. But such an expression could never go unnoticed for more than a second or two. She smiled at herself in the glass, a sweet understanding smile, a smile of comfort and commiseration. Poor Edward, how could he go on putting up with Laura? And then for the first time Mrs Martell noticed the sweet peas on the dressing-table. How extravagant of her mother when they were still so expensive! But her first feeling had been one of pleasure.

On the lawn at Abbotsmere Laura played with Constantia and Augustus.

'I love you more than anyone in the world,' Laura said to Constantia, who wagged her tail enthusiastically, evidently transported with delight; but it didn't matter what you said to Constantia she always wagged her tail. Augustus didn't, he was more serious.

'You're so much nicer than any children could possibly be'— Laura picked up Augustus—'and you'll never get to the stage when you'll start being horrid to me, you'll just get nicer and nicer as the years go on.'

Augustus struggled to be free and Constantia wagged her tail in passionate agreement.

Hackett was coming out of the house, almost certainly coming to tell her that she was wanted on the telephone; why could one never be peaceful? But if one was peaceful one was also lonely. Regretfully Laura put the puppies back into their play-pen, which had been grudgingly made for them by Mr Seymour. Mr Seymour had once been the house-carpenter, but was now set up for himself as a builder and decorator and didn't really care about doing odd jobs. The cage which he had constructed for Constantia and Augustus had wire-netting sides, and they spent nearly all their time in learning to climb out of it.

'A telephone message from Mr West, madam,' Hackett said. 'He has been detained in London and won't be back this evening.'

'Thank you,' and Laura saw the rest of the afternoon and the evening spreading out into infinity. She was terribly and devastatingly alone, and why had Edward sent a message instead of speaking to her himself?

'Did he say when he was coming back?'

'Tomorrow, madam, I imagine.'

'Thank you,' Laura said again, and was depressed out of all proportion to the cause.

Hackett turned and left her. Laura imagined that there had been disapproval in his voice. She was unfortunate in that she minded so very much what people thought of her.—'But probably everyone minds really, and everyone is afraid.'

'There now,' Ethel said, as Edward came back from using the telephone in the hall, 'I'm sure that's set your mind at rest.'

Edward grinned, somewhat shamefacedly.

'And now, we'll have a nice cup of tea.'

Edward sank down into one of the easy chairs which creaked a little and shifted on its bad leg.

'With a drop of whisky in it,' Ethel promised, 'because you really aren't looking at all grand.'

'It was lucky meeting you like that,' Edward said; 'though what either of us was doing in that store I can't imagine.'

'I'd gone in to get some elastic'—Ethel was taking the tea things off the dresser—'but you're a bad boy to wait until you "happen" to run into me, you ought to come and see me oftener.' She was looking at him as if he were still a child, as if he were still one of her boys—the elder one, the one who's inclined to be delicate, when I first went to them he was no more than a skeleton, poor little chap.

Edward looked fondly at Ethel. She must surely be into her seventies by now; but somehow she didn't seem to look so very different from the way she had when she had walked down Sloane Street with him and Charles and they had shopped for shoes at Peter Yapps. And she had stayed with them through their early schooldays, and then, when Charles was almost ready to go to Eton, she had married. She had married a butler, not their own Mr Hackett but a strange butler from the other side of the Park, and together they had retired to S.W.10 where, in a large grey house, they had let out rooms. They had been doing that ever since, through the years of depression, and the years of plenty, and right through the war and the Blitz and on into the post-war world which appeared to be just a prolonged period of clearing up, with everything temporary and 'for the time being'; only now Mr Belton didn't 'valet' the gentlemen any more, for one thing Mr Belton was getting on and for another the gentlemen no longer seemed to have any money.

'It must be nearly two years,' Ethel said reproachfully as she lit the gas fire. 'I don't believe I've seen you more than twice since your wedding.'

Edward smiled at her with affection; but at the same time he wondered exactly why he should be supposed to see Ethel at regular intervals.—She had been very close to him for fourteen years and afterwards he had stayed at her house from time to time—when it had never been so convenient as it was in rooms where he was not on such intimate terms with the landlady, and where he was not expected to sit in the kitchen or pause on the stairs in order to talk over old times.—Old times which had been talked over so often that there was nothing in the world that remained to be said about them.

'It was a pretty wedding,' Ethel said; 'not that it's any good talking about that now,' and then, 'she was too young for you.'

'Fifteen years isn't such a very great deal.'

'Pity that you couldn't have had it at Abbotsmere,' Ethel said. 'I always think there's something about a wedding in a village.'

'It was easier to have it in London, all our friends were there'—arguing about it as if it mattered, as if it was important that she should be made to see his point of view.

'I don't know what you're to do now, really I don't,' Ethel said; 'she oughtn't ever to have done it.'

'Anything to draw attention to herself, I suppose'—but he didn't know if he believed what he said.

Ethel didn't answer. The kettle had boiled and she was busy making the tea, reaching for the caddy which stood on the mantelpiece (if she wasn't careful they were going to run short of tea again before the end of the month) and measuring out the spoonfuls—one for him and one for me and one for the pot, and another half-spoonful for luck and because it didn't do to be mean. She was upset really, though she wouldn't have admitted it to anyone.—Turning round from the elastic counter like that and seeing Edward just sort of standing there. It had given her a turn and her knees had started to tremble. She had been afraid for a minute that she was going to come over dizzy and would have to ask them for a chair—like that time in Derry and Toms, they had been very kind, but somehow she had never liked to go in there again—she would have hated that to have happened now and with Edward there to see her too. But it had been all right and the feeling had passed.—Silly to get those turns, and it wasn't the sort of thing you could ask a doctor about either, because it was really too silly.—'Hullo, Ethel, you're looking younger than ever'—she couldn't say the same for him, he was looking thoroughly ill if you asked her and . . . and, well, there was no other way of putting it, 'middle-aged.'

They had gone out into the street. Edward had wanted to give her tea in the restaurant but she wasn't going to have that, not when they could be at home in no time at all, and the bus took them almost to the very door. But then, before she could stop him, he had called a taxi. They hadn't talked very much at first, apart from the usual things—'How have you been keeping?' and 'How's Mr Belton?' and 'How's Mrs West, and Abbotsmere, it must be looking lovely?' But then, when they got down to the kitchen, it had all come out. (She didn't believe she had ever known him to talk so much. Even when he was a little boy he had always been secretive.) However, something must have started him off, because suddenly he was telling her about Mrs West not being able to have a baby, (and that was sad too even if there hadn't been Abbotsmere to be inherited) and about her having those doctors down there and telling everyone at the dinner table all about it.—And men didn't like that sort of thing, especially as she'd hinted in front of all of them that it might be Edward's fault that there wasn't a baby. Well, you couldn't expect a man to stand for that sort of thing! It was different for women, women had to get on with things, whatever happened, or whatever was said to upset them. And it had happened a whole week ago, but she could see that he was shaking all over as he sat there in her kitchen. She hadn't known what to say to him.

'Why don't you go away for a holiday?'—'They' always went away when things went wrong for them and there was nothing against it that she could see. It wasn't even as if it was a waste of time; for 'their' time was there to be done as they liked with.

There had been a lot of going away when Edward was a little boy. Brighton and Margate for chicken-pox and for his general state of 'being delicate'.—And deaths were another reason for going away and of course divorce.—Not that Edward's father and mother had ever actually divorced. Ethel, as she plodded up and down the Broad Walk in Hyde Park, or bought vests and pants at Edmunds and Orr, had been spared that humiliation; but there had been times when things had been 'difficult' and then Edward's mother had spent months together in the South of France, or sometimes in America.

'If I were you I should get right away,' Ethel said, and had a sudden realisation of how awful the last week must have been for Edward.—With Laura always there to remind him of the awful thing she had done and of the baby she couldn't have.

'I'm sorry for her,' Edward had said and wondered if he could tell Ethel about Mrs Martell.

'If you were to get right away, you'd probably feel quite different about it.'—He seemed to be calming down now.

And then Edward had surprised her by suddenly getting up and saying might he use the phone—he needn't have troubled to ask, it was a call-box anyhow.

'I don't think I shall go back tonight in any case; I want to think and I can't, when I'm surrounded by people.'

Ethel said that he was quite right and that he'd feel better now that he'd decided on something to do.

She went over to the cupboard for the whisky bottle. She didn't hold with whisky in tea in the usual way, but after one of her turns she somehow seemed to need it. Today it would do them both good.

Edward sat with his head supported on his clasped hands, his thumbnails pressed against the bridge of his nose. Nothing after all mattered so very much.

He watched Ethel as she came towards him, the white cup and saucer in her hand. The reflections from the electric light sparkled on the china.

'Thank you.' Edward put out a hand and took the cup from her.

'Are you sure you're feeling all right?' Ethel looked at him anxiously. 'Your eyes look heavy to me.'

That's what she used to say when she thought he had a cold coming on. And when the cold had run its course there was cod-liver oil and malt and then, after every second or third cold, the visit to Margate or Brighton.

—You need to get right away but not to Brighton or Margate. He might go up to Scotland, or, better still, he might get hold of old George Stimpson and go down to Hampshire. George had some very good fishing. Yes, he thought he would try ringing up George.

'If I were you,' Ethel said, 'I should go to Paris.'

The afternoon having become suddenly chilly, Laura carried Constantia and Augustus into the house. With Edward away she could set up their cage, well lined with newspapers, at the end of the library. The library was preferable to the drawing-rooms, preferable to her own sitting-room; it seemed somehow to be less empty. 'And I can read,' Laura thought, 'I can read and read and forget about absolutely everything,' but the trouble was that she never could get lost in a book, unless there was something else very exciting that she ought to be doing.

She wondered if she should go and tell Nelly that Edward wasn't coming back this evening so not to bother about dinner. But Hackett would have been sure to have told her already; and they would have commented on it and wondered at the reason.— As if they cared, Laura thought impatiently; and there isn't any reason why I shouldn't go and tell Nelly that I'll have dinner on a tray. And so, because she couldn't bear to be alone, she went down to the kitchen.

Mrs Martell finished her unpacking, or as much of it as she intended to do, and went out to join her mother. Fortunately the Colonel and his wife had disappeared, but the roller had been left in the middle of the grass, waiting for them to continue their labours. Mrs Martell sat down and looked out over the parade at the sea. It was an afternoon of clear light, but not of particular beauty. The sea was part of the furnishings of a south coast resort, and not something of freedom and adventure. It was diminished within the limits of a picture postcard, pretty but not exciting; not conducing to anything or anyhow not conducing Mrs Martell to thoughts of freedom.

'And I shall venture forth across the sea,' only it wasn't that kind of an afternoon. Dull, dull, dull, something to look at throughout years of tedious retirement. Or years of perambulator-pushing, or endless dreary terms at endless dull and uninspiring schools. A school procession passed along the parade, the children two by two, chattering in high toneless voices and at the end of the procession a bright games-mistress walking between her two admirers.—'May I walk with you this afternoon, Miss Smith?' and Miss Smith, of course, was only too delighted.

'Mother,' Mrs Martell said, 'I'm expecting a friend down on Sunday.'

'Oh.' Mrs Hartley-James considered the information, putting it against the amount and quality of the food in the larder and the meat-safe. She would have to go shopping again tomorrow; and she had thought that she had finished the shopping for the week-end.

'You won't have to bother about food; we shall probably go out.'

'Oh,' and Mrs Hartley-James was disappointed, 'I had asked Mrs Willis and Daphne to supper. Daphne isn't coming until tomorrow, otherwise you might have travelled down together.'

'Oh, Mother, how *could* you?'

'I have to ask Mrs Willis sometimes; and Daphne is very clever, I thought you liked her.'

Mrs Martell shrugged her shoulders. All her mother's friends were bores; how, in a place like this, could they be anything else? It wasn't even worth arguing about.

'Will your friend be staying the night?'

'I expect so; I'll have to see about getting him a room at the Queen's.'

—Him; Mrs Hartley-James became rather more interested. Perhaps Cathie was thinking of getting married again. Mrs Hartley-James always hoped that Cathie would remarry, it would cover up the scar left by the divorce.

Mrs Martell was well aware of the trend of her mother's thoughts, and very unfairly despised her for it. She didn't offer any details about Mr Hardy, or even disclose his name. Her mouth was drawn into its primmest lines.

'I had thought that if you weren't too tired, we might go down to the Pavilion this evening.'—Mrs Hartley-James was offering the only cultural pursuit which was (this evening) locally available, the Court Repertory Company.

Mrs Martell suppressed a yawn, and asked what they were 'doing'.

'A play called "The Glass something or other". Mrs Willis saw it on Tuesday and she said it was really quite good. Of course it isn't the same as London, but they're really quite "good".'

Mrs Martell graciously accepted to go and see the glass something or other; and then, an almost unprecedented concession, she offered to help Mrs Hartley-James get the tea ready.

Mrs Hartley-James was delighted and suggested that they should each have a boiled egg.—'Then we needn't bother about supper until we come back, but we might have a little cocktail just before we start,' and they were happily united in domesticity.

7

NELLY SAT at the kitchen table smoking, and drinking a cup of nice strong tea. There were no signs of 'that girl' or of the odious Jimmy. Laura came into the kitchen and told her the news about dinner. Nelly said that she'd already heard from Mr Hackett. She added that it was a pity because of the salmon.

'Couldn't you make it into kedgeree?' Laura said, vaguely, because that wasn't the point.

Nelly asked Laura if she wasn't ready for a cup of tea, and got up to make the drawing-room tea in the china teapot which, together with a cup and saucer, a plate of cucumber sandwiches, and a fruit cake, stood ready on a tray.

'Couldn't I just have a cup with you?'—and Laura sat down, putting her elbows on the table, and was pleasantly reminded of the war.

Nelly, who was also thinking of the war, sat down again, and said that for her part she always said that there wasn't anything like a brown teapot for a really *good* cup of tea.

'Those urns,' Laura said, 'weren't they absolutely disgusting?'

'Never cleaned them out,' Nelly said, 'that was the trouble, but we were all right in our department in the end, because we used to make our own. On the electric fire, turned upside down.'

Laura looked incuriously round the untidy kitchen; and thought how nice the two red geraniums, which stood in one of the windows, looked. Mrs Lacy had never had geraniums; nor would Mrs Lacy ever have allowed her to have tea in the kitchen.

'Don't you ever get bored?' she asked Nelly, 'or are the refugees good company?'

'They might be if I could understand a word they said, but as I don't, I usually give them their meals outside. No, I don't get bored particularly, but you couldn't say it was lively.'

Laura agreed with her, and she couldn't imagine Abbotsmere ever being lively again; not until it was turned into something else. A school perhaps or some kind of an institution.

'When my mother-in-law lived here they used to have about fifteen servants, and enormous house-parties.'

'That's like the place I was scullery-maid in before the war, Mrs Northcote's; I don't suppose that we'll ever see those days again.'

'I don't think I particularly want to,' Laura said.

'That's right,' Nelly agreed, and added that everything had to *change*—during the war Nelly had attended three out of a course of six lectures on political economy, and the fact that 'everything had to change' was one of the few things she remembered about it.—Everything has to change, the water goes on getting hotter and hotter and eventually the kettle boils.—She was uncomfortably aware that she had a wonderful opportunity, with Laura installed so comfortably in the kitchen, of 'dropping a word' about Mrs Martell.—'I wouldn't trust her further than I could see her', or, more elaborately, 'there's *one* change that wouldn't be for the better', but she hadn't got the courage.

They went on chatting about things of no importance.—The refugees; Nelly's suspicion that 'young Norah' might be going to have another baby. 'She denies it of course, but then so she did the last one until it was practically on the doorstep.' At one moment, unseen by either of them, Mr Hackett put his head round the door and withdrew, walking back to the pantry with disapproval. Nelly said that there was a fair going on at a neighbouring village.

'Only the two evenings, so if there isn't a dinner tonight, I thought I might get Arthur to take me over.'

A fair! Laura had only the happiest memories of fairs. Treats to Olympia and Ranelagh when she was a child; warm summer evenings in country villages; and once, unforgettably, a fair on the quay in a Cornish fishing village with the lights reflected in the still waters of the harbour and the familiar garish music sounding over the little houses and the tall fish stores to lose itself in the blue-black of the night.

'How are you going?' she asked Nelly.—But they would be going on Arthur's motor-bicycle, no excuse to offer to drive them over in the car. But she was lucky. Arthur's motor-bicycle was out of order. He and Nelly would be catching the bus. Immediately, Laura suggested the car, not listening when Nelly said that if she didn't want the bother of going out Arthur could drive it. How very much easier to forget one's own thoughts at a fair than sitting alone in the library reading a book. But ought they to offer to take any of the others? Mr and Mrs Hackett, or the refugees? Hadn't one always heard about the wonderful fairs in Poland; so probably the refugees would love to go to the fair, or wouldn't it be good enough for them? No performing bears, no exotic confectionery sold from trays by peasants in fancy dress, no bearded coachmen, no dance of the nursemaids—she had been thinking of Petrushka, of course; modern fairs, even in Poland, could no longer be like that.

She didn't dare suggest that the odious Jimmy should be left behind; obviously Nelly and Arthur would consider this a treat especially designed for him. Nelly went out to the room which had once been the servants' hall, but which was now exclusively used as a dining-room by the refugees, banished from the kitchen because of their lack of English.—She came back with the news that the refugees were very very grateful, but that, mysteriously, they were going to the fair the following evening, with friends—no one had known that the refugees had any friends.

'And they're in there, sewing away like maniacs,' Nelly reported, 'making themselves ball-dresses, I suppose.'

'Perhaps they'd like to look after Constantia and Augustus while we're out.'

Nelly said that she would tell them to do so.

Jimmy came in to know, what about his tea? and Laura went upstairs. She would have dinner early, and at eight o'clock they would start. Only three hours during which she would have to be alone.

Laura didn't realise that she had got into the way of counting each day in this manner; only four hours alone, only two hours until I am due to go out to dinner, only three hours until I can go to bed and sleep, forget everything in dreamless oblivion; only that much of stated time during which I can think.

'Paris!' Edward said to Ethel; 'what would I do in Paris?'

'That's up to you entirely, of course, but you said you wanted to be somewhere where you wouldn't be disturbed, where you could get off by yourself and think things out.—Or he could go down to Redbourne and see Cathie. Cathie could comfort him and make him feel that he wasn't a fool. That he wasn't weak and middle-aged and a failure.—'I want to speak today to those who have lost heart,' that had been a clergyman on the Light Programme, but 'the ones who had lost heart' were supposed to have had some very good reason for doing so. They faced death and irreparable disaster and, with the saints, they were to offer their sufferings to God.—But it was not to be supposed that the humiliation of Sir Henry and Mr Gideon could be offered to God. God, like Robert and Diana, would undoubtedly find it funny.—And the fact that Laura couldn't have a child? . . . Oh, what was the use, and hadn't he and Cathie talked endlessly round the whole thing at Abbotsmere?

He might telephone to Cathie, he might even go down and see her, take her by surprise; she would like that—and Edward imagined Cathie sitting rather sadly in her mother's flat—he had never seen it, so in his imagination he made it a little more dreary, a little smaller and a little more shabby than it actually was. Cathie would be sitting on a sofa—an old-fashioned horse-hair sofa. She would be sad and lonely and would, of course, be thinking of Edward; and then the doorbell would ring and he would be shown into the sitting-room.—At this point the flat became slightly larger in order to make room for a little maid in a starched cap and apron. The sort of little maid who had been employed in the lodgings at Brighton and Margate where Edward had stayed with Ethel when he was a child. He would be shown into the room and Cathie would jump up from the sofa, all the tedium of Sunday afternoon disappearing on the instant.—But why particularly Sunday, that was two days ahead. Anyway he arrived and she ran into his arms, and then . . . and then what? Nothing had been solved. There was nothing to be said that could alter anything at all.—He was suddenly sick and tired of the whole idea. What he needed was to get away. To go to his club, to go to a boxing match, to a public-house, or, as Ethel had suggested, to Paris. He was sick and tired of wom-en.—'I had sixpence, jolly, jolly sixpence'—he remembered the discordant voices of the men, and the stuffy sweaty smell of the room. It was in a saloon bar, somewhere near Bath, sometime during the war.

'More tea?' Ethel asked, 'or haven't you finished that yet?'

—Edward hurriedly gulped it down.

'It doesn't do,' Ethel said, 'to let things get on top of you; whenever I feel things getting on top of me, I say to myself "don't".'

—She could do that of course. She was an old woman who kept a lodging house and whose greatest dissipation was a drop of whisky in her tea.

'That was the trouble with your mother,' Ethel said, 'always worry, worry, worry.'

Edward frowned, he didn't want to think about his mother, not now, when he was tired of all women, not ever perhaps. He had been very fond of her but she had preferred Charles.—The fascinating, the almost perfect Mrs West, who had been so clever and wise, wise in what she faced and in what she chose to ignore and, whenever things became such that it was impossible any longer to ignore them, retiring discreetly to America to 'abroad'. Her life had not been easy, but it had held two compensations, a great love and Charles.

'Fascinating and clever,' and only the servants in her own house had known that she worried. 'The fascinating and beautiful Mrs West', that's what Cathie wanted to be. She thought that he didn't know that. She thought that she was being very clever, but she wasn't as clever as he was.

He got up, 'Well, Ethel, I must be off.'

'Already?' The old woman, broken off in the midst of her reminiscences, was disappointed, and yet perhaps it was just as well. There was the supper to get, and a letter to be written to her sister, as well as those socks, which ought to have been done this morning, to be washed through.

'You'll let me know what happens; you won't leave it so long the next time?'—But he would, he'd mean to get in touch with her, but he'd put it off and off until perhaps he wanted something (but that was foolishness, there was nothing nowadays that she could do for him) or they happened to meet accidentally like today. And then one day she'd see him and it would be for the last time. They'd neither of them know that it was the last time, but it would be.

Edward stooped to kiss her cheek. 'Of course I'll let you know, I'll send you a postcard from Paris'—but he hadn't decided yet if he would go there. 'Don't bother to see me out.'

But she was walking behind him up the stairs.

'Give my love to Abbotsmere when you get back.'

'I shall; why don't you come down there sometime for a holiday?'

'Perhaps I will.'

He was in the street.—The long rows of grey houses, the sooty gardens, and there was nowhere in the world where he had to be, they were not expecting him in Paris or at Abbotsmere or at his club, nor was Cathie expecting him at Redbourne, his time, all time, was utterly and entirely his own. He turned in at the doors of a public-house and ordered a double whisky. Green leather upholstery and blatant Tudor decorations, an old man sitting at a table sipping his beer with gentility, two genteel young men on stools at the bar, an ugly girl in a plum-coloured dress and hat sitting in a corner, her feet pressed close together, who watched for her young man. It wasn't what he wanted; if he had had anything in mind it wasn't this.

Edward finished his drink and ordered another. It was best to start an evening on a firm foundation.

There was the music, there were the jostling crowds, the smell of trampled grass, the smell of beer; but it wasn't dark yet; the fair could be seen for what it was; a collection of booths and tents set up in a field. There was an old-fashioned merry-go-round, and a tower down which you could slide sitting on a small coconut fibre mat.

Laura parked the car, and she and Nelly and Arthur walked towards the fairground. Nelly said that there seemed to be quite a lot of people. Arthur said that they were lucky in the weather. Laura came near to regretting that Jimmy had been left behind—he, at least, would not have been self-conscious.

They stopped in front of a shooting gallery, 'Like to try your luck?' Arthur asked. Nelly and Laura tried their luck, they did quite well, but not well enough to win a prize; neither, to his annoyance, did Arthur. He muttered that the whole thing was a ramp, and had another shillings-worth; a gang of small boys gathered to watch him.

The merry-go-round was slowing down, the brazen music died away; now there were only the little sharp noises from the shooting-gallery and the voices of the hucksters.

'Might as well have a ride,' Nelly said, but Arthur remained obstinately shooting at the little cardboard targets.

The music started again, the merry-go-round gathered speed. The young man in charge of it went between the riders collecting the fares. Laura, holding on to the twisted brass rod, was carried back more than twenty years.—Children's Day at Ranelagh, the hot afternoon, and Mr Pemberthy, and Mrs Pemberthy's friend, and the little girl who had been chosen to share this treat. There was a queue for the merry-go-round. Laura, looking up at the beige-coloured wool dress immediately in front of her, hated the wearer with unreasoning intensity, and there were large buttons down the back of the dress. As long as she lived, Laura would never have a dress of that colour, that horrible non-colour. All around her children were laughing and talking, but Laura stood in the queue, hot, and apprehensive of the ordeal which lay ahead of her, the curtseying grey horses; and always that oatmeal-coloured dress, shutting out the view, shutting out the air. And then at last, it was their turn, the close-ly-packed queue surged forward, they were climbing on to the horses, she was free for ever from the oatmeal dress and yet not free, for when she went down into hell there would be some-one in the crowd, immensely tall, wearing that dress. Only Mrs Pemberthy had said not to worry about hell, because quite likely it didn't exist at all. But Laura never worried about hell, why should she? The grey horses were very high above the ground. Tomorrow she and Mrs Pemberthy would be travelling back to Yorkshire where everything was much safer. The square house set behind the stone wall; and Miss Wilson would have returned from her holidays, and they would start again on long division; and after tea Mrs Pemberthy, wearing a mackintosh, would water *her* part of the garden as distinct from the part which be-longed to the gardeners. And Laura and Miss Wilson would go for long walks on the moors, and through the park which be-longed to Uncle Henry and Aunt Louisa. And there would be European History and the counties of England. European His-tory was quite incomprehensible—'Prepare for tomorrow', and Miss Wilson would smile brightly; and later, while Miss Wilson was busy with her embroidery, Laura would struggle to read two pages of small print—Frederick the Great, the Spanish Suc-cession, Richelieu—there was no meaning to it—'In some ways Laura is a very stupid little girl'—'Meanwhile in England . . .' but even England ceased to have any reality when it was muddled up with the history of Europe.

The merry-go-round was going faster and faster; terrified, Laura clung to the brass rod, but her hands were wet and sticky, she couldn't get a firm grip; she would not be able to hold on very much longer, already she was slipping sideways.

'Aunt Anne, when I am older, will I be able to go away to school?'

Mrs Pemberthy didn't think so; but there was plenty of time, they would have to see. In fact, Laura never did go to school. She remained with Aunt Anne (who was not her aunt) in the house in Yorkshire; and Miss Wilson stayed with them until Laura was seventeen. Twice every year for a fortnight at a time they came to London; the dentist, new clothes and 'treats' suitable to her age. Children's Day at Ranelagh, the pantomime, and Olympia, either the Military Tournament or the Circus. Later it was an Aldwych farce and an occasional concert, but Laura was not musical. She never met her own father and mother or her sisters. At first it had been decided that such a meeting would not be good for her, and when she was fifteen she had come to hate them; these strangers, who should not have been strangers, and who had deserted her. On the whole she was happy. She did not realise that she was very lonely, or that her upbringing was unusual. Mrs Pemberthy was not a recluse; people came to stay with her; but they were not young people. When she was away on visits Laura was left behind with Miss Wilson. Sometimes she would be asked to tea by Uncle Henry and Aunt Louisa; they were both immensely old, and Aunt Louisa had a tortoise-shell ear-trumpet and smelled of lavender water.

It was no use, her hands were slipping from the brass rod; she shut her eyes, waiting to fall; this was the end of everything.

'Now then, now then.' The voice was rough and admonitory.

She had not, after all, fallen into revolving space, and for one brief instant she was sorry.

She was being pushed back on to the grey horse and the ordeal was not over, would probably never be over, and she had lost her way of escape.

'Now then, now then.' The voice belonged to the man in shirt-sleeves who was in charge of the merry-go-round.

Laura burst into tears of which she was bitterly ashamed.

How long ago was it, over twenty years anyhow. But the same horses still revolved, the same music sounded in her ears. But they were going faster and faster, faster even than they had done at Ranelagh; and she began to feel giddy.

'I should never have married him,' Laura thought, 'I should never have married anyone,' but that wasn't true, there were people in the world with whom she could be happy. 'If only,' Laura thought, 'if only I wasn't frightened.' There was a dull pain in her head and eyes—'perhaps I am going to faint,' but you couldn't faint in the open air; only once, when she had been out shooting with Edward, she very nearly had fainted.—But it isn't that, it can't possibly be that.—A stuporous condition—dementia—and Aunt Anne lying in the dimly-lit room—tumour of the brain—but it had been worse before, before she had admitted to being ill.

Why hadn't Edward come back from London, why had he spoken to Hackett instead of to her?—They were going faster and faster; but suddenly her head cleared. A clot passing through the brain? But it couldn't do that without killing you.—When Byron died they found that he had the brain of an old man. But she wasn't as old as Byron. He had told them that he had the brain of an old man; but they hadn't believed him; when he died they found out that he had been right.

The air was cool against her face; the light was beginning to fade. She could so easily be happy. She had been happy during the war.

Sitting alone on the grass above the cliff, the sun beating down on bare arms and legs. And at other times surrounded by companions; going with them to the pub, and the jokes which had seemed so wildly funny. And Michael. She had imagined herself to be deeply in love with him. Perhaps she had been, she would never know. What way was there of judging what was 'deeply in love' and what was a passing infatuation; either way it was only words. Words arranged by the poets, or by women's magazines.—'Let me not to the marriage of true minds.' But what in fact, in actual fact, were true minds, and how could you recognise them? Recognise them without any possibility of being mistaken. At the time she had loved him; but she had made many mistakes.—'Which alters when it alteration finds.' He had begged her to marry him and she had refused. Later, when she had loved him most . . .—'Which bends with the remover to remove'—lying in the darkness, and endeavouring, at least, not to cry aloud; and then the war was over and she had met Edward again. He was much older than Michael, more serious, and far richer. But I didn't marry him for his money, truly I didn't do that. 'It wouldn't work,' Michael had said, and 'I am not good enough for you,' but that was only an excuse. And she had loved Edward, she still loved him; but she was terribly unhappy. 'Wherefore is light given to him that is in misery, and life unto the bitter in soul.'

They were revolving more slowly now and the music was dying away. Ahead of her Laura could see Nelly, who exchanged pleasantries with an unknown young man whose horse rose and fell beside hers. Looking across at the shooting gallery she could just make out Arthur. The music stopped and she climbed down. Nelly called that she was staying on for another go—and so, it appeared, was the young man. Laura shook her head, it would never do to feel faint again.

She wandered over to the stall where pennies were being rolled down little wooden contrivances on to squared oilcloth. If your penny fell fairly into a square without touching its edges it was returned to you with two or three others, sometimes with sixpence. It wasn't as exciting as a casino, but it was something.

'If only I knew what was happening,' Laura thought. But she was not thinking of Edward or of Mrs Martell. She was not thinking of Aunt Anne or of Michael. She was thinking of what was happening in her own mind; and that, of course, she would never know. If there is an answer it must be a mathematical one. Mathematics start somewhere near long division; and few people are able to follow them very much further than that.

Laura offered the young woman in charge of the stall a sixpenny piece, and received seven pennies in exchange. She thought it was a mistake, but the young woman said, no, they always gave change in that way at this stall. Laura put the pennies in a little pile beside her, and started rolling them on to the oil-cloth.

8

'PLATFORM SEVENTEEN, but I doubt whether you've the time to make it,' and then, or so it seemed to Mr Hardy, the booking clerk had been as slow as possible over issuing the ticket and giving him his change.

In spite of running all the way to platform seventeen Mr Hardy only just managed to fling himself into one of the last carriages as the train started to move. Mr Hardy was triumphant, but also very breathless and his heart thumped uncomfortably. He wondered, with annoyance, if he perhaps wasn't as young as he had been; and the thought did not give him pleasure.

He went out into the corridor in order that he might recover his breath in comparative privacy. Thirty, well thirty-one really, was no age at all. It was not an age at which one ought to give up running for trains, or at which one had to begin to be careful of one's health. On the other hand there was no doubt that his body demanded more of his attention now than it had done ten years ago. He had been guiltily aware for some time now that his stomach was not as flat as it had been in early youth, and only last week one of his colleagues had described it as a pot; it hadn't really reached that stage yet, of course, but it definitely wasn't flat.

He lit a cigarette. Perhaps he ought to start doing exercises; but to do exercises would be to admit the necessity for them and doing exercises alone in one's bedroom was surely the very sign, symbol or indication of approaching middle-age. Exercises done in company and called P.T. were not the same thing.— Compulsory P.T., usually a punishment for too many late nights and over-heavy drinking.

To hell with it anyhow, he was very well as he was, and Mr Hardy smiled rather smugly and with a simple pride, for was he not the reporter usually chosen to go after the difficult stories?

Mr Hardy's mother, proudly following his career from a vicarage in Devonshire, might have been surprised had she known how much of his modest success depended upon his physical appearance, and how little on his literary gifts. On the other hand she might not have been, for she was no fool. And although she loved her son she never joined with her husband in regretting that Dicky was not on the staff of *The Times*.

Mr Hardy, now breathing quite normally, returned to the carriage. He looked without interest at the holidaymakers who were his fellow travellers—too young and healthy, with clear bright eyes, and starved emaciated bodies. He opened his detective story; he wondered if getting up so terribly early on a Sunday morning in order to catch this train was going to prove worth while.

Sunday at the seaside with children playing on the beach and young couples and family parties cluttering up the parade. Luncheon at an expensive and probably not very good hotel; a night spent at the same hotel—Cathie had engaged a room for him, and then on Monday this same boring journey in reverse. At the moment, and with a slight hangover, he wasn't sure that Cathie was worth all the trouble.

On Wednesday, or at least on Thursday morning, it had seemed that no trouble in the world would be too much for the sake of being with her again; but that had been three and a half days ago.

The play he had taken her to had been terrible; but Cathie, because it was a first night, had enjoyed it, and had made a lot of what sounded like very intelligent criticisms of it (some of which he had been able to remember and to work into the three lines of copy which the *Sunday World Post* demanded in exchange for their two free seats). He had found himself giving her supper at the Savoy Grill, he had found himself ordering champagne. She had talked to him about himself and his career. He had found himself ordering 'just a teeny brandy.' She was wondering if one day he wouldn't perhaps be on *The Times*; she had several friends who were on *The Times*; she must get them to meet him. Just when he felt that he couldn't bear it a moment longer he found that she was ready to leave. They had returned to Baker Street and the photograph albums. As before there had been a quarter of a bottle of gin. In turning over the pages of the album their hands had met and had not parted again. In examining a photograph their heads had come together. Mrs Martell leant across Mr Hardy and switched out the light. This time Mrs Martell did *not* say that it was terribly naughty of them; and it was hours and hours before she withdrew to the far end of the sofa.

Mr Hardy looked back on the evening with pleasure, and, as he considered it in detail, his present journey seemed less tedious. Cathie was a very wonderful woman, and for her sake it was worth getting up early on a Sunday morning; it had been worth quarrelling with Janet, who had expected to spend the weekend with him—and who was Janet anyhow when compared with Cathie? Just another reporter like himself, who in no way added to his prestige or feelings of self-importance.

The train was drawing into Eastbourne and the holidaymakers were preparing to leave the carriage. Mr Hardy alone would travel on to Redbourne. He wondered if Cathie would meet him at the station, but she had given him directions for finding his hotel so probably she wouldn't. But just in case she should, he would go along to the restaurant car and get himself a drink.

'O come let us sing unto the Lord': Mr Hardy's mother leading the female portion of the choir, turned to frown at a gawky girl of about sixteen who was singing far too loudly; probably she was out of tune as well, but Mr Hardy's mother, not being particularly musical, couldn't be absolutely certain.

'Let us come before his presence with thanksgiving': the frown had not had its effect, Doreen's voice sounded loudly above everyone else's. Mr Hardy's mother frowned again but without much authority, for all she really cared Doreen and the rest of them could scream their heads off, or else remain in complete silence throughout the duration of the service.

'In his hands are all the corners of the earth': but Mrs Hardy, as she so often did, was thinking about Dicky.—Dicky was the youngest of her three children and the one who was nearest her heart; this she admitted to herself and to God, but never to anyone else—not even to Harold. For all her children were equally beloved, and for all had she made equal sacrifices. Only secretly was Dicky preferred above the others, and in doing so, she felt that she committed a sin. But Dicky was the youngest and the one who had always seemed to be most in need of protection. And then, but even to God she could not admit that this had anything to do with her feelings, he was the most beautiful. Agnes Hardy sighed deeply and wondered if Dicky was really all right. There was no reason why he shouldn't be, but it seemed a very long time since she had had a letter from him; only really it wasn't such a very long time, for Dicky was a dutiful son and wrote home quite fairly regularly. Lavinia, who was now a school-teacher in Rhodesia, and John, who was a tea-planter in Ceylon, wrote fairly regularly too, for the Hardys were that rare thing, a very devoted family.

'Forty years long was I grieved with this generation.'—(Obviously Doreen must be doing it on purpose, and something would have to be done about her.)

Mrs Hardy wondered if Dicky wasn't thinking about getting married. He was over thirty—how incredible that seemed—and it didn't do to leave it too long. When she was up in London in the spring Dicky had introduced her to Janet; ever since Mrs Hardy had wondered if Dicky and Janet were going to be married. Janet had seemed a very nice kind of girl, adequately pretty, and she would probably prove to be a steadying influence. Not that it was certain that Dicky needed to be steadied, but there was always the possibility. It was better for a man to be married, and Mrs Hardy looked forward with a vague pleasure to Dicky's children.—'And this is my little granddaughter,' but as, in her imagination, she formed the words, Mrs Hardy looked upwards instead of down, for she had travelled back over fifty odd years of time.—'As it was in the beginning, is now and ever shall be.'

'Redbourne.' Mr Hardy gulped down the remainder of his whisky and soda, grasped his bag, and hurried out of the train. He was always afraid of being left on trains and carried on to unknown destinations; such a thing had never happened to him, but he always feared that one day it would. With the rest of the passengers he walked up the ramp which led from the platform. There was no sign of Cathie. As he gave up his ticket, Mr Hardy was resentful, she might at least have taken the trouble to come and meet him.—'As you come out of the station you turn to the right,' but why on earth should he?

Cathie Martell sat in the enormous lounge of the hotel and waited for Mr Hardy. She was taking advantage of the occasion to read the latest number of the *Tatler*. She wore a cream linen suit and a rust-coloured blouse, into which was pinned the diamond brooch given her by an infatuated Mr Martell during the first weeks of their engagement. As a concession to the informality of the seaside she was not wearing her hat made of rust-coloured silk but had placed it on the little table in front of her. An elderly waiter who had first come to the hotel in about 1920 and had never since found the energy to leave, approached and asked if he could get her anything to drink. Mrs Martell said that she was waiting for a friend, and the waiter wearily retired on his flat feet across the several miles of carpet, a glass door swung to behind him and the enormous lounge was again empty. Mrs Martell looked at her watch, and wondered with irritation whether Dicky had missed his train. But he couldn't possibly have done that, he would be far too anxious to be with her. She closed her eyes with the idea of remembering some of the delightful things he had said to her, and was surprised when she could not call any of them to mind. It was very odd, for of course there was no doubt but that he was desperately in love with her. She opened her eyes only to be confronted by the photograph of the beautiful daughter of a duke who had just become suitably engaged to be married. The lips slightly parted, the eyes gazing into a, presumably, roseate future; and the whole cleverly lighted to catch the glint of the pearl necklace—a present from the bridegroom? Mrs Martell turned over the page.—On Wednesday, or rather on Thursday morning it had seemed that no trouble in the world would be too much for the sake of seeing Mr Hardy again. But now she wasn't so sure.—He had his advantages—tickets for first nights, for instance. But was he worth the risks she was taking for his sake, and was he serious enough? If poor Edward ever found out about Mr Hardy he would be very, very hurt, and she imagined poor Edward sitting in the library at Abbotsmere. He was tired and dispirited—depressed because she wasn't there to amuse him.—He had a glass in his hand, because she wasn't there to amuse him he would drink too much; he never got drunk, of course, but when he was depressed he drank solidly and far, far too much.—She wondered if she had been right to leave Abbotsmere on Wednesday morning. If she had stayed on she would have missed the first night and that would have been a pity, and there were other considerations. She had suspected for some time that when she was away Ruth entertained men in the flat, perhaps even in the sitting-room! The idea was disturbing and repugnant. It mightn't be a bad idea to go back to London without warning Ruth of her coming. If there was 'anything going on' she would have to be got rid of immediately. And Mrs Martell was very sorry for herself, was she never to be allowed any peace or tranquillity of mind? She had returned to London—it mightn't anyhow be a bad thing for Edward not to feel too sure of her—and because Ruth's young man had been ordered to Birmingham for two days on an outside job Mrs Martell found everything at the flat was perfectly in order with Ruth sitting primly at the kitchen table engaged in mending a pair of Mrs Martell's knickers.—However, to return to Edward, she imagined him sitting rather sadly in the library at Abbotsmere.—If she had known that he was *not* at Abbotsmere on that Sunday, her tranquillity of mind might have suffered a considerable disturbance.

Mrs Martell turned over a page of the *Tatler*—heaps and heaps of people having a good time at Ascot.—'And our little girl stays single,' but it wasn't true, and very soon now she would be married to Edward. 'The beautiful Mrs Edward West'—'A party at Abbotsmere'—'Mrs West had the honour of entertaining . . .'—'Mrs West enjoying a joke with His Royal Highness'—the past was merged with the future, the actualities of the present were forgotten.

'I believe you have a room reserved for me.' Mr Hardy put his bag down in front of the reception desk.

Reception, represented by an anaemic middle-aged woman, rose slowly to its feet and consulted an enormous ledger—everything in the hotel was enormous, dating from the time when there had been many visitors.

A porter in a gold-braided uniform shuffled forward.

Reception, without looking up from its ledger said, 'Will you register, please, and I believe there is a lady waiting for you in the lounge.'

It was Mr Hardy's last chance of freedom. If he had had any sense he would have picked up his bag there and then, left the hotel, and taken the first train back to London; as he took up a pen with which to sign the register, instinct told him to do just that. He hesitated, the pen poised over the ink-well; what could it possibly matter what the receptionist thought of him, or the porter either for that matter. He hesitated, and then he was writing his name in the register, 'Richard L. Hardy.' It was very unwise of him.

'Darling,' Mr Hardy was saying and then again, 'darling'. His voice was thick with emotion and he was long past being sensible.

Mrs Martell, watching him through half-closed eyes, was very well satisfied. Her lashes fluttered on her cheeks.

'You're so beautiful,' Mr Hardy said, and then, 'why can't we always be together like this?'

Why not indeed, and Mrs Martell sighed deeply; now; she was on well-tried ground, soon she would be telling him how cruel and un-understanding was the world.

Mr Hardy, who had only the vaguest idea of how closely he was keeping to the book, said, who cared about the world?

'Oh, my dear!' and Mrs Martell sighed with the weight of her knowledge of the world. Surreptitiously she glanced at her wristwatch, soon the chambermaid would be due to turn down the bed, and Mrs Martell had no idea of being caught by the chambermaid.

'You're so beautiful,' Mr Hardy said again, and didn't appear to notice that he repeated himself.

Mrs Martell, looking down at her body through half-closed eyes, could not but agree with him.—Skin the colour of ripe apricots, long beautiful legs and all the rest of it. She smiled sphinx-like, making no reply. Who was it who had told her that she resembled a beautiful Egyptian cat? She could not remember.

Mr Hardy sat up and lit a cigarette. 'I should like,' he said unexpectedly, 'to have you meet my mother.'

Without thinking, Mrs Martell pulled the sheet up to her chin. 'I'm sure she's very nice.'

'I think you'd like her,' Mr Hardy said thoughtfully; 'of course she's lived nearly all her life in the country, but I think you'd get on together. I'm very fond of my mother.'

'I'm very fond of mine.'

'Do you know Devonshire at all?' Mr Hardy asked.

Mrs Martell said that she didn't.

'Of course it's awfully dull down there; except for the fishing there's nothing to do at all. If mother didn't get away to Switzerland every year, I think she'd go mad.'

'Doesn't she ever come to London?'

'Not often, of course she's awfully good about all the parish things, but I don't think they really interest her. Mothers' Meetings and the choir, you know, and of course she has to go to all the services so that there shall be someone to say the responses.'

Mrs Martell said it sounded awful.

'Well, you know what a country parish is like.'

Mrs Martell said that she didn't and suggested that it was time they got up.

'Wouldn't you like me to order some tea?'

Mrs Martell was scandalised. To spend a long afternoon in Mr Hardy's bedroom was one thing, to have the chambermaid and the whole of the hotel staff know that she had done so was another.

'I shouldn't think they'd be interested,' Mr Hardy said. Mrs Martell, on her way to the bathroom, looked at him disdainfully.

Later, she sat in front of the dressing-table putting on the rust silk hat; informality was at an end. When she was ready she made Mr Hardy go out into the corridor to make sure that there was no one about. There wasn't, of course, and she gave him orders to wait in his room for five minutes, and then to join her in the lounge. Mr Hardy found the whole performance unnecessarily elaborate, but he did as he was told.

He drew back the curtain, and stood looking out of the window. After the previous dimness of the room, his eyes blinked in the bright light of the afternoon sun.

'Mother, this is Cathie.' In his imagination Mr Hardy was standing in the doorway of the vicarage drawing-room. Mrs Martell in her cream suit, the rust-coloured blouse and the diamond brooch was by his side. Mr Hardy's mother got up from the sofa on which she had been sitting. She had crossed the room, she was kissing her future daughter-in-law on the cheek. Mr Hardy's father, filling his pipe, was coming towards them across the lawn, in a moment he would have reached the french windows, he would have entered the room, it was a moment charged with emotion and deep happiness; but no one, except Mr Hardy, actually spoke, Mr Hardy couldn't think of anything for them to say.

'You haven't met my wife, have you?' Mr Hardy was in a London pub, introducing Mrs Martell to an unspecified circle of his friends. Mrs Martell (still wearing the cream-coloured suit) was being welcomed by them. Mr Hardy was intensely proud of her; and then, although he had not intended her to be there, he saw Janet.—'I don't think you've met my wife.'—But the whole scene had vanished and he was in the window of the hotel bedroom looking out at the sea. Janet had been expecting that he would marry her, there was no doubt as to that. They had talked about it quite often. A small flat (if only they could find one) and she would continue on her paper. A daily woman and potatoes peeled and left standing in a saucepan of cold water—not that they would often be in to meals anyhow.—'I don't think you've met my wife.' The five minutes must be up by now. He would go downstairs and rejoin Cathie. How beautiful she was; whatever happened now he would never marry Janet. It would have been such a sensible marriage. Janet was such a nice girl, would have made such a good wife and mother; their two children would have gone to nursery school in order that Janet might go on with her work. They would have taken out insurance policies against their education. Later the boy would have gone to Rugby or to Greshams, perhaps it would have been rather a struggle to send him there; but Janet would have managed it; girls are cheaper to educate.—'This is my little grand-daughter.'

Mrs Martell, waiting in the lounge, was in a very happy state of mind. She had had a very enjoyable afternoon, and Mr Hardy was completely in her power. If everything else failed she could marry Mr Hardy. But, of course, everything else would not fail her. She would sit at the end of the long dining-room table. She would stand aside to allow Royalty to precede her into the drawing-room.—'This is rather an interesting little table, Ma'am.'— 'Her Royal Highness will be arriving just before five o'clock.' She and Edward would be in the hall to receive her—or wouldn't that be correct, would they wait in the drawing-room and have Her Highness brought to them there by Hackett, and there would be the lady-in-waiting and perhaps a gentleman in attendance.

It was all very far removed from the antiquated lounge of the Redbourne Hotel.—'Would you care to see your room, Ma'am?' or, to the lady-in-waiting, 'Would Her Highness care to see her room?'—The best bedroom in the middle of the house, with the blue hangings to the bed and the blue window-curtains, the bathroom leading out of it and opposite the door into the dressing-room. No need to apologise for such a room—the view of the mere and of the park.—'So difficult to keep up in these days.' But would it ever be like that? 'The beautiful Mrs Edward West.' The whole thing was a dream. And it was very wrong to think like that; for Laura stood in the way of the realisation of the dream. How beautiful everything would have been if only she had met Edward long, long ago. But what chance had she ever had of meeting people?—Mrs Hartley-James' lack of important and fashionable friends. Mrs Hartley-James' selfish determination to go on living in Redbourne. For Cathie there had been Madame Sondheim's, but there had been no London season, how could there have been? A job at Madame Sondheim's, that had been her only way of even so much as getting to London. And even that had been begrudged her. If Cathie would take Mrs Hartley-James' advice she would remain in Redbourne and work in the local beauty parlour which produced excellent results at a lower cost than anything which could exist in London. When Cathie had not taken her mother's advice Mrs Hartley-James, somewhat to her surprise, had been secretly rather relieved. Cathie had become too discontented, too selfish to make a very pleasant companion with whom to share her uneventful life in a small flat.

From then on, of course, Cathie had made her own way. She had done the best she could for herself.—If she had not done spectacularly well; she had, at least, progressed beyond her point of departure—a small flat in a seaside town, the friendship of Mrs Willis and Daphne. Marrying Mr Martell had perhaps been a mistake; Mrs Hartley-James was inclined now to think that it had been. She forgot that at the time she had been delighted.

'I only want what is best for all of us.' Cathie said the words under her breath.—Somehow, in the end, it would all come right. But would Edward see 'the best' in the same way as she did? She couldn't be sure of him as she was now sure of Mr Hardy. If everything else failed she would marry Mr Hardy and she smiled graciously up at him as he came to her across the lounge and suggested that they could do with some tea.

She was at peace with herself again, but of course she didn't know that Edward was *not* at Abbotsmere, was *not* sitting sadly in his library wishing that she were with him.

In Paris Edward lay on the bed in his hotel room. The brass bedstead and the shabby furniture which might have come out of one of those boarding houses in Margate or Brighton. There was the mock bamboo table covered with a white cloth and the dressing-table which had been designed without any feeling for form.

They had existed through all these years, Margate or Brighton or now, nearly half a century later, in the centre of Paris.

It was a very respectable, a very well-thought-of hotel. Within two minutes' walk of the Ritz Bar—the man in the club who had recommended it to Edward had spoken very highly of it.—Not pretentious you know, but clean and cheap, and, with all the difficulties about currency, cheapness had become terribly important. Edward shifted unhappily on the bed and wished that he was at the Ritz. It had been a mistake anyhow to come. His eyes filled with tears and he was reassured by this proof of his own unhappiness.—'You can't take it with you'—'You can't run away from it.' He looked at the leather travelling clock which stood on the table beside the bed. Four o'clock! God, he felt terrible. He supposed he ought to get up. He'd probably feel better after a bath, after he was shaved, after he was brushed and dressed.

It had been a mistake to come.—'Get away to Paris or somewhere and forget about it.' But it hadn't worked.

The last two days were blurred in his memory. Ethel and the grim house in S.W.10. Had *she* suggested that he should go to Paris? The pub in the Fulham Road, then he had gone to his club.—'A quiet evening at the club.' Someone, was it Macdonald, had told him about this hotel. Then the brothel, or was it only a flat, over a dairy. He couldn't remember much about it, only that there had been a girl with red hair. He had never liked red hair. The last time he had been inside a brothel he was seventeen, trying to find out about life.

He had gone to the Turkish Baths and later in the morning he had rung up Laura and told her that he wouldn't be going down to Abbotsmere until after the week-end. Then he had taken the plane to Paris.

But Paris hadn't solved anything for him. He had made a fool of himself, that was all, and he would be very lucky if he didn't end by being blackmailed.

Half-past four, he really must get up, he must have a bath and it was ridiculous to think about blackmail; you couldn't be blackmailed for sitting in a bar and crying. It was ridiculous, it was undignified, but there was nothing criminal about it. They had tried to comfort him in the bar, they had been very kind and at the time he had been grateful to them. In the end they had put him into a taxi and sent him back to his hotel. How had they known which hotel he was staying at? But now he remembered, he had given the address to the taxi-driver himself. Anyhow it didn't matter, he would go home to England and it would all be forgotten. He must have been very upset to behave in such a manner. In a way so alien to his nature.—He would go home this evening and very soon he would forget all about it. But, as he reached for the telephone, he thought of his comforters in the bar and was deeply ashamed.

The telephone was ringing loudly in the flat which had been Miss Codrington's and was now Mrs Keble's.—Mrs Keble woke reluctantly from her Sunday afternoon nap. In her dreams she had been back in India; the nap was a siesta; soon the boy would come with her tea. Everything was spoiled by the telephone. She was in Baker Street; if she wanted tea she would have to boil the kettle herself on the gas stove in the squalid little kitchen. She picked her way across the room to the telephone. The room was overcrowded with furniture, antiques which had proved to be unsaleable.

Mrs Keble lifted the receiver.

'I'm terribly sorry, I do hope I'm not disturbing you. I'm Laura West, Cathie Martell's cousin. I met you at Cathie's flat last week.'

'But of course.' Mrs Keble was pleased. She had liked Laura, who had been more sympathetic than the others about the rent; and who had done her best to protect Mrs Keble from the probing questions of Mr Hardy.

'I'm terribly sorry to bother you; but have you any idea when Cathie will be back in London?'

'Not until tomorrow.' Mrs Keble was quite certain about that for Ruth was entertaining her young man on the floor above.—If Mrs Martell had been expected back Ruth and the young man would have gone out.

'Couldn't you get any answer from Ruth?'

'No,' Laura said, 'perhaps the telephone was out of order.'

'I'm so sorry,' Mrs Keble said, and, 'is there anything I can do?'

'I don't think so,' Laura said; 'has your sister arrived from Bombay yet?'

Mrs Keble was pleased with Laura for remembering about the sister from Bombay.—'Her plane's due in tomorrow; there's nothing like one's own people when one's in trouble, is there?'

As she had done last week Laura agreed and again wondered which of her own relations could be thought of as 'one's own people' in that particular sense. There wasn't anyone at all, that was why she clung to Cathie. Cathie was so helpful and, usually, so kind. Laura didn't allow herself to think too much about the times when Cathie had not been kind, it was asking too much of herself, it wasn't possible to live in a world where there wasn't one person whom one could trust. Edward? she ought to be able to trust Edward; but she was afraid of him. She never knew when he would become withdrawn and aloof; or suddenly displeased with her.

'Are you sure there isn't anything I can do?' Mrs Keble asked.

'No,' Laura said, 'no, it's very kind of you, but there isn't anything really.'

'If you're in London, why don't you come round and have tea with me?'—It wouldn't be any trouble making tea if there was someone to drink it with, and there were those little sugar cakes left over from yesterday.

Laura hesitated, only for a moment, and then she accepted. She could be with Mrs Keble in less than ten minutes. She replaced the receiver and got up from the bed. It had been foolish of her to come to London; but this morning she had felt that she couldn't face another long day alone at Abbotsmere. Friday had been all right and she had enjoyed the fair. But when on Saturday Edward had telephoned to say that he would be away for the whole week-end; she had known something very like despair.

He had run into old George Stimpson at the club. George had asked him down to Hampshire. Laura wouldn't mind, would she? George owned some of the best fishing in that part of England. There had been no explanation of, no apology for, his failure to return the previous evening. He would be back at Abbotsmere on Tuesday or Wednesday, he would let her know. He sounded cold and unapproachable. It was ten o'clock in the morning; she was faced with three, possibly four, days during which she would be entirely alone. It wasn't even as if she had any friends who lived nearby. Robert and Diana? But she had always been alarmed by Robert and Diana; and after the dinner party with Sir Henry and Mr Gideon she didn't feel that she ever wanted to see them again.—The Templetons? There was nothing alarming about the kind Templetons and their egg-faced daughter. But what was the point? So she spent Saturday alone with Constantia and Augustus. If only it hadn't been the weekend there would have been Nelly; but on Saturdays and Sundays Nelly was almost exclusively occupied by her husband and son. By Sunday Laura couldn't bear it any longer. She would go up to London. Constantia and Augustus were left in the care of Nelly. Laura chose a slow train; she arrived in London at about four o'clock. But it had been a mistake. In London she was more alone than she had been at Abbotsmere.

She sat in her hotel bedroom and telephoned; from most of the numbers she tried there was no reply. As a last resort she looked up Miss Codrington's number in the book and rang up Mrs Keble. Mrs Keble might be able to tell her whether Cathie was expected back this evening. It was a slender hope. Mrs Keble's invitation came as a surprise.

She could be with Mrs Keble in less than ten minutes. 'But how can she?' Laura thought, 'how can she go on living in that place where her sister was murdered?' Laura sat down again trembling. 'I can't possibly go.' She had spoken the words aloud and was frightened by them.

Ten minutes later she was ringing the doorbell in Baker Street. Mrs Keble, who had been standing in the kitchen, waiting for the kettle to boil, started violently. Laura was expected, but Mrs Keble had been so long alone that she had not believed that she would come. Living in the shadows, real people as well as phantoms had become a legend. All were ghosts, having no substance but in her thoughts. 'My sister from India will be with me tomorrow,' but she will never come, any more than my other sister will come from beyond the grave.

Mrs Keble took one last anxious look at the kettle and hurried down the stairs.

Laura and Mrs Keble got on splendidly together. Here were two people who were very unhappy; but who strove to hide their unhappiness from each other.

They spoke only of things which could not give pain.—Constantia and Augustus, how sweet they were.—The goings on of Ruth and her young man.

'But she's not a bad girl,' Mrs Keble said, 'and I must say she keeps that flat beautifully. We all have to have compensations.'

It was understood that the compensations were for the disagreeableness of all work generally and not specifically for the hell of having to look after Mrs Martell.

Laura refused the last of the sugar cakes which was being unselfishly offered her by Mrs Keble. There was a little pause in their conversation. They had each of them passed through bitter experiences—'as who had not,' Laura thought, afraid even to allow her unhappiness a place which should be uniquely its own.—'In some ways Laura is a very stupid little girl; and if it hadn't been for Mrs Pemberthy goodness knows what would have happened to her. She has nothing of her own, you know, only what her guardian chooses to give her.'—The governess hadn't really been sure that Laura had heard her; but there had been so much frustration in her own life that her desire to hurt others was almost uncontrollable.

Mrs Keble suggested that they should go round to the club and have a drink.

'It's only just round the corner, and it isn't a bad little place.'

Laura started to refuse, but if she didn't go with Mrs Keble she would be alone. She would go back to her hotel bedroom and ring up numbers from which there was never, could never, be a reply.

'It's not a bad little place,' Mrs Keble said persuasively, 'and it's run by quite a nice girl, you wouldn't think it, but her father's a clergyman.'

'Why wouldn't you think it?'

'She's got backing, of course.' Mrs Keble carefully wiped the coffee-coloured sugar from the last of the cakes from her fingers. 'She says she's going to marry him, but I don't know, I don't think he's good enough for her.'

Laura didn't answer.

'He's all right in his way,' Mrs Keble went on, 'and he's a gentleman, I'll say that for him; but he must be at least twice her age.'

'Oh dear.' Laura nodded sympathetically, prepared to agree that these strangers were probably making a mess of their lives.

Mrs Keble rambled on a little about gentlemen; and about the inadvisability of most marriages; ending up with a regret that she herself was no longer married.

'I tried it twice,' Mrs Keble said, 'and I very nearly tried it a third time; if I'd had any sense I would have stuck to my first, even though he was more like a father to me.*

Laura continued to agree with her and to be softly sympathetic.

The club when they reached it was very much what Laura had expected, and very typical of its kind; that is to say it was situated in a basement, for the rents of basements are relatively low, and who in any case wants light, other than artificial light, by which to drink.

'This is Gladys,' Mrs Keble said. With a proprietary air she introduced the young woman behind the bar.

The clergyman's daughter was pleased to meet them.

Mrs Keble ordered drinks and said that business didn't seem to be very brisk.

Gladys said that it was early yet, and, having served them, retired to the other end of the bar, where she had been talking to a gentleman.

Mrs Keble whispered loudly to Laura that that was 'him'.

Time wore on and Mrs Keble ordered more drinks. She had a lot to say about marriage. Marriage was always difficult. They were nearly always jealous; they drank and then behaved abominably; either that or they were old enough to be one's father.

She told Laura about the trouble in India, he had been very handsome and brutal. Laura waited for the part where Mr Keble blew out his own brains in an access of rage and jealousy; she had heard all about that from Ruth, it would be more interesting to hear it from Mrs Keble, but it was only hinted at.

'I was never one to make trouble, but if you want a word of advice, you look out for that cousin of yours.' Laura looked at Mrs Keble in startled bewilderment.

'Now listen,' Mrs Keble was saying, 'I'm a much older woman than you are; and all I'm doing is to warn you to look out. I'm not saying that there is anything wrong. But you can take it from me that she's no friend of yours.'

Laura felt the blood rushing to her face, 'I don't know what you mean.' She must get away from here. Mrs Keble was drunk; it would serve no purpose to have a row with her. Laura stood up; Mrs Keble put out a detaining hand.

'Now don't take me wrong, dear, I didn't mean to upset you; but do believe me when I tell you that that woman isn't up to any good. She's a bitch if ever there was one.'

'How dare you.' Laura was very frightened.

'Very well,' and Mrs Keble's voice was no longer propitiatory, 'if you don't believe me ask Gladys. She's come in here often enough and discussed you with Gladys; and what she's said hasn't been very nice.'

'It isn't true and I don't want to hear it.' Laura was standing up and several people were looking at her with curiosity.

Suddenly, looking at Laura's face, Mrs Keble regretted what she had done. It never did to interfere, not even with the best will in the world, it was so easy to make things even worse than they were already.

Laura was moving towards the door. Mrs Keble got up and followed her. Without looking back Laura walked up the stairs. Mrs Keble followed closely behind her. When they reached the street she touched Laura on the arm.

'I'm sorry, I'd no idea that you'd be so upset.'

Laura swung round to face her. 'You'd absolutely no right to say things like that about Cathie.'

'I'm sorry,' Mrs Keble repeated humbly.

9

EUSTON STATION on the eleventh of August was no longer the glorious spectacle that it had been before the war. Then the night train to Inverness had been run in seven parts. Line after line of sleeping cars with their attendants in the plum-coloured uniforms and little plum-coloured caps, a modification of the caps which had been worn by firing parties in the Franco-Prussian war. Rich and harassed travellers sweltering in the tweeds which would be so appropriate the following morning. Retrievers with their tongues hanging out, rolled tartan rugs, gun-cases, fishing-rods and bags of golf-clubs.—'You wait here and I will go and see about the tickets, the retrievers, the dining-car reservations.—There is Eloise, there are the Underwaters, there are the Remington-Rands.'

Americans seem to make up the majority of the travellers, but many of them will have English guests who will be staying with them. There are a few Scots, less betweeded, with, on average, fewer tartan rugs than the Americans.—'There are the Underwaters again, there is a girl wearing pale blue brogues.'

Today the night train is run in one part only, a few sleeping coaches have been added, but that is all. The travellers are still harassed, but there are fewer of them. 'What fun it used to be in the old days, when the Underwaters, the Remington-Rands and Eloise all had shooting lodges.' 'You wait here, and I will go and see about the dining-car reservations and the tickets.'

The porter has gone to look for a barrow, he has been gone for a quarter of an hour. Barrows are scarce round here, the porter said so; there do not seem to be any left over from the days when the night train ran in seven parts. Perhaps they were requisitioned during the war. Edward is very angry with the porter. It is to this that the nationalisation of the railways has brought us.

Laura sat on the pile of suitcases and waited. She agreed with Edward about the incompetence of British Railways. It wasn't worth arguing about. It seemed that it was a general rule of life that things deteriorated after a war.

'Oh, aren't they sweet'—the fat mother of two small children had stopped to admire Constantia and Augustus sitting defiantly in their travelling baskets.

Constantia immediately rose to her hind legs and let out a high falsetto bark.

The fat mother giggled shrilly, calling to her young to share her enjoyment. Edward glared at her. He did not care to be treated as part of a free side-show, a foretaste of the delights that she would find on the beach at Blackpool. Laura called upon Constantia to hush, and at that moment their porter reappeared with a very small barrow.

They walked for nearly a quarter of a mile. Their train, with its extra coaches, was drawn up at one of the farthest platforms. Edward repeated his remarks about the awfulness of British Railways. The porter was too busy pushing the barrow, and, at the same time, trying to prevent Constantia and Augustus, the fishing-rods and most of the suitcases from sliding off it, to have breath left for conversation, so Edward's remarks went uncommented upon.

At last they reached their sleepers. Constantia and Augustus, in spite of protests from Laura, were taken away to the van.

'But they've travelled so very little, they'll be terrified.'

'You should have thought of that before you dragged them up to London.' Edward was not inclined to be sympathetic. 'It would have been far better to have left them at Abbotsmere.'

'But it's going to be their holidays,' Laura said. 'I couldn't possibly have come without them.'

Edward didn't answer, he was busy searching in his case for a flask of brandy.

Laura sat on her bed and wished that she were anywhere but here. She didn't want to go to Scotland. She told herself that she hated Scotland, but what she really hated was the thought of having to entertain her brother-in-law's friends.

'Did you let Charles know that you were bringing those dogs?' Edward asked presently.

'Oh, yes,' Laura said, secure in the knowledge that yesterday she had sent Charles a postcard which would almost certainly not arrive in Sutherland for another two days.

'Very good of him to agree to it,' and Edward rang the bell for the attendant, who, being further down the car attending to some people in one of the other sleepers, neither heard it nor answered it.

Edward, unlike Laura, was looking forward to Scotland. He liked salmon fishing, he liked shooting and he was glad that Charles's rich American wife was away in America attending on the deathbed of her rich and aged father. Not that he had anything particularly against Georgette; but with her away, he and Laura became more important to Charles. It was because of Georgette's absence that they were invited for the whole of the two months for which the lodge had been rented. Otherwise the duration of their visit would probably have been far shorter. The present arrangement was more satisfactory.

'And if Laura would just give an eye to the housekeeping,' Charles had written—'and, of course, during the Princess's visit it will be far easier if there is a hostess.'

Laura, when the letter was shown to her, had been appalled; not by the thought of the elderly mid-European Princess, but by the horrifying idea that she would be expected to keep an eye on the autocratic, the unbending, the terrible Mrs Osborne who was Georgette's cook. But she had not dared to refuse. Charles's letter had arrived just after Edward's return from Hampshire; just after the horrible five days that Laura had spent alone at Abbotsmere and in London. Edward had come back from Hampshire (Laura never doubted but that he had spent the whole of the five days in Hampshire) in a good temper with himself—the fishing, he told her, had been excellent—and in a bad temper with Laura. Abbotsmere, he said unfairly as well as untruly, was run disgracefully. Laura had no idea of civilised behaviour, and in fact made a fool of him in front of his friends; the whole episode of Robert and Diana and the dinner party with the doctors was gone over again. Laura's behaviour in everything was irresponsible and childish. Laura had sincerely agreed with everything that Edward said. She was irresponsible, she was childish, she was inadequate. But once, in spite of all these deficiencies, Edward had loved her; and that night Laura had retired to bed in tears. The next morning the letter from Charles had arrived. Laura was touched and surprised that Edward should want her to go to Scotland with him; should judge her capable of acting as hostess to the Princess and of 'keeping an eye on the housekeeping'. She would have liked to refuse; but if Edward's confidence in her had mysteriously returned, it would be unwise to disturb it by telling him that she would rather do anything in the world than that which he had suggested.

'What fun,' she had forced herself to say, and again, 'what fun,' and, 'how very kind of Charles.'

Looking at her across the dining-room table Edward had thought how lovely she was. His ill-temper of the night before was forgotten.

'He isn't really unkind,' Laura thought, and he has a great deal to put up with; and then she thought how nice it would have been if Edward had said he was sorry for having made her cry, and for having seemed so unkind. But Edward never did say he was sorry; why should he, when he was never in the wrong?

The train started and Edward said that they might as well go along to the dining-car. Even if dinner was not ready it might at least be possible to get a drink. That damned attendant, doomed to inefficiency by the nationalisation of the railways, was evidently never going to answer the bell and satisfy Edward's need for soda water.

Mrs Martell was spending the eleventh of August in Redbourne and she was not pleased about it. Other people went to the South of France; other people went to grand house parties in Berkshire, other people went to Scotland, especially they went to Scotland, and Cathie Martell dabbed angrily at the abstract work of art she was creating. What was the use of anything when one was condemned to spend August in Redbourne.

'Cathie, you haven't forgotten that Mrs Willis and Daphne are coming to supper?' and Mrs Hartley-James opened the door of her daughter's room.

'No,' Mrs Martell said, 'I haven't forgotten.'

Mrs Hartley-James came nearer and looked over Cathie's shoulder, peering uncertainly at the work of art.

'That's very nice, dear.'

Mrs Martell didn't even bother to reply.

Mrs Hartley-James, discouraged, went out of the room murmuring something about starting to get supper, and about running a bath. Cathie was left alone with her little tubes of paint and her thoughts of Scotland. It wasn't fair that Laura at this moment was in a first-class sleeper *en route* for Scotland, that she should be with Edward, that she should be going to stay with Charles.

Mrs Martell dabbed again at the work of art and added a little thick plastic squiggle to the right-hand corner. But it would take more than a little squiggle to arouse her from her present mood of despondency. Abstracts, whatever they may look like to others, are of the stuff that dreams are made of, and they are at the same time a wonderful release for the subconscious, or so Mrs Martell had understood from one of the many fascinating interviews she had had with her psychologist. It was a pity that the psychologist was so expensive, otherwise she would have gone to him much oftener. The restful atmosphere of his Harley Street office, his quiet reassuring voice and the way he agreed with everything she said to him were all points in Dr Grostein's favour; what was not in his favour was that he was at present fishing in Scotland. Mrs Martell frowned slightly and returned to her abstract, poking at it with a little wooden instrument shaped rather like a nail file. Her fingers were sticky from the paint and varnish. She must go and wash her hands, and make up her face, and put on a crêpe-de-chine dress because Mrs Willis and Daphne were coming to supper; but because it was only Mrs Willis and Daphne it wasn't worth while having a bath. She got up reluctantly, the subconscious would have to remain, for the time being, unreleased. She glanced briefly out of the window; the beastly holiday-makers were milling up and down the front. Mrs Martell's cup was filled to overflowing with discontent.

Edward and Laura had breakfast at the station hotel at Inverness. Edward, who had slept well, was in a good temper, and even prepared to countenance the existence upon this earth of Constantia and Augustus. Constantia and Augustus were in hilarious spirits and so was Laura. She had temporarily forgotten that she hated Scotland, or that she was afraid of Charles, his cook and his guests.

After breakfast they travelled on to Inverlochie by the slow train, and there they were met by Charles's chauffeur, or more precisely by Georgette's chauffeur, and were driven the remaining forty miles to the lodge which Charles had rented.

'My heart is in the Highlands a-chasing the deer.' Looking out of the car window, Laura reflected that there was nothing that could reasonably be found fault with in the Highlands; considered only as scenery they were very nearly perfect. If only the Highlands were as empty and deserted as they appeared to be; but hidden in the folds of so many of the hills, standing on the shores of so many of the lochs, were those horrible shooting lodges.

The lodge which Charles had rented stood on the shores of a loch; like all the others it was badly built and uncomfortably furnished. The salmon fishing and the deer stalking which went with it were superb and the rent was perfectly enormous.

On the second night at dinner Laura looked down the table and was filled with envy of Cathie spending the summer comfortably at Redbourne. At Redbourne the sun was probably shining, one could take the dogs for picnics on the beach, and, Mrs Hartley-James' flat being small, there would be no guests to mar one's pleasure.

The moment had almost arrived when she must catch Lady Forston's eye and shepherd the ladies out of the dining-room; but Lady Forston was engaged in an animated conversation with Charles. Laura rather admired Lady Forston who had so much jewellery and so much conversation. The jewellery consisted mostly of rubies which were internationally famous, and the conversation of scandal. Lady Forston was in fact a period piece. Her age for many years had been a closely guarded secret, she had tiny hands and feet and she resembled a chicken, particularly in her little bright eyes and about the neck and throat. Having failed with Lady Forston, Laura tried to get the attention of Mrs Johnston Manningham seated on Charles's other side. Mrs Johnston Manningham proved more amenable and the ladies rose from the table.

In the drawing-room there was a great collecting of petit-point and various pieces of embroidery. Mrs Johnston Manningham was working on the eleventh of a set of imitation Jacobean chairbacks that she was making for Mr Johnston Manningham's stately home near Maidenhead. The other ladies agreed in admiring it and in exclaiming at Mrs Manningham's industry. Only Lady Forston did not join in the general chorus, and gave it as her opinion that Mrs Manningham was wasting her time.

Georgette's butler came in with the coffee tray. Constantia and Augustus came in to beg for lumps of sugar. Lady Forston wanted to know why Georgette had so many children and all of them girls, such a pity.

'There are only four,' Laura said.

Lady Forston said that that was too many. Then she wanted to know what everyone thought of these dreadful jewel robberies on the Riviera. She had heard from poor Annette only this morning, poor Annette had lost practically everything.

'Dreadful,' Mrs Johnston Manningham said, 'quite dreadful; I think I shall write to her.'

Lady Forston looked suspicious; she didn't believe that Mrs Manningham knew Annette, anyhow she didn't know her well enough to call her by her first name.

'Though it's ridiculous for her to say that there was twenty thousand pounds worth.' Lady Forston was indignant. 'Annette never *had* twenty thousand pounds worth of jewellery. You know that as well as I do, Barbara.'

Thus appealed to, Barbara Waverly said that she supposed not, and returned to counting the stitches on the sock that she was knitting for her fourth husband.

There was a little more desultory conversation, and, at last, the men began coming out of the dining-room. The first to appear was Mr Johnston Manningham. Mrs Manningham looked lovingly up at him. They had been married for fifteen years and she now considered him to be entirely her own creation. Without her constant help, guidance and nagging he might still have been nothing more than a country solicitor. Now, he was a coming man; the director of more than one company and a newly-elected member of Parliament (on the Conservative side, naturally). And it was she who had done everything for him, everything, including keeping him out of the late war.

Mr Manningham sank into a chair; he looked as if he were already half asleep, which wasn't surprising for as a sedentary worker he was unaccustomed to the open air or to any form of exercise. Mrs Manningham frowned a warning; he was not yet important enough to fall asleep in other people's drawing-rooms.

David Waverly, Mrs Waverly's husband, came and sat by Laura; he occupied himself with trying to teach Constantia to jump over his foot. He was a charming young man several years younger than his wife, and he earned part of his living by working in a publisher's office. From a financial point of view it was no longer necessary for him to do this, for Mrs Waverly was very, very rich, having been born a Waldorf or an Astoria or something of that kind.

The party was completed by Edward and Charles and by Mr Reggie Hodgson, one of those fashionable middle-aged bachelors who are always to be found in every house party that ever takes place in England or Scotland.

Nobody was asked what they would like to do; the poker table was set out, and poker was to be their amusement this evening, and every other evening that they remained here. Only Mr Johnston Manningham would not play; he would go into the other sitting-room in order to read an important white paper, in other words he would go to sleep.

The chips were counted out by Charles; they were very elegant chips with the denomination marked on them on one side in gold, and, on the reverse, Georgette's monogram, also in gold.

At Redbourne Mrs Martell lay on her bed thinking, among other things, about the state of her health. In spite of the morning exercises and the morning glass of hot water she did not believe that her intestines were all that they should be. There was a nagging pain which insisted in her side, and from time to time she suffered from an excruciating pain in her back. She wondered if she ought not perhaps to consult another doctor. Idly, she started on some deep breathing exercises; they were part of a system in which she had been deeply interested a few years before, and were said to form part of the Yogi philosophy.—In through the nose, and down the backbone, now the whole body was flooded with health and sunlight, it was at the centre of the universe and connected with everything else in the world by an arrangement of invisible telephone wires.—In through the nose and down the backbone, if only one kept it up for long enough one would begin to feel oneself floating a few feet above one's bed. One was at the exact centre of the universe. There were times when she actually hated Edward, he was so selfish, so self-centred, considered nobody's comfort but his own. Last week at Abbotsmere he had been very sweet to her, but there was no denying that he had seemed quite happy about going to Scotland for two whole months, and leaving her quite alone. But she wasn't alone, there was Dick Hardy. Edward didn't know about Dick; anyhow he didn't know quite how desperately Dick had fallen in love with her. Cathie had only hinted at it to Edward; she had hinted very cautiously, trying to find out whether the existence of a rival would be useful or not to her designs. Disappointingly, Edward had not seemed particularly interested. But Edward didn't know all, he didn't know that Mr Hardy had so lost all sense of self-preservation that he had suggested to Mrs Martell that they should get married.

In through the nose and down the backbone, now her body was flooded with health, her back no longer ached, and if she wasn't actually floating about in the air she was certainly the centre of the universe. Mrs Martell smiled indulgently, rather pityingly, as she thought of Dick. She couldn't marry him of course, but perhaps, after all, she would.

Then her expression changed and for a few moments she was unrecognisable, for without having quite to undergo the humiliation of admitting it to herself, she knew that she had only a short time in which to make up her mind. If she was to marry Dick she must do it soon, before he thought better of the whole idea.

At Millhill the poker game went on until nearly two o'clock in the morning; by which time Mrs Johnston Manningham had lost a hundred pounds and was very frightened.

'Lots of time to get your revenge.' Charles was entering the winnings and losings in a washing book. He had no idea, as indeed nobody else had, how closely the Manninghams lived to the outside limit of their resources, and they had no capital at all; nobody knew that either.

Mrs Manningham smiled and lit a cigarette; as he had said, time was on her side. She fingered one of the diamond brooches pinned to her dress. Did anyone know that this jewellery was not her own; was in fact hired from the same department store as the Manningham fishing-rods and guns.

'What a lovely brooch.' Laura, who nearly always admired other people's jewellery, was looking at Mrs Manningham's large beringed hand.

'Oh, this.' Mrs Manningham considered the brooch.

'Johnnie gave it to me for my birthday.'

Laura was impressed and smiled at Mrs Manningham, whom she was beginning to like. When you got to know them, these people weren't really frightening after all. Only Lady Forston, perhaps, remained as a potential source of danger. But the Waverlys were charming, especially the husband. She looked across at Edward. Edward seemed to be in a very good mood, he had been in a good mood all the evening. She smiled at him, but he was occupied in helping Charles with his arithmetic, and didn't notice her. It's going to be all right, Laura thought. We shall start all over again and it will be all right. I shall be exactly like everyone else and we shall be very happy together. Then she remembered her duties and asked Lady Forston if she didn't think it was time for bed. Lady Forston thought it was, and half an hour later Laura was in bed and reading a children's book which she had found on one of the bookshelves. At the back of her mind was the thought that everything was going to be all right. In the past she had been very silly and childish, but now all that would be changed. She would think before she spoke, she would be quite different, and Edward would be proud of her. He would feel that he could depend on her and everything would be all right. She was just about to switch off the light when Edward came in; he was still wearing his dinner-jacket.

'Hullo, darling, I'm reading my favourite book.'

'Oh, yes.' Edward went and stood by the dressing-table, not looking at her.

'*The Secret Garden*, I haven't seen it for years; did you have it when you were a child?'

'No, I don't think so.'

'It's *fascinating*, shall I read you some of it?'

Edward turned to face her, then he came slowly across the room until he reached the foot of the bed. He leant on the old-fashioned iron foot-rail and looked at her intently. Laura looked back at him, already she was rather frightened. Edward continued to stare.—'Everything's going to be all right,' Laura thought desperately; she clung to the phrase as if there was some kind of charm in it.—'Everything's going to be all right.—He's drunk,' she thought; 'I hadn't noticed it downstairs, but he's drunk.' She stared into his eyes. Then Edward shrugged his shoulders and turned away.

'You little fool.'

It was a relief that he had spoken, but she no longer thought that he was drunk. He was quite sober and he hated her.

'You must be mad,' Edward said.

'Everything's going to be all right.'—A few moments ago she had been happy. She had managed to comfort herself. Her eyes were fixed on Edward. She wanted for him to destroy her.

When he left the room she lay perfectly still. If she lay quite still it was as if she was dead. The room was hideous, the furniture shoddy and the curtains faded, it was a house which was intended only for the occupation of strangers, it was more impersonal even than a hotel bedroom. The top of the deal wardrobe was decorated with a fretwork frieze.

She was mad. Edward had not been angry with her or shouted at her. He had been cold, detached. She was mad, it was apparent in everything that she said and did. She had been very rude to him downstairs; if she was not aware of it, it was because she was mad.

'But what did I say?' Laura didn't know; she had been afraid to ask Edward in case it should be something so terrible that she would not be able to bear the thought of it.

And that wasn't all, she had made a fool of herself with young Waverly, trying to flirt with him. Waverly had been disgusted.

But she hadn't, she knew that she hadn't. Only, if she were mad, how could she possibly know what she had said or done?

'I didn't flirt with David Waverly. I wasn't rude to Edward'; but already she doubted. There was no point in Edward saying these things if they were not so. Why decorate all the furniture with fretwork scrolls, wasn't it hideous enough without that? It wasn't safe just to enjoy herself, she must never allow herself to relax again. 'But what was going to happen now?' Edward had said that he couldn't go on very much longer. Did that mean that he would leave her, or that he would turn her out of his house, and if he did where would she go? Edward had said that this life was making both of them miserable, but she had thought that he was happy.

Perhaps, after all, it was Edward who was mad. He told her that everyone was disgusted at her in order to torture her. But Edward was not mad, or cruel. She lay quite still, trying to think only of the shapes of the furniture.

If I'd had any sense, Laura thought, I wouldn't be here. I should be a Sister in a hospital, or I should be on the stage. I was a fool, but he said he loved me, and I married him. If I'd thought of it from his point of view I'd never have done it. I am the one who is to blame for everything. She switched off the light and lay staring into the darkness.

10

STRANGELY ENOUGH, the next day was quite fine, and fine days in Scotland, despite anything that the Scots themselves may say, are extremely rare.

Those members of the house party who had come down to breakfast were in extremely good tempers, and those who had remained in bed were in even better ones.

'Wonderful day, what?' Charles approached the sideboard, rubbing his hands together. Porridge, bacon and eggs and cold grouse; it was the sort of breakfast Charles liked. He was glad to see that there was no iced orange juice, with Georgette in America, the servants had returned to civilised habits.

'Splendid day.' Edward had joined his brother at the sideboard.—Porridge, bacon and eggs and cold grouse, it was exactly the kind of breakfast he liked.

Bessie, Charles's elderly retriever, sat staring up at them; she was interested only in the grouse, anyone who liked could have the bacon and eggs.

"Morning, Manningham,' Charles said; 'you've got a good day for it.'

Mr Manningham smiled, but not completely wholeheartedly. He was to be fobbed off with some of the best salmon fishing in Scotland, whereas the others were going to shoot grouse. In a conversation with Charles the previous evening he had somehow been manoeuvred into saying that he preferred to fish. Afterwards, Mr Manningham hadn't quite been able to see how this had happened. It was the sort of thing that happened to him in the House of Commons and at meetings with his constituents, and Mr Manningham never did see how it happened.

'Those dogs arrived all right, I suppose?' Edward asked Charles; 'awful nuisance having to hire dogs, they're never satisfactory.'

Charles agreed that hired dogs were the devil, and the brothers settled down to their breakfast.

Looking at them across the table, Mr Hodgson thought, not for the first time, how extraordinarily alike they were. He had noticed it first when he had come to stay at Abbotsmere more than thirty years ago. Then Edward and Charles had been schoolboys and Mr Hodgson had been one of the very young men who seemed to be in continual attendance on their mother. How beautiful she had been, and Mr Hodgson sighed deeply; but it was all a very long time ago and he continued with his breakfast. Things changed, old loves were not replaced by new, but still there were compensations, and he thought of the beautifully printed treatise on certain aspects of some minor eighteenth-century poets which was due to come out next month, and was content, for he still had his work.

Georgette's butler came into the room to tell Charles that the car was at the door. And Charles said that when everyone was ready they ought to be making a start.

David Waverly, who had only just appeared, began to eat very fast; and Bessie, slowly, because of her rheumatism, rose to her feet, and stood by the door wagging her tail.

'Laura will be meeting us for lunch,' Charles said, and smiled at his sister-in-law. 'You know where it is? Anyhow Macdonald will be able to tell you.'

Macdonald was the ghillie who was going to take Mr Johnston Manningham fishing. Laura supposed that he was somewhere around the house. Probably in the decaying shed that was given over to fishing-rods and waders and all the rest of the cumbersome paraphernalia of this life.

The four men and Bessie with one of the keepers from the high-ground and two alien pointers were packed into the car. Laura and Mr Johnston Manningham were left in quiet possession of the dining-room.

Mr. Manningham lit a cigarette, and wondered if he should air his grievance about the shooting to Laura, but decided against it. Presently, they were joined by Mrs Manningham, who had breakfasted in bed. She was wearing a tweed fishing costume and was eager to be started.

Macdonald was found, the Manninghams were provided with packets of sandwiches, Mr Manningham's flask was filled with whisky, and to the benefit of the household another two guests were disposed of. There remained only Lady Forston and Barbara Waverly, both of whom were still in bed. Laura retired to the sitting-room in order to be out of the way of Georgette's butler, but she was not allowed to remain long in peace, for she was followed there by Georgette's cook.

Mrs Osborne was a masterful woman, able, but not at all willing, to take responsibility. Laura alone must think of things for them to have for dinner; must take all the thought for the luncheon that was to be carried out to the guns. The only concession made by Mrs Osborne was the admission that she had prepared the cases for the patties.

Edward, on the outside with Mr Hodgson a little way away to his right, tramped determinedly through the heather. They had tramped for about two hours now and Edward was far too hot. The morning had not gone at all well, and Edward had reached a stage where he was admitting to himself that he would have been happier elsewhere, doing something quite different. Far away on the horizon, he could see two dots which plodded slowly forwards, Charles and David Waverly.—Charles had been made a fool of when he had been induced to rent this moor, that was the only thought that, at the moment, gave Edward any satisfaction. The moor was bereft of grouse, that had been perfectly clear for some time, and if there had been any, they would have been free to have gone openly about their business, unnoticed and unharassed by those fools of dogs. Crossly, Edward thought of some of the other ways in which he might have been spending this very beautiful morning. Sitting under a tree and being brought a long cool drink by a waiter in a white coat. Or sitting under the awning of a yacht moored in the harbour at Cannes; this evening an enormous car would drive them to the casino; tomorrow they would sail out to the islands. And why the hell wasn't he there? He could have been perfectly well; the Grants had invited him, he had all but accepted, and then, to please Charles, he had come to Scotland. And what had he got for it? A damned dull party, and a long hot walk through a lot of beastly heather.

The dog working in front of Edward had stopped. The keeper was waving to him and Mr Hodgson to come up. Edward was slightly mollified; perhaps, after all, the morning was not going to be an entire waste of time. The trouble was that he was getting soft. He didn't take enough exercise, and he was putting on weight; but only temporarily, he insisted to himself as he plodded on, only the plodding was easier now that there was a promise of a reward for his labours.—Wonderful how old Eddie had lasted, he must be all of sixty-five; but he was as active as ever. He remembered how he and Charles had despised Eddie when they were boys; the tame pussy, the perpetual hanger-on, very little better than a gigolo; but Eddie had survived and he had his little reputation as a litterateur.

—Why on earth wasn't that covey getting up? It ought to be by now, they were very nearly on top of it. Had that blasted fool of a dog made a mistake, standing there as if it were playing grandmother's steps. Another few yards and the grouse would have to get up, that is if they didn't want to be trampled under foot.

Another few yards and there was a terrific agitation, a terrific fluttering of wings, and a lark rose straight out of the heather.

'Damn and blast!' Edward lowered his gun. He was very angry, and what is more, he was justified in his anger.

'What a perfectly heavenly day.' Lady Forston stood by the open window of the sitting-room and took a deep breath of air; a sample, as it were, of the day's beauty.

Seen by daylight, Lady Forston appeared to be even more brittle than she did in artificial light. She would break quite easily, Laura thought; but in this she was wrong, for Lady Forston was extremely tough, she had had to be.

Lady Forston took another tentative breath of air, and then came over to the fireplace. She told Laura that it was time that they were starting.

'Do you think so?' Laura got up immediately. 'I'll go and see if Mrs Waverly is ready.'

She would also have to see if luncheon was ready; Mrs Osborne had threatened that it might be late.

Lady Forston did not miss the look of anxiety on Laura's face, and she was faintly amused. Fear, in any form whatsoever, was not an emotion for which Irene Forston had any time. Fear must be broken down, concealed and forgotten; if it were not, life would be impossible. That was a good sound principle, and it had brought Irene (*née* Annie) all the way from Chicago to, well to where she was. It had brought her across all the years that lay between herself as she now was, and the little timid girl who had entered seventh grade some time in the late eighties.

She considered Laura with contempt. Here was someone who was not making the best of their opportunities. 'Fool', Irene thought and smiled at Laura.

Mrs Osborne had relented, and luncheon was after all ready on time. Georgette's butler packed it and Lady Forston, Laura and the pekes into the shooting brake, where they sat and waited for Barbara Waverly.

Lady Forston was afraid that this present marriage of Barbara's was not going any better than her previous ones.

'And it can't always be the fault of husband after husband.' Lady Forston was severe.

'I suppose not.' Laura was depressed, thinking about her own marriage to Edward.

Lady Forston started on a diatribe upon the advantages of a happy home life led for the most part in Grosvenor Square, but she was the only speaker, she did not give Laura an opportunity to join in. 'I chose,' Lady Forston said, to marry an Englishman and to live in this country; but I could have done anything I liked.'

Laura could well believe her.

'And I have known all the important people of my time.'

But she spoke of a world which had already passed away.

'I am so terribly sorry to have kept you waiting.' Barbara Waverly was hurrying out to the car.

Laura looked at her with some respect; here was someone who had failed, not in one marriage, but in four.

Laura started the engine and they drove towards the moors. Their arrival there was exceedingly unfortunate. Either Macdonald had done it on purpose, or else Laura had mistaken his directions for reaching the area which Charles had thought the guns would have reached by lunch time. However it was, Laura, Lady Forston, Barbara Waverly and, even more unfortunately, Constantia and Augustus appeared out of the heather at exactly the right moment to put up a covey of grouse which Edward and Mr Hodgson had been patiently pursuing for the last hour. This was to have been the reward for their morning's exertions, this was to have compensated them for the lark, and it was all spoilt by Laura's stupidity, and by the happy barking of Constantia and Augustus. The covey, rising into the air, swung away to the left, only to alight when they had reached a part of the moor which belonged to an American gentleman who had rented the next-door lodge. Laura, quite unaware of the enormity that she had committed, waved at Edward. The puppies bounced awkwardly through the heather, their movements reminiscent of extremely heavy-weight hunters, or perhaps more exactly of old-fashioned rocking horses. Naturally, Edward was extremely angry; so was Mr Hodgson, who, unlike Edward, did not feel that he was able to say so.

'But Macdonald said we were to come this way, Charles said to ask Macdonald where to come and he said here.'

'That's quite impossible.'

'But he *did* say it.' Laura turned for corroboration to Lady Forston, who had not been present at the interview with Macdonald.

'Anyhow you could *see* us, couldn't you?' With at; terrific effort, Edward managed to stop himself from shouting at his wife, and was rather pleased with his own forbearance; another man . . . another man would probably have killed her.

'No,' Laura said, 'we couldn't see you, because you were just behind that little slope.'

—This was the sheerest idiocy; if they hadn't seen him and Reggie Hodgson with their attendant keepers, at least they must have seen Charles and David Waverly on the, other side of the shallow valley.

'Considering you've ruined the entire day for everybody, you ought to be satisfied.'

'I saw you,' Barbara Waverly said, 'but I didn't think it could be you—I mean, I was expecting you to be walking the other way.'

'And those blasted little dogs.' Edward had become suddenly aware of the presence of Constantia and Augustus.

'At least you might have known not to bring them out on a moor.'

'You see,' Lady Forston said quietly, 'I did tell you.'

It was precisely at this moment that one of the hired dogs so far forgot itself as to join Constantia and Augustus in chasing each other round a large clump of heather, both Constantia and Augustus were delighted by this addition to their party; they showed their delight by yelps and squeals of mock terror.

All Edward's fury was now turned on this dog and on the man who was supposed to be in charge of it.

The dog changed its mind about the whole thing being a game, from somewhere underneath the dog Augustus screamed to the world for help; Constantia crept away into the heather. Augustus was rescued and caught up in Laura's arms, where he continued to scream for some minutes, although apparently quite unhurt. Constantia reappeared and stood smugly wagging her tail, looking up trustfully at the angry human beings by whom she was surrounded.

But it was only Edward who was seriously angry. The others were prepared to forget the whole thing and have luncheon, for it was, after all, a very beautiful day. Lady Forston was relieved to see that on the other side of the valley Charles had called a halt; he and David Waverly were walking towards the road where the station wagon was parked. Bessie, released from duty, lumbered behind them.

'You *are* mad,' Edward said. He and Laura stood alone, facing each other.

'I don't care if I am.' Laura heard her own voice ending in a sob. Augustus, still badly frightened, whimpered in sympathy.

'Do you want everyone to hear you?' Edward spoke very quietly, hardly above a whisper.

'I don't care,' Laura said desperately, and now she was sobbing quite loudly.

Edward took a step towards her and grasped her wrist.—'Control yourself, can't you.'

'I can't,' Laura said, 'I've tried and I can't. Everything I do is wrong and I don't care. Go and have lunch with your beastly friends, or Charles's beastly friends. But leave me alone, because I can't stand any more of you.' She turned away from him, stumbling blindly.

Edward was extremely put out, and uncertain as to what to do next. He could see Lady Forston looking back at them over her shoulder; and, only too clearly, he could imagine Irene as she would look when describing this scene. She would be sitting in the large tapestried chair which stood in her drawing-room; one small white wrinkled hand resting on the arm, the other poised at an angle, holding her long old-fashioned cigarette holder.

Laura was still only a few paces away from him. He called on her to stop.

'What the hell do you think you're doing?'

'I don't care.'

'Control yourself,' Edward said, and then, 'pull yourself together,' but his voice was not as certain as it had been a few moments ago.

It was quite obvious that Laura was incapable of pulling herself together. He caught up with her and saw that tears were running down her cheeks. Constantia played happily in the heather, and Augustus struggled to get out of Laura's arms.

'Leave me alone.'

Edward hesitated for a moment and then turned his back on her. Why should he care what Irene thought? Irene was nothing but a silly gossiping old woman—so was Reggie Hodgson if it came to that. Defiantly he started after the others. Why did Charles have to surround himself with such dreary people? But then Charles always had been a pompous ass.

Luncheon, when the picnic baskets were at length unpacked, was not an easy occasion. Edward's announcement that Laura seemed to be upset and was going for a walk was received rather nervously.

Charles hoped that she wouldn't go and lose herself.

Lady Forston gave it as her opinion that it was a great mistake for people to allow things to upset them; and there was a glint of malice in the expression on her little wizened face.

Barbara Waverly, helping to unpack the baskets, was much touched when she came across two small parcels of minced meat wrapped in grease-proof paper and respectively labelled 'Connie' and 'Aug'.

Although, in front of his guests, Charles had expressed the sympathetic hope that Laura would not go and lose herself on the moor, he was actually extremely annoyed with her.

During the long hot afternoon, as unproductive of sport as the long hot morning, he had plenty of time in which to brood over his anger. Laura was being very tiresome, and even if Edward didn't care, Charles very definitely did.

He wasn't unreasonable, he quite realised that Georgette's father wasn't dying on purpose; but it was inconvenient that Georgette should be away. Very inconvenient. And in a few days the Grand Duchess would be arriving; to be confronted with a hostess who ran away and hid in the heather! Edward should have learnt by now to keep his wife in better order! Something very definite would have to be done about it. And Charles scowled and his thoughts turned towards the Stock Exchange; but there was no comfort to be found there either.

By six o'clock he had worked himself up into a state of righteous indignation. The Government, Georgette's father, the

Stock Exchange, Laura, but Laura was the only one which he could actually do anything about. He started to do it as soon as he got back to the house. He went straight up to his bedroom and sent for Edward. He also sent for a decanter of whisky.

'Ghastly, isn't it?' Edward said as he came into the room; 'the fellow ought to be sued for false pretences.'

Charles said that there had been plenty of grouse on the moor the year before.

Edward helped himself to whisky.

'Look here,' Charles said, 'I'm not going to beat about the bush with you—is there anything the matter with Laura?'

'Oh that,' and Edward sat down on the bed; 'well you know what she is.'

He seemed to have forgotten how angry he himself had been with Laura both last night and this morning.

'Well, I won't have it,' Charles said, 'anyhow not in *my* house. Has she come in, by the way, or is she still wandering about on the moor with her bloody dogs? Why did you let her bring those dogs anyhow? You must have known I wouldn't like it.'

'Really, Charles, you get more pompous every time I see you.'

'Well, has she come in?'

'As far as I know.'

'Very well, and you say there's nothing the matter with her?'

'Why should there be anything the matter with her?'

Perversely, Edward would not admit or perhaps he could no longer see, that there had been anything amiss in Laura's recent behaviour. Charles was still the pompous little ass he had always been. Always trying to impress people and terrified of what they would think of him. Edward remembered with amusement that time at their private school when he had told everyone who would listen to him that the Wests were an old Jewish family and were just about to emigrate to Palestine. Charles had been furious, terrified that his friends would believe it—quite a few of them had.

'Now look here,' Charles began again from the beginning, 'I don't want to beat about the bush. I think Laura's suffering from nerves or something; and we can't have her going on like that when the Grand Duchess arrives. I mean to say, it's embarrassing for everybody.'

'Do you remember when we were an old Jewish family?' Edward asked.

'It's no good trying to be funny,' Charles said, 'and I'm damn sorry for you. I should think everybody's sorry for you; but something's got to be done about it.'

'What would you suggest?'

'Well we might . . .' and Charles paused; he found it difficult actually to put into words the fact that he would prefer his sister-in-law to leave his house.

'Well?' Edward had got up and was standing by the fireplace looking down at Charles with the amused rather pitying smile of an elder brother.

Charles shifted in his chair. 'It's damned awkward.'

'Aren't you making rather a mountain out of a molehill?'

'No,' Charles said decisively; 'no, I'm not.'

'Good.' Edward helped himself to another whisky.

Charles was considerably put out. He was no longer used to being thwarted in anything at all. The obedient and rich Georgette was accustomed to obey him, a mere hint was enough and she would remove every obstacle (or crumpled rose leaf) from his path.

She had taught his children and the servants to obey him instantly.—Any troubles, complaints, or attacks of insubordination must be brought to Georgette. Charles was beyond criticism and must be protected from everything that was disagreeable. His health had saved him from having to take any active part in the war.—Exactly what was the matter with him was never quite clear—too weak for war, but strong enough for grouse shooting.

With Georgette in America and Edward and Laura in Scotland Charles was no longer protected.—Why, he asked himself, had he ever invited them? It had been a mistake; but at the time he had thought that, as members of his family, they would act as his protectors.

He passed his hand across his forehead, momentarily closing his eyes. It was well known that he wasn't strong; that he got tired very easily. If Edward and Laura were to leave, things would not really be much better, for then the entertainment of his guests would fall entirely upon himself; and who would show the Grand Duchess to her rooms? It was too bad that he had never had a sister, that his aunts, who hadn't been of much use when they were alive, were now dead.

But there was, of course, an answer ready to hand. It came out in hints and half-hints. Edward, to his credit, was rather against it.—As soon as that was clearly established, Charles became insistent.

Mrs Martell was Laura's cousin, wasn't she? That made her more or less a cousin to all of them. Nobody would think it odd if she came up to Scotland; in order to be with poor Laura, who really wasn't at all well. (Generously, Charles was allowing Laura to join him in his private sanctuary of mild invalidism.) Nobody would think it odd if Cathie were to take as much of the entertaining as possible off poor Laura's shoulders. Nobody would think it odd if Cathie showed the Grand Duchess to her room.

'Very well, if you are determined on it,' and Edward helped himself to a third whisky and soda.

'Now be reasonable,' Charles said, 'it's by far the best plan'— and then, because he was not really ungenerous, he said that he was sorry for what he had said about Constantia and Augustus, and that if they were kept under proper control, he saw no reason why they might not remain at Millhill.

Mrs Martell, messing about at Redbourne with her barbola work, was agreeably surprised when the telephone started to ring. And it couldn't possibly be Mrs Willis or Daphne, for after a prolonged tea with Mrs Hartley-James; they had only just left the house.—Mrs Martell had heard their departure through the closed door of her room. She had heard the prolonged search for Mrs Willis's galoshes' (unlike Scotland the south coast of England was undergoing a period of unremitting rain). She had heard Mrs Hartley- James' apologies for her daughter's absence from the tea-party, which apologies had been unwisely mixed with explanations in which important work, a headache and absence from home had been indiscriminately intermingled.

'Yes!' Mrs Hartley-James had managed to get to the telephone before her daughter. She was excited when she heard that the call was from Scotland. Disappointed when she learnt that it was not for herself.

Cathie, coming to the telephone, was disappointed to hear Charles's voice instead of Edward's. But when she heard what he had to say, the whole world became immediately delightful. A delight which would have been perfectly pure had it not been mixed with triumph.

She must take the night train to Scotland tomorrow. She would be at Millhill the following morning. Yes, she would try and get a sleeper, but if one were not available it really didn't matter. She sent her love to Edward and to Laura.

Dinner that evening was, anyhow to Laura, as dull, or alternatively as terrible, as it had been the evening before. She hadn't seen Edward alone since they had parted on the moors. When, having dressed, she came down to the drawing-room, Edward, deep in conversation with Mrs Waverly and Lady Forston, pretended not to notice her.

The conversation went on. Laura stood a little apart from the others. She had not even the support of Constantia and Augustus; it had been part of her afternoon's resolutions that they should be kept as much as possible out of the way.

David Waverly came across and spoke to her; but what did she care for David Waverly?

Suddenly, Edward looked up. 'Ah, Laura, I didn't see you come in.' The look he gave her was of private hate and of social welcome.

Laura smiled back; perhaps after all everything was going to be all right.

'Where are the dogs?' Charles asked and his voice was kindly.

'They're upstairs,' Laura said.

But Charles hadn't expected an answer.

'Perhaps after all,' Laura thought, 'everything was going to be all right.' A short while ago she had despaired; but now she was confident. Even the Johnston Manninghams became delightful companions. And only very faintly, and in the background, was the voice that continued to pray for 'all this' to go on for ever.

—Please, oh please, let me never be unhappy again. Please I will be good. Please let me be happy.—'If you stopped for one moment thinking about yourself you would be happy, you have everything to make you so.' That was another voice, it was Edward's but she hardly recognised it. And all the time that these voices were going on she was talking to David Waverly about the theatre.—But they weren't really voices, for they were without sound.—'If you stopped thinking about yourself.' But didn't everybody think about themselves? Even if you thought about something entirely impersonal, like a problem in algebra, for instance, there was only one's own mind with which to think. And here, Laura smiled very charmingly at David and agreed with him that *she* had never enjoyed *Twelfth Night* very much either.

—'If only you could tell what people were thinking as well as what they were saying.' Some people claimed that they could; but Laura didn't believe them. Of course there was the quite simple case where someone said, 'Thank you very much, I'd love to,' and you knew perfectly well that they'd rather not. But below that there were so many layers of thought,—how do you spell a certain word,—or the spelling of the word running meaninglessly through one's head—what am I going to do tomorrow?—What if so-and-so doing now?—What is the meaning of life?—and the difficulties of imagining Elizabethan England, when one had to think away the hedges.

David Waverly was talking about *Hamlet*, a very long play, and *Macbeth*, which was the best 'theatre'. |

Laura had had this conversation before. It left her perfectly free to continue to think about herself.

But in one way and another they were all thinking about themselves.

'Yes, and no, and yes,' but all the time Mr Johnston Manningham was thinking about his constituency.—If only he had a decent agent; Baker was a good fellow, but really he had no idea! And it still rankled with him that he should have been sent fishing when the others were on the moors.

Mrs Manningham, giving a lecture on parliamentary procedure to Charles, continued to worry about her clothes. What exactly was wrong with them? She couldn't be sure; but they were 'wrong', of that she was certain. She looked across at Barbara Waverly. Barbara would have been able to tell her about her clothes; but Mrs Manningham would always be too proud to ask her.—And it wasn't simply that they weren't expensive enough, for she had paid a great deal of money for them.

—The relative merits of the performances given by Alec Guinness and Gielgud—David Waverly was getting on well now. He was concentrating entirely upon what he was saying. It would be several minutes before he would start worrying again about Barbara.

But Laura was hardly listening; it wasn't necessary anyhow, for she really was very accustomed to this conversation. She was watching and listening to Edward as he talked to Lady Forston.

Edward was leaning slightly forward looking into that crabbed little face with every appearance of admiration.

How well he did it, Laura thought irritably, the smile, the slight suggestion of deference.

'. . . but, my dear Irene, we don't have to worry about that.'

—What hadn't they to worry about? Laura hadn't heard the beginning of the sentence.

'But I don't see at all that it was necessary.' Lady Forston threw out her tiny hands in a gesture of exaggerated bewilderment.

Edward laughed softly.

'As who should say, what a child you are, Irene,' Laura thought, and was struck unpleasantly by her own maliciousness.

And then she realised that Edward had gone on, he was telling Irene that Cathie would be arriving the day after tomorrow.

'But who is this very sudden cousin; why have I never heard of her?'

—But of course Lady Forston had heard of Cathie. Laura was seized with a sudden, an almost uncontrollable, anger.

Gielgud and Alec Guinness and *Hamlet*, and never for one moment must one forget *Richard III*.

—Why hadn't they told her that they had invited Cathie up here, and *when* had she been invited anyhow? Why, Charles hardly knew her!

Mrs Manningham decided on a sudden that her real trouble lay in flowered crêpe-de-chine.

—I don't care, Laura told herself, and looked very much as if she were going to cry.

But David Waverly, although he was looking directly at her, didn't notice anything.

—And I wish she were dead.—No, I don't, one mustn't wish for anyone to be dead. It's wicked—or it comes back on oneself.

Laura looked wildly round the table and was rewarded by a frown from Charles. She had been very near to forgetting that the time had come for the ladies to leave the dining-room.

11

'LEAN *AVAY* from the hill.' Now you are travelling faster and faster. Try not to think about anything at all. How cold the air is.—This is what flying *ought* to be like. How beautiful it is with the sun shining on the snow.

'Lean *avay* from the hill.' Very soon there will be the corner; it is very icy there and it will be difficult to turn. 'Lean *avay* from the hill.' You take in a great breath of icy air. And now unbelievably you are falling.—If this were a dream, I would wake up before I reached the bottom.

This can't possibly be happening to me. Sliding down the side of a mountain and at the bottom there is a precipice.

And then, for no reason that was apparent to her, Laura came to rest with her face buried in soft snow. She shook herself free and sat up rather carefully. The edge of the precipice was still quite a long way away.

She looked upwards at the heights from which she had descended. Small figures flashed along the side of the mountain;

as she watched, one of them, having apparently lost all sense of reason, suddenly threw its arms in the air and began an utterly uncontrolled descent. It was travelling very fast and Laura was terrified that it would reach the edge of the precipice and disappear over the edge.

There was a roar of fury from above, 'I say you should lean *away* from the hill.'

The other figure now lay spread-eagled in the snow; its skis, pointing in opposite directions, made it look like some defunct insect. It had stopped much nearer to the edge of the ravine than Laura.

'Are you all right?' Laura called ineffectively; if the insect really was dead there was nothing she could do about it. If it was alive and wanted help it would undoubtedly be better served by the guide.

'You do as I say, you lean *away* from the hill.' The guide, Hans, with an unnecessarily expert flourish, came to a standstill beside Laura. He stood looking down at her, making no attempt to help her to her feet.

'I think,' Laura said, 'that that gentleman is hurt.'

Hans shrugged his shoulders. Laura was his pupil and the hurt gentleman was no affair of his.

The hurt gentleman struggled and sat up. He was in great pain; but he didn't know yet that he had fractured his collar-bone.

'Are you all right?' Laura called.

'No,' Mr Hardy called back, 'I'm not all right at all.'

'You see,' Laura said admonishingly to the guide. But Hans had already relented and was making his way across to Mr Hardy.

'Such a shame to break something at the beginning of the fortnight.' The elderly lady who had waylaid Laura in the hall of the hotel clicked anxiously over her knitting-needles.

'Yes,' Laura agreed, 'oh, yes.'

'When I was out here with my boys *last* year, we had two broken legs; but only on the very last day.'

'Even so, it must have been dreadful.'

'Of course they didn't both belong to us. What does the doctor think of your friend? I always think that Swiss doctors all excellent; that is if they have time to come at all. When my daughter had influenza, or at least we thought it was influenza, the doctor never came near her. Just sent a message to say he was busy doing something else.'

'How dreadful.'

'Indeed it was, and the room filled with bluebottles. How they manage to *live* in this climate, I can't imagine.'

'Isn't it extraordinary, there are heaps of bluebottles in my bedroom every evening.'

'The doctor isn't keeping your friend in bed, is he?'

'Only for this evening because of the shock. He says he can get up tomorrow.'

The lady nodded her agreement; collar-bones, that is to say clavicles, ought never to be kept in bed. They mended quicker if the patient was walking about. But it took time and there would be no question of the friend skiing again for the rest of his holiday.

'And I suppose you and your husband feel partly responsible for him?'—This was a shot in the dark. The lady had been curious about this party ever since its arrival three days ago.— Which of the two men—if either—was married to Laura? And what relation to any of them was the older lady, and that girl of about fifteen? Then there was that other rather grim-looking woman whom Mrs Marsh somehow thought wasn't quite nice, and the men; it was the men in whom she was interested.

'My husband,' Laura said, obligingly playing right into Mrs Marsh's hand. 'Oh, he isn't responsible at all, he's in England.'

'Not able to get away, I suppose?'

'I suppose not.'

Mrs Marsh suddenly began to count the stitches on her needles; a quite unnecessary operation really, as she had just come to one of those straight pieces on her knitting—

'Continue until the garment measures thirteen inches from the beginning of the ribbing.'

Laura drifted away.—Should she go and have a nice hot bath before dinner; or go and find Mrs Hardy and have a long talk about the collar-bone? She decided on the bath.

Laura walked upstairs to her bedroom which was on the top and third floor. Halfway along her corridor she met Rosemary, Mr Hardy's niece by marriage.

'I've just been in to see him, and he says it isn't hurting nearly so much now.'

It was Rosemary's habit of speaking of everyone as 'he' or 'she' and addressing them as 'you' which had frustrated Mrs Marsh in her efforts to identify their relationships.

'I'm glad,' Laura said, she didn't really care about Rosemary.

'Are you going to have a bath, because if you are, can I have the water after you've finished?'

'I should think so'—and Laura went on into her bedroom.

Asking to use other people's bath water after they had finished was, Laura thought, one of the worst of Rosemary's irritating habits. If one agreed to such an arrangement one felt that one had, in honour, to keep the water as clean and hot as possible—not an ideal way of having a bath—and not to agree put one in the position of being intolerably selfish. Either way it was maddening and it was the greatest pity that baths were an 'extra' and extremely expensive.

Laura rang the bell for Trudi, who would unlock the bathroom, run the water and find towels. All of which took at least a quarter of an hour, even if Trudi didn't happen to be busy performing the same services for somebody else.

Laura took off her jacket and kneeling down, began to unlace her ski boots. She did it slowly, regretfully. It was like taking off a disguise or putting aside one's armour.

Trudi knocked at the door to know if it was Laura who had rung; she was young and fresh-faced and spoke practically nothing but German. Her English consisted of such basic words as 'bath' and 'early morning tea'.

Laura put on a dressing-gown and settled down to wait. It was a new woollen dressing-gown especially bought for Switzerland.

She looked round the carefully austere bedroom, the scrubbed floor, the grey painted bedstead, the flowered wallpaper. The small high sofa with, in front of it, a solid wooden table. The sort of table at which one ought to write a book, Laura thought. How wonderful it would be just to stay here. This room and the view of the mountains. Artists and writers buried themselves in places like this for months at a time. The stage and the setting, but there was no central character. Just an English lady recovering from a long illness. Laura, wrapped in the beige anonymity of her dressing-gown, was suddenly depressed. A lady whose relations had arranged for her to live abroad. But it wasn't like that at all. She was a member of a jolly party who were in Switzerland for the winter sports.

It had been kind of the Hardys to include her; but of course the whole thing had been arranged by Cathie.

Cathie had been wonderful through everything. She had been wonderful at Millhill, protecting Laura from all those people.

And then when Laura had gone into the London nursing home she had been wonderful again. Going to see her nearly every day. And it was such miles away, Laura thought, and I was there for so long. The doctors never had found out what was the matter with her. Just those terrible headaches and the high fevers.

—They say that you can't remember pain. Lying in bed crying helplessly and waiting for the night Sister to come and unlock the drug cupboard. And then being roughly wakened in the night by a nurse who said that she had been screaming and could be heard right the other end of the building. The nurse had seemed to be very angry and now they would have to wait for the Sister to come and give them the pills which would send Laura to sleep again.

In the end she had got better. The headaches had come to be bearable. One night a patient from across the corridor had come into Laura's room and started telling her about a lot of duchesses. The patient had an idea that Laura might be related to some of them. One of the duchesses had jumped out of a window in Eaton Square.

'Was she killed?'

But at this point a nurse had appeared and started to hustle the patient out of the door.

'You know perfectly well, Mrs Smith, that you are not allowed out of your room.'

It was after this incident that Laura had begun seriously to wonder whether she was in a lunatic asylum.—But she couldn't be, because the patient next door to her was suffering from two broken legs and a fractured pelvis. She had broken them in Africa and had been flown to this London suburb in order that they might be mended. Matron said that she made a wonderful patient.—If next-door has a fractured pelvis, I can't be in a lunatic asylum.—But the woman who had talked about the duchesses had seemed to be very mad.—And they haven't told me what is the matter with me.

Edward came to see her about two or three times a week, bringing fruit and flowers; he was very kind, but somehow Laura's headaches were always worse on the evenings which followed on Edward's visits. Then, when she was getting better, he went down to Abbotsmere and she didn't see him for nearly a fortnight. And it was during that time that Cathie caught influenza and Laura didn't see her either for several days. Laura missed Cathie very much and realised that she had come to rely on her, to trust to Cathie's advice in everything.

Then the doctor told her that in a day or two she would be well enough to go home and after he had left the room, Laura dissolved into tears. That evening her temperature was up again to a hundred and four. Matron appeared and said that they would keep her for as long as she wanted to stay, Laura mustn't think that they wanted to get rid of her.

A few weeks later the doctor again said that she was almost well enough to leave; and this time Laura took it more calmly. The doctor said that what she needed was sea air.

'If you could get away to Italy now, or perhaps the South of France.' The doctor had seen service abroad during the war and it had left him dissatisfied with England.

But Cathie arranged that Laura should go to Brighton.

'You just remember that you have been very ill; time enough to think about going abroad when you are stronger.'

'You don't think I ought to go home?'

But apparently the doctor had told Cathie that he didn't think Laura ought to go to Abbotsmere at the moment.

'Why not?'

'He doesn't think that you are up to it,' and Cathie repeated that Laura was to remember that she had been very ill.

Cathie and Laura travelled down to Brighton together. Cathie playing the part of the solicitous friend.—Laura must put her feet on the footstool. She must try and drink just a little coffee and eat just one of those delicious digestive biscuits.

They had rooms at one of the smaller hotels on the front. Horrible rooms which had been cut down, by means of plywood partitions, from larger ones.

Cathie managed to hire a bath-chair, and for two afternoons she pushed Laura, blue with cold, along the parade. On the third afternoon Laura refused to get into the chair and said she would rather walk. Cathie took it upon herself to be offended. She let it be understood that Laura was lacking in gratitude: and after everything that had been done for her! They walked slowly to the nearest shelter and there, Cathie told Laura about the arrangements which had been made for her.

'Dr Heseltine thinks that it will be quite a long time before you are able to go home, but, of course, you mustn't allow it to upset you.'

'No,' Laura agreed, and then suggested that if they were going to be in Brighton for a long time it might be nice to send for Constantia and Augustus.

'I think you'd find them rather difficult to manage in the hotel; anyhow, I don't believe dogs are allowed.'

'Then perhaps we could move to somewhere else.'

Cathie frowned; they were becoming entangled in a side issue.

'We didn't necessarily think that you should stay indefinitely in Brighton. But Dr Heseltine does think that you need a complete change—of people, as well as of surroundings,' and Mrs

Martell smiled very sweetly, consciously remembering that she was dealing with somebody who had been very ill.

'You mean,' Laura said, 'that Edward doesn't want me back?'

'Now then, it's not going to do any good to talk like that,' and Mrs Martell smiled even more kindly and leant over and rearranged the rug which she had insisted upon bringing for Laura.

'But that's what you're trying to tell me.'

'You're being foolish,' Mrs Martell said. 'Dr Heseltine and Dr Johnstone were both agreed that what you needed now was a complete change.'

'Then why didn't they tell me so?'

'If you don't believe me . . .' Mrs Martell was becoming impatient, it was a real effort to keep the smile in place.

'Oh, I believe you,' Laura said; 'I just thought it was funny, that's all.'

'Perhaps it would be a good thing if we got Dr Heseltine to come down here; he would explain it all so much better than I can.' She was in control again now, and the smile was easy and self-assured.

'If I'm not to stay in Brighton and I'm not to go home, where am I to go?' Laura asked, and added hastily, in case Cathie should become annoyed again, that she was only wondering.

'Well, we did have a little plan, but if you don't like it you only have to say so and we'll think of something else.' The smile now was of the cosy motherly variety.

Laura, who felt suddenly very tired, didn't say anything.

'Well now,' and Mrs Martell paused to frown discouragement at an elderly gentleman seated at the other end of the shelter. She suspected him of listening to the conversation, but she needn't have worried for the elderly gentleman was practically stone deaf.

Cathie crossed her beautiful slim ankles and paused again as she admired them. She was very happy, this was just the kind of conversation she most enjoyed, a long heart-to-heart with herself doing all the talking. She was about to be wise and understanding and reasonable. She was about to get her own way. Kindly and reasonably she told Laura about the perfectly splendid little plan for sending her off to Switzerland with the Hardy family.

'You remember Dick, you met him with me in London.'

Rather dazedly Laura agreed that she remembered Dick.

Mrs Martell smiled encouragement and continued; she was being so completely understanding, so entirely sympathetic, that she quite failed to notice that Laura was exhausted and very cold. Only the elderly gentleman, as he watched them, wondered if the young lady might not be going to faint. The plan was quite simple. For sever weeks every year (when there was no European war going on) Mrs Hardy, that is to say Dick's mother, was in the habit of abandoning her parish duties and the choir, and going with a party of young people to Switzerland.

'Cheerful company,' Mrs Martell said, and 'a complete change, and of course with a certificate from Dr Heseltine there will be no difficulty about getting additional currency.'

Laura tried the experiment of not listening. If only, she thought, people who were well would realise that the most tiring thing in the world is a discussion of little plans.—'You can do this, or this, it would be an even better idea to do that.'—If only they could understand that it isn't possible to make any decisions when the brain has become only a burning lump of metal. But Cathie continued inexorably.

One day when she was coming out of the door of the nursing home she had met Dick quite by accident; he had been sent down to Hammersmith to cover the story of a haunted house. They had had tea together. He had been terribly sorry to hear of Laura's illness.—She didn't mention that he had wanted to know when Cathie was going to spend another week-end with him. Cathie had been deeply shocked; the incident at the hotel at Redbourne had certainly not been a week-end (and anyhow it had been a long time ago). Well, if she didn't think it had been a week-end it hadn't been, Mr Hardy for his part was willing to let it go at that. Rather too willing, Mrs Martell thought, for was he not the second string to her bow? The smile she gave him was intended to be provocative and full of promise. Her eyelashes fluttered on her cheeks. To cover what might have been an awkwardness, they spoke of Laura.

'And he told me about his mother going to Switzerland, and it all seemed to fit in so beautifully. As she goes there every year they give her special rates; and then of course they are sure to give her an allowance on the people she brings so you don't have to be at all grateful to her.'

'I don't mind being grateful.' Laura had realised that simply 'not listening' was no defence against Cathie.

'Anyhow she's longing to have you.'

'So it's already arranged?'

'Not if you don't want to go.' Cathie was becoming impatient again; Laura *had* been ill of course, but really it was time that she tried to make an effort.

'I don't think that you ought to have written to her without telling me.'

But the protest was not a serious one and that evening Laura, having her supper in bed, was agreeing with Cathie that Switzerland with the Hardys would be delightful.

'Dick may even be going himself.' It was Cathie's final reward for acquiescence. Secretly she considered it the only flaw in her plan.

Three weeks later Edward and Cathie were seeing Laura off at Victoria station. Laura was a member of a jolly party which was going to Switzerland for the winter sports. Edward had been charming and helpful. Looking at him as he talked to Mrs Hardy Laura wondered exactly why Dr Heseltine had considered it best for her to be separated from him.

'Take care of yourself and come back well and strong,' and he had bent to kiss her cheek.

'You'll write to me?'

'Every day,' Edward had promised, but as he never wrote any letters at all it wasn't, Laura thought sadly, a promise that he was likely to keep.

As the train drew out of the station she watched him and Cathie as they stood together on the platform. Slowly, they dissolved into the fog which hangs for ever over Victoria Station.

Laura turned her face away from the window, looking, without interest, at her travelling companions. The hearty young men, she disliked particularly the one with the moustache, and the child Rosemary, and Mrs Hardy had already begun the occupation which was to last her the duration of the journey; that of counting the various pieces of luggage for which she considered herself to be responsible.

The journey had been without incident and the channel had been smooth. At Calais there was the excitement which comes with the boarding of a foreign train. An excitement which is never more than partially dissipated by the fact that every sleeping berth is inevitably occupied by the English.

Then the disappointment the following morning on finding that Switzerland, unlike London, is without snow. And the slow ascent by funicular railway and the unbelievable beauty of snow and mountains and frozen waterfalls.

The arrival at the small, clean hotel, the welcome from the proprietor and his wife, the introduction to the bedroom with the scrubbed floor and the gay wallpaper, the discovery that, despite all of Mrs Hardy's efforts, a suitcase has been left behind at Wengen.

Laura looked out of her bedroom window at the mountains and wished that she could stay here for ever.

There was a knock on the door; it was Trudi who announced that the bath was now ready.

Regretfully, Laura got up, collected her towel and sponge and started down the corridor. As she came to Rosemary's door, Rosemary, who had been waiting for her, shot out of it.

'You won't forget that you're going to leave the water for me?'

'No, I won't forget.'

'I'll come and knock on the door in about ten minutes, shall I?' And Rosemary smiled happily, seemingly quite unaware of what a bore she was being.

12

CATHIE, TRAVELLING OUT to Switzerland, began her journey with elation; but long before she had reached the end of it the mood had changed and she was filled with misgivings. To begin with she seemed, amongst the crowds of holiday-makers, to be the only person to be travelling alone and this in itself was depressing. There should amongst all those people have been one tall handsome stranger of suitable age. He should have been placed at her table in the dining-car of the French train. He should, in the natural course of conversation, have asked her to share a bottle of wine with him; and the story should have gone on from there; but her story couldn't have gone on from there, for it was already written.

Even so, an encounter with a tall and handsome stranger would have been a pleasant interlude, but alas, he did not appear. Once, in the corridor, and right at the beginning of the journey, she thought she had found him; but later when he came into the dining-car he was surrounded by a gaggle of five or six bright adolescents all of whom addressed him as 'Daddy'; and they were accompanied by a depressed middle-aged woman who inevitably was Mother; impossible to imagine her as having ever been anything else.

Mrs Martell had only her sense of self-righteousness with which to sustain herself throughout the long journey. She was right, she was brave and she was also beautiful. But the face which she saw reflected in the early morning in the mirror over the washbasin was grey and anxious. That would not do, this was not how she must appear to other people. Mrs Martell frowned, a last private indulgence. When the girl who shared her compartment returned to it a few moments later, Mrs Martell, as serene and beautiful as ever, was putting the finishing touches to her make-up.

The girl smiled uncertainly. The evening before she had been alarmed by the prospect of having to share the sleeper with this elegant woman. She had interpreted Cathie's silences as implied

reproof of herself; and had fled to the security of the compart-
ments occupied by her relations, only returning to her own after
Cathie was in bed.

But this morning Cathie turned to her with a radiant smile. It
was the smile which was to limber her up for the day, the smile
of which the morning exercises (one, two, three and *heave*) were
the physical equivalent.

But the girl didn't know this, she took it as implied approval
of herself.

'They're going to put the breakfast car on in half an hour.'

Cathie smiled again indulgently, for she needed nothing in
the world but weak tea and toast.

The girl, who had been greedily looking forward to eggs and
bacon, was abashed.

'I suppose you can ski already? It must be wonderful.'

Cathie agreed that it was, St. Moritz before the war, the girl
could have no idea.—But Wengen, and Cathie looked doubtful.
It was a place, wasn't it, to which tours went? Seven or fourteen
inclusive days. Probably it was very nice in its way and probably
in the evenings they had very nice little dances in the hotels.

'Daddy says it's a wonderful ski centre.'

Cathie allowed with a gesture of her hands that that was possible. 'But I shall probably only be there for one night.'

'And then you're going on somewhere else?'

'And then I shall be going back to England.'

'Oh,' and the girl was silenced.

Suddenly bored with her, Cathie turned away to the window.

Laura leaned back against the yoke of the ski-lift. How
strange it felt to be pulled up the hill like this slowly and silently;
her companion a strange young Swiss with whom, as he spoke
only German, there was no possibility of conversation. She
looked upwards at the mountain, the pairs of skiers attached to
the lift and sliding, against all the rules of nature, 'up' the slope.
This particular lift had only been installed last year; before
that those who wished to make either of the two runs from the
summit of Jungden had first to climb slowly up into the moun-

tain with skins attached to their skis; people who had possessed the necessary amount of endurance to do so, much resented the installation of the lift.

At the top the guide waited, surrounded by a little group of his pupils.

'You will lean avay from the hill.'

The pupils smiled sheepishly. They were the third class in the ski-school; there was one below them, a little group, who, so far, were only allowed to fall about on the nursery slopes; to them the third class was vastly superior; its members were allowed to fall about on Jungden and get in the way of the expert skiers, many of whom were practising for the championships.

The bulk of the experts were allowed to get away; shouting gaily to each other in German they shot straight down the mountainside, turning and twisting at the corners in a flurry of snow, but never for a moment seeming to lose speed. The class standing together shivering a little in the cold, watched them with a kind of helpless envy. Now there was a lull in the numbers of skiers being borne up to them by the lift; and the pause would continue until the next train arrived from Wengen.

'You are ready?' The guide spoke to all of them; but most particularly to the rather pretty girl who was his star pupil: tomorrow she would be leaving for the second class; but it didn't matter, he was not interested in girls.

'You follow me and you lean away from the hill.' He took off choosing a simple traverse; they had only to lean away from the hill and there was no need for any of them to fall. Down and up, skimming the side of the slope, never travelling very fast, and then a simple slow turn, which, if properly executed, would bring them to a second slow traverse. The snow—there had been a fall during the night—was dry and powdery and there was no ice; conditions were ideal.

One, two, three, four, five, six; and now it was Laura's turn. Down and up and down, knees slightly flexed, leaning away from the hill, the weight on the outside foot. The Winged Victory of Samothrace, the turn and a moment of apprehension, but the weight was safely transferred to the other foot; the Winged

Victory raced onwards. Down and up and down, then upwards again and over a sharp shoulder of the hill; another turn, another change of weight, 'Lean away from the hill', for ever and for ever and for ever; it ended, it had to come to an end, not at the next turn but at the one after, spoilt, as usual, by the mind which hesitated over trivialities.

Later in the morning, Laura sat at one of the little, green-painted tables by the ice rink. At all the tables there were skiers who ate their luncheons out of paper bags and ordered drinks from the waiters who passed between the tables. On the rink itself old gentlemen in Scottish tweeds bent low over their curling stones, or danced backwards in a traditional shuffle as they swept a pathway for the stones; and there were little traditional cries which went with the game and which were not to be understood by outsiders.

'So that is what the Scotch do when we leave them alone in Scotland for the winter'—and Ralph Brandon (he was the one with the moustache) turned from contemplating the curlers and signed to the waiter, who came immediately.

Laura began to unpack her luncheon and hurriedly decided against the tomato which had become frost-bitten.

Mr Brandon—he was far nicer than Laura had thought on first seeing him in the train—ordered a round of *Glühwein* for the six people who sat at the table.

This unwonted piece of generosity was received by the others with gratified misgivings. For was not the hoarding and counting of Swiss francs, together with the paying back to each other of borrowed centimes, the chief intellectual pursuit of all the English visitors?

Mr Brandon was very well aware of the impression he had created. He explained expansively that the *Glühwein* would warm them all up.

'Quite a nip in the air in spite of the sun.'

Mrs Hardy, wrapped up in her old and respectable fur coat, agreed that indeed there was.

Rosemary—why was it inevitable that Rosemary should always be with them?—giggled, in anticipation of the wine.

The young man whom they had inadvertently picked up at the ski-school didn't say anything. He was wondering if he had got himself mixed up with a party of black marketeers.

Josephine Manley (the woman whom the old lady in the hotel had somehow thought wasn't quite nice) said that the next round must be on her.

Rosemary giggled again, the ultra-sophistication of a second round was altogether too much for her.

The waiter appeared with a trayful of steaming glasses. At the entrance to the hotel a young Swiss started to play a piano-accordion. Another funicular arrived from Wengen and now nearly all the little tables were occupied. Through the plate-glass windows of the hotel residents could be seen at luncheon. Looking at them Mrs Hardy remarked that it was a mystery to her how they could manage on the allowance.

The young man from the ski-school—in real life he was an officer in the merchant navy—decided that perhaps Mrs Hardy wasn't a black marketeer after all.

There was a strangled cry from Rosemary.

'Do you see who's coming out of the hotel!'

The person to whom she referred was a tall, fair man who was standing at the top of the three long steps which led up to the hotel entrance; he was deep in conversation with another man who stood just behind him.

'I don't see anyone,' Mrs Hardy said, 'unless,' she conceded, 'you mean those people standing on the steps?'

'But don't you know who it *is*?' Rosemary asked.

Mrs Hardy looked again. 'Yes, dear, it's Robert Daniel, the composer you know.' She was thinking that Rosemary really was a very silly little girl but supposed, not for the first time, that nothing could now be done about it.

'It *is*, isn't it?' Rosemary turned for confirmation to the Merchant Navy officer, to Miss Manley and to Miss Brandon. Laura was still watching the curlers and hadn't even bothered to turn round.

The Merchant Navy officer (he was called Mr Jones) remembered that he had seen something about it in the *Daily Mail*; but it had only said an unknown destination in the Swiss Alps.

'Do you think I could get his autograph,' Rosemary said, 'do you think I could?'

'Oh, that reminds me'—and Mrs Hardy began to search in her bag—'he gave it to me for you.' She produced one of the hotel envelopes and handed it to Rosemary. On it was written, 'For Rosemary, with best wishes from Robert Daniel.'

'But you don't *know* him?' Rosemary's mouth had fallen slightly open; she looked quite idiotic.

'Certainly not, but I recognised him just now while I was waiting for you, and I thought it would be interesting to talk to him.'

'But . . . oh, what did you talk about?'

'About him, those people are all the same, and that's what they like, and I asked him how he composed his music. It appears that his hands do it by themselves while he's improvising on the piano.'

'How very, *very* interesting.'

'And then, I told him about the difficulties we've been having with the choir, always singing too loudly you know; I thought, as he had once been a chorister, it might interest him, and of course, I told him how very much I had enjoyed his last opera, *Heloise and Abelard*—that *was* the name of it, wasn't it? There were the two contraltos, such an unusual arrangement, I thought,' she finished anxiously, flushing a little, because, in spite of anything which she might have implied to the contrary, Mrs Hardy had been very pleased by her encounter with the famous Robert Daniel.—'Britain's best-loved composer,' who wrote not only 'serious' music, but music for the theatre which anyone could enjoy.

'There was a profile of him in the *Sunday Times* about two weeks ago,' Miss Manley said.

'A bit overdone, I thought.' Mr Brandon didn't like Miss Manley.

'Have you kept it, can I read it?' Rosemary asked.

'They told me down at the hotel that I should probably find you here.'

At the sound of the clear modulated voice, Laura jumped up from her seat. It couldn't possibly be Cathie, not out here, and yet, horribly, it was. For the last half-minute she had been aware that it was Cathie who had descended from the funicular, Cathie who was approaching them, and Cathie who would eventually come upon them and make escape impossible.

In the flurry of introductions and exclamations of surprise, the celebrated figure on the steps ceased for the moment to hold the whole attention even of Rosemary.

'This is indeed very pleasant.' But even as she said the words, Mrs Hardy felt certain misgivings. She wasn't really at all certain that Cathie's unheralded arrival on the ice rink was so very pleasant after all.

'Do you know who's here?' Rosemary was determined to be first with the news. 'Robert Daniel, *himself*, and Grandmother has actually talked to him.'

'Really,' and Mrs Martell looked vaguely in the direction indicated by Rosemary.

'Oh, he's 'gone.''

'Did you see his opera?' Miss Manley asked.

And it seemed that everybody had except Cathie.

'Oh, you should have, it was wonderful,' Rosemary gloated.

Mrs Martell said that of course some of his music was all right, but if she was going to be perfectly honest, she must say that she thought it disgraceful that someone who was capable of writing serious music should lower himself in order to write theatre music.

'Not theatre music, exactly, "music for the theatre", it's rather different, isn't it?' Mrs Hardy said.

Mrs Martell said that of course he wasn't as good as any of the top foreign composers, but then one couldn't expect him to be, the English weren't a musical nation, were they?

'Oh, don't you think so?' Miss Manley asked.

'He writes for the films too, you know,' Rosemary said.

Mrs Hardy said that she never felt that was the same thing, and had Mrs Martell spoken to the hotel about a room, because she was practically certain they hadn't got one.

Mrs Martell said, oh yes, she had wired to them last week and they had given her a very nice room with a private bath.

Mrs Hardy said, oh, in a rather disapproving voice.

'But you never let us know you were coming,' Laura said.

Mrs Martell smiled enigmatically and said that the sun was really wonderful, wasn't it?

The Merchant Navy officer murmured something about getting one of his skis fixed and if they would excuse him; he trailed off towards the ski shop.

Earlier in the day, Rosemary, who had fallen desperately in love with him for the sake of his fair wavy hair, would certainly have found that there was something the matter with her skis as well. But now, with the unexpected arrival of Mrs Martell and the existence somewhere quite close to them of Robert Daniel, she was content to let Mr Jones go on his way unmolested and unregretted.

Mr Brandon said that time was getting on and that if he was going to make the run down to Grindelwaldt he had better be starting.

Laura half rose as if to follow him and then, thinking better of it, sank back into her chair.

Miss Manley also remained where she was.

'Hadn't you better be getting your skis on, dear?' Mrs Hardy spoke briskly to Rosemary.

But Rosemary, as usual unco-operative, said no, her ankles ached terribly and she thought she wouldn't ski any more today but just go back quietly in the funicular with Mrs Hardy when she was ready to go.

Mrs Hardy, who had planned to go back alone in the funicular with Mrs Martell and find out exactly why the woman was here, was not pleased.

'Do you think *He* went back into the hotel when he disappeared?'

Mrs Hardy said that she had really no idea, and why didn't Rosemary go and ask the concierge?

Rosemary hesitated, but finally decided to remain where she was. There was obviously some mystery connected with Mrs Martell and if she were to leave the others alone now she might never learn what it was. She might of course never learn what it was anyhow, but there was no point in wantonly cutting herself off from the possibility of information.

'And how about you?' Mrs Hardy turned her attention to Miss Manley. 'Aren't you going to ski or anything? It seems a pity to waste a lovely afternoon like this.'

Miss Manley, after first glancing at Laura, said that she wasn't sure, but she didn't think anyhow that she'd go with the class—'It's not a very interesting run.'

'What a pity,' Mrs Hardy said and frowned. She was beginning to be quite certain that she didn't like Miss Manley, that was the worst of taking people who had only been recommended to you and whom you didn't know personally. 'Of course she's all right,' Mrs Hardy told herself firmly; trying not to think the worst, trying to be charitable; but she *hasn't* got an agreeable expression, and, whatever she may say, I'm positive that she's more than twenty-eight; and then a far-away look came into Mrs Hardy's eyes; she was thinking over the possibilities of looking at Miss Manley's passport.

Mrs Martell continued to talk pleasantly about the sun and the snow, and the discomforts of her journey. She also told them that they were all looking very well; especially Laura. Didn't Mrs Hardy think that Laura was looking remarkably well?

Mrs Hardy agreed and wondered about Dick. Was it for his sake that this woman had come out here? Well, if it were, she couldn't do anything about it. Only hope that everything would come right in the end. Things quite often did she had noticed, and anyhow wasn't everything in God's hands? She sent up a hurried confused prayer for Dick's safety and eventual happiness and continued to worry.

What with one thing and another, and especially Rosemary, it was quite late in the evening before Mrs Martell found an opportunity of being alone with Laura. They were in Mrs Martell's bedroom where ostensibly Laura was to admire the view of the moon shining on the mountains. The view was exactly the same as the one from Laura's own room on the floor above.

Obediently, Laura stood by the window and waited.

Mrs Martell lit a cigarette and sat down in the armchair.

'I want to talk to you.'

'About you and Edward?'

Mrs Martell was put out. She had planned the opening sentences of this conversation very carefully and now she was being interrupted.

'You needn't bother to tell me, because I know.'

'How can you possibly know?'

'I should think everybody did; do you want me to divorce him?' Laura had turned away from the window and stood looking across the room at her cousin.

It was all going much faster than Mrs Martell had planned. The news was to have been broken slowly with tears and solicitude. And a plan for Laura's future was to have been sketched in. Edward was prepared to settle a very handsome allowance on her—personally, Mrs Martell thought that it was unnecessarily handsome, but that wasn't the point. Laura would be able to live in the country with her dogs, and perhaps she could take to dog breeding; she would like that, wouldn't she, and it would give her an interest. And of course they would find somebody who would live with her, for naturally she mustn't be lonely. And Laura mustn't think that Cathie wasn't still very fond of her, because she was, only this was one of those things that do happen in life. One of those things which it is outside the power of anyone to control.

That was what Mrs Martell would have said. She had thought it all out so many times; lying on her bed in Baker Street, staying at Abbotsmere, or sitting on the verandah at Redbourne. Then, the whole thing, herself and Edward, had been only a dream; now at last, it had come true.

Edward had asked her to marry him.—'If only I were free we could be married.'—Now, there was only Laura who stood between Cathie and her happiness.—Who stood between them and their happiness. And Cathie had been sure that Laura could be 'managed'.—'You must let me go to Switzerland and tell her.'—Edward hadn't been sure about that. Laura wasn't well, oughtn't she to be given a little longer in which to recover? And when the time came to tell her, he must do it himself, to allow Cathie to do so would be altogether wrong. Sitting on the floor at his feet, Cathie had been furious, but Edward had never known it; she had been sweet and gentle; and in the end it had been her will which had prevailed.—'I can manage her, Edward, please do believe that it will be far less hard for her if it is done like this.' She hadn't said that one had to be cruel in order to be kind, she hadn't gone as far as that; but she had said that their present situation was one which it was outside the power of any human being to control. But, alone with Laura, Cathie felt that somewhere something had gone wrong.

'Do you want me to divorce him?' Laura's words still hung in the air, and Laura was standing by the window, and speaking without any emotion; there was no sign of tears, or even of a particular interest.

'But don't you mind?'

'Did you want me to?'

'Now then,' and Mrs Martell recovered herself, 'you must know perfectly well that all this is terribly painful to me. Because I am fond of you, Laura, and you must never believe anything else.'

This time Laura didn't say anything; she still stood looking at Cathie, waiting for her to go on.

And Cathie did go on, making the prepared speech, saying all the things which, in her imagination, she had said often before.

At the end of it, Laura said that she didn't think she would care for breeding dogs.

'That isn't the point.' Cathie was finding it more difficult to keep her temper with Laura than she had with Edward.—'It isn't even as if you had given him a child.'

'Do you want to be cited in the case?'

'I suppose so'—but before leaving London she had decided that, in the interests of them all, there had better be an unknown woman.

'Then I'll write to the solicitors.' Laura turned to leave the room. 'I suppose you'll be leaving in the morning?'

'Laura,' Cathie said, 'Laura.' But Laura had gone and the door was shut behind her.

13

THREE DAYS LATER Mrs Martell sat at the Louis Seize writing-table in the small drawing-room at Abbotsmere. 'My dearest Mother.' She paused and dipped her pen into the ormolu inkstand; she smiled secretly and continued. 'Perhaps you will not be surprised to hear that Edward and I are to be married, we have loved each other for a very long time'—she paused again, the 'secret' smile was very nearly a grin—'of course poor Laura has never really been a wife to him, and since her breakdown things have been terribly difficult. Naturally I am desperately sorry for her; but of course one has always known that she is completely unstable. I have just returned from Switzerland, where she is staying with that clergyman's family, she is well and as happy as I suppose she can ever hope to be. Edward is to make an extremely handsome provision for her; and I suppose that everything will be arranged and we will be married sometime in the summer.' She paused; she had said what she wanted to say without dragging in the word 'divorce'. How beautiful this room was, the perfect setting.

The smile still hovered round her lips and, with her chin supported in her hand, she thought of the goodness of God. She had been very patient and forbearing and in the end God had not deserted her. 'I was beset by mine enemies but the Lord has comforted me, he has led me into green pastures, and here she looked out of the window from which there was a very good view of the park and the lake. In the end goodness is always rewarded, one had only to ask in order to receive. She got up from the writing-table and roamed round the room. She ran her fingers along the edge of the Adam mantelpiece; the marble was cool to her touch, white and green marble. There was a French enamelled clock set with brilliants; if only it had been little later in the year there would have been a great bowl of roses. The smile never left her lips. She returned to the table in order to finish her letter to Mrs Hartley-James.

'Oh, there you are, darling.'

Mrs Martell looked up to smile lovingly and possessively at Edward.

At about the same time Mrs Hardy was sitting at one of the little tables beside the ice rink waiting for the member of her party to join her. It wouldn't have been exactly true to say that she was lying in wait for Robert Daniel, only if he were to appear it would be very pleasant.

Yesterday and the day before they had had such stimulating talks. He's nice, Mrs Hardy thought and, without knowing that she did so, she started to hum, not at all in tune, the opening bars of one of Mr Daniel's easier arias. And how extraordinary that he should be interested in spiritualism; not, of course, that she could possibly approve of it; but there was no denying that very extraordinary things did seem to happen. Mr Daniel and his secretary Mr Wyman had actually been at séances where things had *happened*. Levitation, and roses thrown into the middle of a circle of people, and Mr Daniel's mother speaking out of the darkness, telling him things that only she could have known. It wasn't 'right' of course, but it was certainly interesting.

She looked at her watch; the time was getting on; it had been earlier than this yesterday when Mr Daniel and that secretary of his had joined her at her table and they had drunk glasses of lemonade together. It had been very pleasant and she had been quite sorry when Rosemary and Laura with Miss Manley had joined them.

'One never grows old, not really', Mrs Hardy thought sadly, 'one only looks old.' And for one wild moment she wondered if perhaps after all she hadn't wasted her life; if the 'goodness' after which she had striven did really matter so very much.

'I'm being very foolish'—and Mrs Hardy made a sincere effort to 'pull herself together'. 'Jealousy', Mrs Hardy told herself, 'at my age, isn't even wicked any more, it's only silly. And, of course, it was less interesting for Mr Daniel to talk to me than to Laura who is young and pretty. And of course, being who she is, they have friends in common and interests in common. It isn't even', Mrs Hardy thought (remembering her failures with the choir), 'as if I were musical.—But Mr Daniel isn't particularly young himself' (in spite of all her efforts, her thoughts were refusing to be controlled); 'I should say that forty-five is the very *least* he could be. And dancing,' Mrs Hardy thought, 'why did he have to invite Laura and Miss Manley up here to dance until two o'clock in the morning, and they had had to come back to the hotel on skis, because the funicular ceased to run after six o'clock in the evening?'

'Agnes!' Mrs Hardy said to herself, using the voice of a governess who had died many years ago, 'you're to stop it immediately!'

She looked at her watch again. Probably today Mr Daniel wouldn't appear at all and anyhow it was nearly lunch-time. From sheer habit she went on to worry about Dick. It was bad luck that he had broken his collar-bone and he was being so good about it. She had been afraid that that woman was going to get hold of him. It had been reassuring when Mrs Martell had stayed at Wengen only one night and then gone back to England. Clearly her object in coming had been to see Laura; none of it had anything to do with Dick. 'All the same I don't trust her,' Mrs Hardy thought. Laura hadn't seemed to be upset by Mrs Martell's visit; but all the same Mrs Hardy was sure that there was 'something'.

She looked around her at the people sitting at the tables; there was no sign of Mr Daniel. Then she looked up towards the mountain, trying to identify some of the little distant figures which moved against its side. She wondered if it was worth while going on waiting for lunch. There was one slow-moving group which she thought might possibly contain members of her party. She decided to wait.

'You're making a great mistake,' Miss Manley said to Laura, as they leant back against the yoke of the ski lift, 'if you think that he's interested in you.'

She was pursuing a line of argument which she had followed with interruptions ever since their return from the dance the previous evening. Laura wished that she would be quiet.

'Whatever he may have told you,' Miss Manley continued vindictively, 'he's sailing under false colours, I'm only telling you so that you mayn't be hurt.' Unlike Mrs Hardy, she made no attempt whatever to wrestle with her jealousy. Neither did she make any attempt to stick to the truth.

'Don't be silly,' Laura said; 'he didn't tell me anything at all.'

Miss Manley allowed herself to look quizzical, but they had reached the top of the lift and, in the business of getting themselves disentangled from it, Laura didn't notice anything, only she wondered if Miss Manley, who had seemed so nice up to now, wasn't really rather a bore.

They stood in a little knot waiting for the guide to tell them to move off. Miss Manley didn't say anything further about Mr Daniel, she had gone back to thinking about Mrs Martell; *why* had she come out to Switzerland only for one night, simply in order to see Laura? It was very mysterious, or perhaps it wasn't mysterious at all. And, in spite of several hints that she should give some explanation, Laura had refused to say anything about it.

'You follow me and you lean away from the hill.' The guide took off, choosing a simple traverse.

One, two, three, four, and now it was Laura's turn, down and up and down, following in the wake of Mr Jones. The class had improved considerably during the last three days; several minutes elapsed before any of them fell.

This was the nearest thing in the world to flying, this was so much more important than Cathie and her terrible announcement. For, 'the announcement must have been terrible only I didn't feel anything at all.'

Now she was coming to the turn; 'lean avay from the hill'; a moment of uncertainty and she had recovered her balance. She hadn't felt anything personal at all, only a slight dispassionate contempt of Cathie. Down and up and down; 'To thine own self be true'—and Cathie was being true to herself.

'And yet, I ought to have felt something.' This seemingly complete immunity from pain could not last for ever. Or could it? Could peace come suddenly like this, without one having done anything to earn it?

'I don't know, I'm sure'—and Nelly Brewster stirred the sugar into the first of her mid-morning cups of tea. She looked round the Abbotsmere kitchen which was as untidy and cheerful as usual.

On the other side of the table young Norah ran her brand-new wedding-ring up and down her finger.

'And what's going to happen now, we don't know.'

Young Norah didn't know either, but she wasn't much interested for in a few weeks she would be leaving to have the baby, and most probably she wouldn't be coming back in any case, for this time Mum had said definitely that she wasn't going to be landed with it. Now that Norah was a married woman she could look after her own children.—Perhaps when they're a bit older I'll be able to come out to work again, Norah thought, but it didn't seem that there was really much hope of that, for by the time that this lot were ready for school, there would almost certainly be others. Norah sighed deeply and considered her destiny without enthusiasm.

'The old bitch,' Nelly said; 'but it isn't as if I hadn't known for months that it was coming, because I have.'

'I expect there'll be some changes,' Norah said.

'You bet there'll be some changes.' Nelly held out her hand for Norah's cup. 'There won't be any more of, *can I take just one tiny biscuit*, from now on they'll all be her biscuits.'

Norah said that her Auntie had been divorced; it was during the war and her husband had come home unexpectedly on his leave and found her with another man. There hadn't half been a fuss and her Auntie had had to run out of the house in her nightdress, just as she was.

'You told me about that before.'

'Mum says it isn't fair, not where there's children.'

'I could have warned her months ago,' Nelly said, 'but somehow . . . I don't know, and then I kept on hoping it would blow over; not that there was much chance of that with *her* always in the house.'

'Will she stay here while the divorce is going on?'

'I shouldn't be surprised, she's brazen enough for anything; and now that she's sure of him life won't be worthy living—that is if we don't all get the sack the day after tomorrow.'

Young Norah looked alarmed; she had counted on at least another three weeks' money before her retirement into the lying-in hospital—and lucky to get a bed, they didn't usually take you in, not for a second baby. 'She couldn't do that, not before she's married to him.'

'She can do anything she wants; haven't you noticed the change since she came back from abroad, ringing the bells nineteen to the dozen and looking at you as if you didn't exist?'

'I didn't know she'd been abroad'—and Norah leant down to offer a lump of sugar to Augustus, who had been patiently begging ever since they had sat down to their tea.

'You know, he is a dear little dog; and Con's a dear little dog too,' she added hastily in case Constantia, who was dancing agitatedly about demanding sugar and attention, should be offended. 'And what's going to happen to you if your missus isn't coming down here any more, you won't like that now, will you?'

'He'll know the difference when he's married to her,' Nelly said; 'you'd think a man of his age would have more sense. Mr Hackett was terribly upset when he told him; he said he hardly knew how to get out of the room.'

'I shouldn't have thought it would have made much difference to Mr Hackett.' Norah was still thinking about the three weeks' money which perhaps now she wouldn't get.

'If it wasn't for Arthur and young Jimmy, I'd walk out of the house this afternoon; 'and I'd tell her what I thought of her before I went.'

'Mum says she thinks it's wonderful the way you've got that old laundry. She says she never would have believed it could look so nice.'

'It'll be difficult finding anywhere else'—and Nelly flushed with pleasure. It wasn't often that Norah's mother was so generous.

'Perhaps you won't have to go; cooks aren't all that easy to find nowadays, and they'll have to have somebody.'

'I wouldn't stay with her here, not even if she asked me. All I'm hoping is that she'll give us time to find something else. Cup of tea, Mr Hackett, or is it too near your dinner time?'

Mr Hackett, who had put his head round the door, hesitated; he very much wanted someone to talk to, but he had hoped to find Nelly alone. He didn't approve of young Norah at the best of times, and now with her enormously protruding abdomen, he found her positively offensive. In his day kitchenmaids who got themselves into trouble were sent about their business as soon as there was anything noticeable. The fact that this time young Norah had managed to get herself married had nothing to do with it; she looked disgusting.

'Come on,' Nelly said, 'it will do you good.'

'Thank you, Mrs Brewster, I think perhaps I will.' Mr Hackett edged round the kitchen table, trying not to look at Norah; he drew up a chair and sat down.

'Ooh, Mr Hackett, isn't it awful!'

Mr Hackett raised his eyebrows and didn't answer; why didn't Mrs Brewster send the girl into the scullery to get on with her work? As nothing happened, he contented himself with telling young Norah that that was enough of that.

Norah pouted, and tossed her head in the air. She didn't think much of old Hackett and neither did Mum, if it earned to that. Always had been stuck up, Mum said, and she should know, because she'd worked in the laundry when old Hackett was a footman. Not that he had always been so respectable, not by a long chalk!

Edward hesitated in the doorway of the small drawing room. 'Darling, Charles and Georgette are here.'

Mrs Martell made a little moue of annoyance. Were she and Edward never to be left in peace?

'They're on their way to somewhere,' Edward said, 'so they've called in.'—He gave the explanation just as it had been offered to him by Georgette.

Mrs Martell got up. Now that she and Edward were to be married (and even Hackett now knew officially that they were to be married) she was the hostess who must be prepared to welcome, and, if necessary, to put in their places and generally sort out, such of Edward's friends and relations who came to the house. Charles, of course, she knew, but somehow or other Georgette's very rare visits to Abbotsmere had never happened to coincide with her own.

'They're in the library,' Edward said, and then, 'I wrote and told them about us a couple of days ago.'

Mrs Martell looked at him lovingly, the 'us' was still very dear to her.

'I think you'll like Georgette,' Edward said.

'I'm quite sure I shall.' Mrs Martell composed her smile, said that she would just run upstairs for a moment and left the room.

'Don't be long,' Edward said, and, 'you'll find us in the library.'

The truth was that he wanted help with Charles, who had arrived in a very truculent mood.

When Edward returned to the library, he found Charles standing with his foot on the fender looking up at the portrait of their great-grandfather. It was a position which Edward himself often adopted and he was subconsciously annoyed. Georgette was sitting on the sofa with a copy of *Country Life*.

'Now then'—and Charles turned to face his brother—'I don't believe in beating about the bush, what's all this about?'

'Cathie will be here in a minute,' Edward said, and lit a cigarette.

'I don't want you to think I'm not sympathetic towards you,' Charles said, 'but this is a very serious step.'

'I know that.' Edward had the feeling that it was not Charles at all but his father who looked across the library at him.

'I didn't know anything about it when we were in Scotland,' Charles went on. 'I noticed that Laura was upset, of course, but I didn't know that there was anything like this going on; if I had I certainly shouldn't have invited Mrs Martell up there.'

'There wasn't anything then,' Edward said.

Georgette looked up quickly; she had one of those small elegant American faces: she was dressed in deep and becoming mourning for her father.

'Charles,' Georgette said, 'I think we might go into that some other time.'

Mrs Martell came into the room. Her face was newly done-up, she looked rather less than thirty-five and her light wool checked dress was just right for a morning in the country. In spite of being perfectly aware of all these things, she was feeling unaccountably nervous. She advanced, hand outstretched towards Georgette.—'What a lovely surprise.'

Edward mumbled an introduction, Georgette said that they were on their way to Chester. Mrs Martell turned to Charles—what ages it was since they had met, and how was dear Lady Forston and the Waverlys?

There was a pause, which was fortunately filled by the arrival of Hackett carrying the drink tray.

Edward said that he trusted Georgette and Charles would be staying to luncheon.

Georgette guessed that there wouldn't be time.

Edward started to mix a Martini.

Cathie waited for something to be said about her forthcoming marriage; when the drinks were fixed would be the time, Charles would raise his glass and say, but what would Charles say? Something charming about the near future when he hoped they would all be relations? To our dear Cathie; a surprise, but an extremely pleasant one and the best of luck to you both. That didn't sound like Charles somehow, but glancing at him Cathie saw that he had already embarked on a whisky and soda, and realised that for the time being anyhow, there were going to be no congratulations—in fact that Charles didn't seem to be at all friendly. It was funny, because in Scotland he had seemed to approve of her, even to like her: had had nothing but admiration for the way she had tackled (there was no other word for describing an encounter with such a personage) the Grand Duchess.—And the tremendously tactful manner in which she had dealt with Laura. Charles had been grateful to her for those things—as well he might be, for without her the party, she was quite sure, would have been a complete failure.

There was a little more desultory conversation: about the weather, about the dear little girls (Georgette was glad to say that they were well), about a recent book of Royal Reminiscences which they had all read and in which their own Grand Duchess had had a very satisfactory mention. Still no one said anything about the forthcoming marriage.

Suddenly, Mrs Martell could bear it no longer, why couldn't any of them say anything?

But Charles was suggesting to Edward that they should go for a walk in the garden.

Edward said that really there was nothing to see at this time of the year; and anyhow, wasn't it rather cold?

Charles, who had remained standing by the fireplace, put down his drink, said that he didn't believe in beating about the bush, and that what he really wanted to do was to talk to Edward alone. As he spoke he pulled out his watch, so perhaps it was true that they were on their way to somewhere else.

Georgette got up from the sofa; but Cathie remained in her chair, looking up at Charles, then she looked at Edward, waiting for him to make a stand.

'Really, Charles'—and Edward smiled without much conviction—'you're making a great many mysteries this morning.'

'There's no mystery,' Charles said crossly; 'it's only that I consider this step that you are contemplating is extremely serious.'

'But surely,' and Cathie's voice was deep with warmth and understanding, 'you can't believe that we haven't fully realised that.'

'And anyhow, Charles, I don't see what it's got to do with you,' Edward said.

'There's no need to take that attitude'—and Charles looked on disapprovingly while Edward helped himself to a second whisky and soda.

Mrs Martell took a deep breath, gathering her forces about her for a possible battle. She was fully convinced that Charles must be brought to see their point of view. Charles must be sympathetic, and the visit must end in amity and loving kindness. She must be loved, not only by Edward, but by his family. It was part of the picture which she had created. The matriarch who dispensed favours, to whose house they all came at Christmas and besides all that (and not clearly represented in the picture) was the very important fact that Charles's and Georgette's friends were now to be her friends. The Grand Duchess, Lady Forston, the Waverlys, it was only through Charles and Georgette that she could bring those people into the interesting life which she intended to make for Edward.

She turned to Charles. 'Of course, I do understand how you feel, but I wonder if you realise quite, quite how difficult things have been. There were no circumstances in which Edward could have gone on with poor Laura. He has been incredibly loyal to her.'

'All the same,' Charles said, 'divorce is a very serious business.'

'But I agree with you entirely'—and Mrs Martell smiled her experienced smile. 'The break-up of a marriage can never be anything but a tragedy.'

'Naturally.' Charles's voice was cold.

Edward got up to refill Georgette's glass.

'I quite understand,' Charles addressed himself to his brother, 'that you can't continue to live with Laura; but is it necessary to rush into a divorce?'

Edward shrugged his shoulders. 'I still can't see, Charles, that it's got anything to do with you.'

'My dear Edward, there's no need to be pompous about it.'

Georgette suggested that perhaps she and Mrs Martell might go into the drawing-room.

But Cathie was not to be warned. Edward needed her support, and he was hers to defend in a situation which called for tact and understanding. As she saw it, Charles was necessary to her plan and therefore Charles must be cajoled into a good humour and into approval.

'Truly, Charles, there is no question of "rushing"; we have thought about this for a long time.'

'But it will look as though you are rushing,' Charles said, 'and what do you think people are going to say?' There, Mrs Martell said, was exactly where he could help them. She knew how close he and Edward were to each other and how much he would want to help, and it was exactly this question of what people would say that had been worrying her. The world, and she was quite certain Charles had noticed it, was cruel; so ready to judge. The world, because it had not had to undergo such things itself, would be only too ready to censure Edward. It could have no idea of the life of misery, even of humiliation, which Edward had been called upon to endure. Edward was too proud, too generous towards Laura ever to explain himself, and it was precisely here that Charles's loyalty would be most useful to him. Charles would explain all these things to the world. Edward might say that he didn't mind what people thought of him, and here Mrs Martell held up her hand to silence a possible interruption; if Edward was too disinterested to think of these things for himself, all the more reason why those who loved him should think of them for him. It was up to them, to her and to Charles, to save him from any adverse criticism which might be aroused by his very lack of self-interest.

Charles said that that was all very well, but things didn't arrange themselves as easily as all that.

'And this may sound strange to you, but I don't personally approve of divorce.'

'But surely,' Mrs Martell said, and stopped. She looked at Edward; he was obviously becoming very angry. She hoped that he would say something that would finally put Charles in his place. Charles had no business to behave like this. And it was not for him to criticise her; to criticise either of them if it came to that. He was Edward's *younger* brother, wasn't he? Very well then!

'Don't you think,' Georgette said, 'it might be better if we left them to discuss it between them?'

Mrs Martell swung round; here was further criticism, and from a source from which she had not expected it. Did Georgette mean to imply that she, Cathie, was not capable of handling all this? Left alone, goodness knew what Edward and Charles would say to each other!—(She didn't allow herself to think for one moment that Edward might be persuaded by Charles into postponing either the divorce or the wedding.) They might quite easily fly at each other's throats, and whatever happened (think of the Grand Duchess, think of Lady Forston) Cathie didn't want a quarrel. No, the whole situation called for a tactful approach, and therefore it called for Cathie.

'I think I agree with Georgette.'

It was the first remark Edward had made for some time and Mrs Martell didn't find it satisfactory. Then she remembered that Georgette was a Catholic and at the thought of it her blood was ready to boil over. People had no right to impose their religious beliefs upon others, that was one of Mrs Martell's most dearly cherished beliefs; she herself would have said that it was her only belief. It wasn't that she had anything against Catholics, or even against religion in general. It was just that she thought that those were a matter of individual conscience. Nobody had the right, especially on moral grounds, to dictate to others what they should or should not do. Nobody had any right dictate to her about anything whatsoever. She cast about for suitable words in which she might explain this to Georgette.

'I don't want you to think,' Charles said to Edward, 'that we're not sympathetic towards you; you know that when it came to it, I'd back you up whatever you did.'

'I know you would,' Edward said.

A smile spread over Mrs Martell's face. *Of course*, why on earth hadn't she thought of it from the beginning! The objections that Charles and Georgette were raising had nothing at all to do with concern for Edward, or what people (Lady Forston and the Grand Duchess) might think of him. They had nothing to do with religion either, or with categoric disapproval of divorce. They objected to his remarrying simply because if he did so, it was reasonable to believe that he might have sons, or anyhow one son.—'I will give you a child.' There would be an heir, a boy walking beside his mother at the fourth of June celebrations at Eton.—'Mr West escorts his mother, Mrs Edward West.'—And in those circumstances what became of Charles's four dear little girls, or their dear little unborn brothers? And here Mrs Martell glanced sharply at Georgette. Could it be, there was no sign, but it was only too likely that it was the case. Cathie was overcome by their perfidiousness, by their bare-faced effrontery, by their deception. So Edward's child was to be denied, not only his rightful heritage, not only Abbotsmere and the fourth of June; but life itself. The thought was appalling. And moreover he was to be denied it for the sake of Charles's criminal selfishness, and for the sake of Charles's unattractive and totally unnecessary children. Mrs Martell could hardly find words in which to voice her disgust, her indignation and her disapproval.

She paused, and as if it were from another world, another plane, she heard Edward's voice saying that there were one or two things he wanted to discuss with Charles—if Georgette and Cathie wouldn't mind? He moved towards his writing-table; there was a paper needing Charles's signature. He had been going to send it to him; there was nothing very much to it, Charles would see for himself. Edward opened one of the drawers of the writing-table.

Georgette was already standing by the door.

Charles was still in front of the fireplace. Self-importantly he waited for the women to leave the room.

Mrs Martell looked at Edward's face bent over some papers which he had placed on top of the desk; how could he be so blind, so pathetically naive?

There was a moment in which she still hesitated, and then suddenly and not quite of her free will she took her decision. Her fury raged against Charles and Georgette, against the Catholic

Church, against society which for so long had contrived to deny her those things which she most wanted.

She got up, and Georgette, mistaking her intention, opened the door.

'Shut that door.' Her voice was harsh, without resonance. She turned to Charles, self-important, conceited oaf! Perhaps he thought that he had won, perhaps he thought that he could really prevent her marrying Edward. Well, he had done for himself now. Very far from ever succeeding to Abbotsmere, he would never see it again. Lady Forston! The Grand Duchess! in this moment of complete sincerity Cathie had forgotten them completely.

'Listen to me,' Cathie said, and now her voice was gaining in volume; 'listen to me, you were talking just now of what people were going to say. As if you minded, as if that mattered to you in the least. Why don't you tell Edward your real objection? Why don't you tell him that you don't want him to marry again, that you don't want him to have children?' She faced Charles, her eyes flashing, her head thrown back. She looked rather splendid.

'That isn't true.' At that moment Charles could have hit her.

Georgette nervously shut the door.—The servants! It was her instant reaction to domestic disagreement.

'Cathie!' Edward said, but she didn't even hear him.

'You must know your real motives.' Cathie was looking straight at Charles; she heard her own voice as the voice of truth, the voice of destiny. And for one sinking second Charles was persuaded that she spoke the truth; the veins swelled in his forehead. She was a vulgar and impossible woman. Where before he had only gently warned Edward now he would do anything to save him from her. Her jealous and incontinent accusations were preposterous.

'Your little sickly girls,' Cathie said and realised that she had gone too far. She stopped abruptly, her mind already busy with the apology she would have to make; à crise de nerfs, only her deep, her overwhelming love of Edward could have brought her to say such things.—She had been living for so long under a terrible, an overwhelming strain. But as she looked at Charles, she realised that it mightn't do.

He saw her for what she was, for what she never allowed herself to see that she was, and he would not be deceived by easy talk of nerves and overwhelming love.

'I think you are the meanest woman I have ever met,' Charles said.

There was a moment of cold, horrible silence, during which Cathie was aware of only one thought.—Edward was not going to come up to scratch. After everything that had been between them. After all that she had given up for him. Edward was going to take Charles's side against her. Charles! If Edward continued to say nothing, Charles would have won. She felt her face flame scarlet; but in fact it did nothing of the kind, the ivory skin remained unchanging, for ever the colour of ripe apricots.

And then, at last, Edward spoke. He had not rushed to her defence, but at least he had not deserted her.

'I think that you forget yourself.' His voice was pompous and, as so often, a little too high. 'You have no business to speak to Cathie like that'; and then, rather pathetically, 'we don't want to quarrel.'

'Not with *you*,' Charles said. 'I hope I shall see you in London.' He took a step away from the fireplace.

'You can't go like this,' Edward said.

'My dear Edward, I think we might go into all that some other time.' His voice was resolute and he moved towards the door.

'Please,' Edward said, 'I'm sure Cathie didn't mean . . .' and he turned towards Cathie, hoping that somehow she would still make everything all right.

But the ivory face was a mask.—She was to be betrayed after all!

'I'll write to you,' Charles said, and opened the door, waiting for Georgette to precede him out of the room.

Georgette, as she described herself afterwards, was very, very disturbed. She had had no experience of leaving a house in anger, and therefore no formula of words which she could bring to her aid.—'It's been just lovely seeing you, and I'd have you know that my children are *not* sickly, nor is my husband an underhand schemer.' You just couldn't say a thing like that. But there must be something kind, and at the same time diplomatic that could have been said. She wanted to comfort Charles and reassure him about the purity of his motives and, if it could be done without in any way annoying Charles, she wanted to comfort Mrs Martell who must assuredly be very unhappy.

Edward rang the bell for Hackett.

'Good-bye.' Georgette held out her hand to Cathie—a slight pressure of the hand and Cathie would understand that, had they been alone together, Georgette, despite the insults which had been offered her, would have spoken words of comfort.

Cathie returned the pressure and in doing so, magnanimously forgave Georgette for the part which she had played in this monstrous affair.

Charles turned on his heel and Edward, following him and Georgette into the hall, realised that this was the first real quarrel he had ever had with Charles.

14

THE JUNE SUNSHINE was pouring into the magnificently furnished office. High-lights were reflected on the shiny cream-coloured desk, on the shiny cream-coloured mantelpiece, on the chromium and cream-coloured table and on the elegant filing cabinets.

The carpet was of that colour which comes somewhere between orange and pink and the whole effect was of an office in a film set, which wasn't particularly surprising, as all the furniture, the carpet and even the curtains had originally been designed and made for a film for which Robert Daniel had written the music.—He had been able to buy them up quite cheaply when the shooting was finished.

'No,' Laura was saying into the telephone, 'I'm afraid Mr Daniel is still in Paris; I won't be able to get in touch with him until late this evening.'

The secretary on the other end of the line continued to be persistent. It was imperative that Mr Daniel should be got in touch with immediately. Mr Kegan, or more exactly the producer of Mr Kegan's latest play, had come up against a lot of trouble over the music. They were three minutes short in the third scene of Act I, the producer had been obliged to make certain changes and Miss Benson's entrance had been delayed; three more minutes were needed *before* Miss Benson—while the Greek Gods were scurrying about Olympus. If Laura would get out the score she would see just what the secretary meant, and it was terribly urgent, the whole company, including the orchestra, were going up to Manchester on Sunday; surely Mr Daniel must be available *somewhere*, if Laura would locate him so that Mr Kegan could have a word with him.—The secretary used the awful name of Mr Kegan as a threat, as a direct edict from the Pope. If Mr Kegan, who was the head of one of the most important Managements in the world, wished to have a word with someone, the direct result must be that that person, though unavailable before, would immediately be forthcoming.

Laura continued to be sorry, she continued not to know at which hotel in Paris Mr Daniel was staying.—She repeated that it would be quite impossible for her to get in touch with him until late this evening, when she would, if she *were* able to get in touch with him, give him Mr Kegan's message.

'We could send an arranger over on the afternoon plane, if Mr Daniel were willing.'

'I suppose that would hurry things up a bit.' Laura was doubtful.

There followed further threats, further invocations of Mr Kegan, but eventually the secretary gave it up and rang off.

Thankfully, Laura put down the receiver. She looked out of the window. It was a pleasant view; the green back gardens, the pale stucco houses, the distant church spires and gasometers.—'The houses in St. John's Wood were built by the Early Victorians for their mistresses'—but there couldn't have been as many mistresses as there were houses?

The garden of Mr Daniel's house was smaller than those of most of its neighbours. From the office window Laura looked down on the flat roof of the enormous studio; it must cover at least half of what had once been the garden.

Half-heartedly, Laura pulled the typewriter towards her, inserted a sheet of writing paper—and two carbons—there must be as many things as possible to put in the filing cabinets—but having done so she turned again to stare out of the window. It was such a very beautiful morning, and, anyhow, there was no particular hurry.

A girl with fair hair came out into the next-door garden and started pegging clothes on to a washing line; she was a very pretty girl and Laura felt instantly sorry for her because she had had to spend this beautiful morning washing clothes, and, probably too, in making the beds and dusting and sweeping.

—And it might so easily have been me, Laura thought if . . . well if I hadn't been adopted and if I hadn't married Edward. It might even have been me if I hadn't met Robert.—I might be doing housework because I hadn't anything else to do, or I might be living somewhere with a lady companion and breeding dogs, and Laura shivered slightly as she thought of the infinitely dreary occupation which had been suggested for her by Cathie.—I have been incredibly lucky.

The telephone was ringing again. It couldn't be Kegan's secretary returning to the attack? She picked up the receiver.

'Is that you, madam? This is Mrs Wilson.'

'How's Constantia?'

'Very well and having a splendid game with Augustus; you'd never think from the way she's going on that those puppies were due today.'

'I suppose it's all right, but the vet did say to keep her quiet, didn't he?'

'Well, then he'd better come and try it, that's all.'

—Incredibly lucky, Laura was thinking, a job that I like and a housekeeper who's kind to Constantia and Augustus and a flat which has a garden for them to play in.

'Excuse me,' Mrs Wilson was saying, and now there was a certain diffidence in her voice, 'but you didn't look at *The Times* this morning, did you?—you left it on the breakfast tray and you hadn't opened it.'

'I meant to bring it to work, but I forgot.'

'Well, it's in,' Mrs Wilson said. 'I thought probably you'd like to know.' She paused, uncertain of what to say next, not sure if she had done the right thing in ringing Laura up.

'You mean the marriage?'

'Yes, shall I read it to you?'

'Do,' Laura said, 'do.'

And so Mrs Wilson, with *The Times* opened at page eight, read how Mr Edward West of Abbotsmere had been quietly married the preceding day in London to Mrs Martell of Baker Street.—It was the announcement for which both Laura and Mrs Wilson had been waiting. For, of course, Mrs Wilson, although she had only been with Laura for a few months, knew all about Edward and Cathie and the divorce. The divorce had been in the papers, too, but discreetly hidden somewhere in the inside pages, no headlines, no photographs, for Edward had known how to arrange it that way. Moving into the flat, appearing in the court, finding Mrs Wilson, it had all happened in the same week; and the following week she had started her job with Mr Daniel.

'Thank you,' Laura said when Mrs Wilson had finished; and wondered why it was that today, of all days, she should have forgotten to look at the paper while she ate her breakfast. There had been several telephone calls, and the *Daily Mirror* to look at and a long discussion with Mrs Wilson as to the advisability of changing the butcher, and Constantia to be made much of— poor darling Constantia, Laura did hope that she was going to be all right.

'I thought you'd like to know,' Mrs Wilson said.

'Oh yes,' Laura said again, and, 'thank you; and you *will* ring up the vet the moment Constantia looks at all likely, won't you?'

'Yes,' Mrs Wilson said, 'and I've got his number written down here beside the telephone. I think I'll take her out with me while I do the shopping so that I can keep an eye on her.'

'Do you think she ought to walk as far as that?'

'She'll get more rest coming quietly round the shops with me, than she will chasing Augustus all over the garden.'

'I suppose so'—and Laura rang off. She put her elbows on the desk and stared again out of the window. The girl in the next-door garden had finished with the clothes line; now she appeared again out of the house; this time she was pushing a perambulator which she wheeled to the far end of the garden, rocking it gently as she went.

—So, he's married to Cathie, Laura thought. She so often wondered how she would feel about it when it actually happened; jealous, or resentful or merely indifferent?—After all he was my husband and I loved him; and she was my friend, or I thought she was.—'I hope they'll be happy,' Laura thought and realised that thought was purely conventional, as though she were merely expressing a polite wish to some third person—the bride's mother, for example.—For really, Laura thought with surprise, I don't feel as though I knew either of them very well, as if I'd ever known them very well.

The girl had left the perambulator in the shade of the cherry tree which grew against the wall dividing her garden from Mr Daniel's. I hope they'll have children, Laura thought, and was totally unable to imagine Cathie with a child.—But there isn't any reason why she shouldn't have one.—How could one live so close to people for so long without retaining *some* personal feeling towards them, without retaining in one's self something that was them?—'I don't understand,' Laura said the words aloud. '*Once they were my whole life, now they are strangers.* I hope they'll be happy, but I don't feel that I know them.

Cathie had woken that morning to a feeling of triumph, which, to her astonishment, was immediately followed by a moment of doubt, or if not quite that, of something that was less than perfect happiness.

She looked round the room, in the grey half light which came from between the curtains—they hadn't been drawn fully across the window—she hadn't noticed that last night. Grey walls, pale green satin curtains lined with pink satin; and the furniture of some kind of pale anonymous wood. Through the door on the left was the green and pink bathroom, the door facing the bed led to the sitting-room. Then she looked at Edward. He lay on his back, his mouth slightly open; he was breathing heavily and he looked older than he did when he was awake. Cathie switched on the pink-shaded bedside light; five minutes to nine by her diamond wrist-watch, two minutes past nine by the electric clock over the mantelpiece—only it wasn't really a clock, just figures engraved on the wall and hands of decorated twisted metal. She looked at Edward again, noticing the heaviness of the skin under his eyes, the growth of beard on his chin and the little bare places where there was no beard. He was hers now. And so was Abbotsmere. It was her home now just as much as it was Edward's. It was hers to alter and to order and to rearrange. Cathie smiled to herself and smiled across at the sleeping Edward; she had, or so she thought, risked everything and she had won.

This afternoon they would be going home—to Abbotsmere! She hadn't been there for several months; Edward had thought it better when the divorce started for her not to go there.—It would make for less talk, and Cathie had been reluctantly compelled to agree with him. So, during the last few months, she had spent long, dull week-ends with Mrs Hartley-James at Redbourne, they had got thoroughly on each other's nerves, and Cathie's 'engagement', which couldn't be a real engagement because of the divorce, had not been a happy one. But now everything had come right, she was the beautiful Mrs West of Abbotsmere. The smile lingered at the corners of her mouth. 'Mr and Mrs West have the honour of entertaining . . .' 'Mrs West enjoying a joke with His Royal Highness.'—'Mrs West and her son strolling on the lawn at Eton on the fourth of June'—but, at the thought of her son, the smile momentarily disappeared; between her and that particular photograph there must be the time when her beautiful body had to become monstrous and swollen—like the bodies of women in grimy overalls who stood and gossiped on the doorsteps of lodging houses. Cathie's mouth set in a hard line.—Better not to think of it and there was plenty of time.

It was wonderful to be going home, but now she wondered if it wouldn't have been even more wonderful if they hadn't had to put off their honeymoon.

It couldn't be helped, of course. Edward had only just been elected chairman to the Road Committee; in a way that was a triumph. Until now its members had consisted of contractors, quarry owners and their satellites, there had never before been an independent chairman, someone who would not benefit financially by wider and more expensive and quite unnecessary roads. Edward couldn't very well start by not appearing at his first committee meeting. And it was right that he should be on the County Council; it was right, if he wouldn't go into national politics, that he should take his part in local government; later on it would be right that he should be Lord Lieutenant.—Cathie had got it all worked out. And wasn't it Cathie who had suggested that he should stand for the Council? Laura had never bothered to do that, she had probably never ever thought of it.

But if it hadn't been for this committee they could have flown to Paris today or yesterday afternoon.

Edward had suggested that they should put off getting married until after the meeting of the committee and the next meeting of the Council. It would only, after all, mean waiting a week or two, perhaps it would be better. But Cathie had not been able to bring herself to agree to that; after all she had been through for his sake he had owed it to her to marry her the very moment the decree had been made absolute.

So yesterday; they had been married at Caxton Hall—just a few friends and afterwards, still with the friends, they had lunched at Claridges and then they had come to this hotel and later they had gone out to a theatre.

It had all been very pleasant and triumphant and civilised, and Cathie would have enjoyed every moment of it if it hadn't been for the discussion about Charles. Charles had been at the wedding and that had been very proper. When he had come to

Abbotsmere he had insulted Cathie; for a time she had been desperately afraid that he had succeeded in persuading Edward to give up the divorce, but Edward had remained loyal to her and the quarrel with Charles had been made up so, if he had not attended the wedding, Cathie would have felt herself to be slighted. But unfortunately, Edward had allowed himself to say, when they were alone together, that it had been very good of Charles to come—it wasn't as if it were an easy time for him to get away.

Good of Charles to attend his brother's wedding! Cathie hadn't said anything, but she had been furious. In her opinion, it would have been just as sensible if *she* had said that it had been good of Mrs Hartley-James, who hadn't been at all well, to come up from Redbourne.

'Very good of him,' Edward, quite unaware of the anger he had aroused, had gone on, 'because he really does disapprove of divorce'; and then, 'I'm very fond of Charles.'

—'He isn't,' Cathie had thought, 'he hates him, but he won't admit it to me.'

'We mayn't always see eye to eye,' Edward had said, 'but I'm very fond of him.'

And Cathie, calling upon all her self-control, had said that he was sweet, because it was still important to her that she should be friends with Charles and Georgette. She had even suggested that she should write and invite them to spend a week-end at Abbotsmere—'before we go to Paris'. And, although she had once sworn to herself that they should never come to Abbotsmere again, there was a triumph in being able to say that *she* would write to Georgette and invite her.

'Oh, I don't know about that,' Edward had said, 'it would probably be difficult for them to get away.'

And, of course, that had spoilt it again.

Cathie got softly out of bed and went into the bathroom. She had to take off the make-up she had put on on going to bed last night, she had to prepare her face for a new day, and she had, in the privacy afforded her by the locked door of the bathroom, to go through a shortened version of one, two, three and *heave*. Altogether, it took her some time and when she came back into the bedroom Edward was awake, sitting propped up against the pillows and smoking.

'Good morning, darling.' She leant over and kissed him, placing her hand behind his head.

Edward, rather impeded by his cigarette, put his arm round her shoulder. He released her almost immediately and said that he had ordered breakfast.

Cathie, offended, drew away. She went round to her own side of the bed and got into it. Last night was the first time they had spent a whole night together. And the traditions, the conventions, of the wedding night, which were surely expected to persist into the next morning, should, if Edward had any idea of the fitness of things, have been respected.

Cathie gave a long-drawn-out sigh.—'The wedding night.'— 'The young bride surrounded by her maidens is brought to her husband, the bed has been made up with scented linen or with silken sheets, the maidens, with many unseemly jokes, retire leaving the married pair alone!'—Was that a description from *Kristin Lavran's Daughter*, or of one of the bridal nights of Henry the Eighth?—Cathie couldn't be sure, but it was all very beautiful and ceremonious—except for the jokes; she wouldn't have approved of those, not upon so sacred a subject.

'Darling,' Edward said, 'I love you.' He had finished smoking and he took her left hand, the one that lay nearest him, turning the wedding ring round and round on her finger.

Cathie was taken by surprise; brooding on her resentment towards Edward she had forgotten about him.

She turned towards him. It was true he did love her. Suddenly she was struck by the wonder of it. A lump came into her throat, tears were very near her eyes. She was completely happy.—But it was a pity about the tears; they were a distraction, and, becoming aware of them, she consciously allowed them to well up into her eyes, to run down her cheeks.

'Darling,' Cathie said, 'oh, darling.'—And there was no reason why he shouldn't love her. After all she had done for him during the last few months, after all she had put up with for his sake, she deserved to be loved.

'We will be very happy,' Edward said; it was a question as well as a promise.

'Of course, my darling.'

There was a knock on the door, and, before Cathie had had time to call to him to come in, a young floor waiter was wheeling a trolley into the room.

'Oh good,' Edward propped himself up higher in bed; he was hungry this morning and he looked at the tray in pleasurable anticipation.

'Over here, sir?' The waiter was wheeling the trolley towards the bed; somehow, he failed to notice one of the pale pink rugs, there was a sudden jolt, the trolley collided with the end of the bed and the coffee spilled itself over the white cloth; in trying to save it he caught his sleeve on the milk jug, it overturned and the hot milk streamed on to the pale green carpet.

The young waiter was horrified; he had only lately been put on floor duty, he was ambitious and he had been considered to be doing well in his profession.

'I'm sorry, sir; I'm sorry, madam.' He felt the blood mounting to his ears as he bent down to start to clear up the mess.

There was a roar from the bed. The young waiter turned a frightened face towards Edward.—'Clumsy,' Edward said—and, 'why can't you look where you're going?' But he wasn't, the waiter noticed with relief, really so very angry. But a torrent of hot milk, a stream of coffee is not a good start to a morning and now there must inevitably be a delay before he could start his breakfast.

'Why don't you get up from your knees and send a *waiter*?' Cathie's voice was clear and modulated.

The young man looked from Edward to her.

'A *real* waiter,' Cathie said.

The young man's face, as well as his ears, flushed crimson.

'It's incredible,' Cathie turned to Edward, 'that in a hotel like this they should send the *boot boy*, or whatever he is, in with the breakfast.'

The waiter, having made good as much of the damage as possible, had almost succeeded in getting himself and the chaos which had been breakfast out of the room.

'Didn't you hear?' Cathie's voice was raised now. 'Get out!'

The waiter shut the door. Edward and Cathie were alone and in the silence which followed Cathie was very frightened.

—Men didn't like scenes—she had known that all her life— but it was the second time that she had lost control.—'Your little sickly girls'—and she was with Charles and Georgette in the library at Abbotsmere. It had taken her months to recover from that scene, to re-establish herself with Edward. Her whole life depended on her control; one slip and the whole illusion, which she had built up over all the years, was destroyed. How did it happen? Over-strain? The inability to play a part for ever and for ever and for ever? The ballerina or the trapeze artiste, the fighter pilot may retire honourably; however long their active career, it will, if they live, come to an end.—'Happily in retirement.' But Cathie could not retire, she had chosen her way of life and there could be no end to it.

'A pity,' Edward said, 'to make that sort of scene.'

But Cathie had recovered her balance, she didn't justify herself. She didn't point out that he too had been angry with the waiter, and had shouted at him.—'Clumsy brute', and, 'why can't you look where you're going?'—For Edward was sure of his own rightness; you could be rude—he could be rude in the 'right' way and there was no shame in it. But to be rude in the 'wrong' way was unforgivable.

'If you hadn't made him nervous by shouting at him, it probably wouldn't have happened.'—He had managed to reconstruct the scene so that it should be wholly to Cathie's disadvantage.

She didn't answer him, only put out a hand to take his.

'I hope that they'll be happy, but I don't feel that I know them.' Laura remained puzzled by that thought for the rest of the day. She in fact went through the rest of the day in a kind of trance and was thus better equipped than she might otherwise have been to withstand the frequent telephonic onslaughts of Mr Kegan's secretary.

She went out to lunch in a nearby restaurant—Mr Daniel's married couple didn't believe in the secretary lunching in the house—they had had enough of that sort of thing with the last secretary—and he had been a man which had made it slightly better; but even so it had been hard on the rations. And when he had ended up by *living* in the house, the married couple, after several months of indecision, had given notice. Nor did the control of an extra ration book do anything to appease them; it wasn't after all as if the grocer, or even the butcher, were so very particular—Mr Daniel being who he was—to stick to the 'exact' rations. But this black market had been instituted for the benefit of Mr Daniel, *not* of his secretary. And Mr Wyman was untidy in his room; having been used to nothing, he never picked anything up. *And* he slopped in the bathroom, *and* he hardly ever bothered to say good morning.

Mr Daniel had been very upset, but in the end, of course, he had sacked Mr Wyman and kept the married couple. And it was mainly on account of this domestic upheaval that he had been in Switzerland. The married couple, having made their stand, were not prepared to spend another week in the house with Mr Wyman.

Mr Wyman, in all fairness, had to be given a month's notice. Cravenly, Mr Daniel had gone to Switzerland taking Mr Wyman with him.

And there, of course, he had met Laura; it had all, probably, turned out for the best. Mr Daniel still wasn't quite sure what had induced him to invite Laura to be his secretary. After he had been picked up by Mrs Hardy he had seen a good deal of her party, and there had been something about Laura which had attracted him, probably her detachment, and what seemed to be her cool self-sufficiency. Mr Daniel was tired of emotions—his own, Mr Wyman's and the married couple's. He had heard Laura talking about getting a job.—Miss Manley had been full of bright suggestions and had harped on about the influence she had with this and that employer.—Mr Daniel, who had taken an instant dislike to Miss Manley, had probably had as one of his motives that of thwarting her. Miss Manley might have *influence* with employers, Mr Daniel *was* an employer. He asked Laura if she could type—it seemed that in the A.T.S. she had hardly done anything else. Without giving the matter any further thought, he had asked Laura if she would like to be his secretary.—Miss Manley had been plainly annoyed and that had been a satisfaction to him. Laura had accepted immediately and, in his own mind, he had at once become doubtful. But if Mr Wyman had to leave anyhow, and it seemed that he had, Mr Daniel had to have *somebody*. And if the arrangement with Laura didn't turn out satisfactorily he could always get rid of her.

The arrangement, so far, had turned out very well indeed. Laura was efficient, she had at once mastered Mr Daniel's very simple filing system (which he liked to think of as intricate), she was tactful with his associates, and, as she was not musical, she didn't say things that irritated him. Also, the married couple liked her.

After luncheon, Laura went back to the office; she walked slowly, it was such a beautiful day. She let herself into the house, in the hall she met Mrs Terrence and they had a nice little chat about what a beautiful day it was—by this time Laura had heard all about Mr Wyman hardly ever bothering to say good morning.

She went on up to the office, where, as usual, the telephone was ringing.

It was Miss Manley; she didn't want to bother Laura if she was busy, she wouldn't keep her a moment, but was Laura doing anything this evening?

Taken off her guard, Laura said no, then she recovered herself and said that there was Constantia, she would probably be having her puppies by this evening.

'I thought she was going to have them at the vets.'

'Well, yes she is, but I'd want to *know*, wouldn't I?'

Miss Manley said that Laura couldn't tie her life down to a dog and that she'd managed to get tickets for a new play that Laura wanted to see and that they'd been very difficult to get and that she'd spent the whole morning on the telephone; but of course if Laura didn't want to go, after Miss Manley had taken all that trouble, she could please herself.

Laura remembered that the last time she had seen Miss Manley she had said something vaguely about the play; but now there was Mr Daniel who had to be rung up in Paris at eight o'clock precisely; she mentioned this difficulty to Miss Manley.

'Please yourself,' Miss Manley said again, 'I shall be at the office until five o'clock; perhaps you could telephone me when you have made up your mind.' She rang off.

Laura was left, as it had been intended that she should be, with the feeling that she had been discourteous and ungrateful. She decided to start on some filing which had been left over from yesterday. Filing, as she had discovered when she was in the A.T.S., was a calming occupation and, whenever possible, she contrived to keep a little filing in reserve for use in emergencies.

I've been very lucky, Laura told herself again, so I can't expect everything to be nice the *whole* time. The miracle was that nowadays things were 'nice' so much of the time.

'And I'm not frightened any more,' Laura thought, or not very often. She never ceased to be aware of this absence of fear and to be almost daily grateful for it. She had been through so much emotion, love and despair; they had nearly overcome her but she had survived and in surviving she had, for a time, been swept clear of all emotion; it was the secret of what Mr Daniel had thought of as her cool detachment. But as long as life goes on emotions can't be for ever done with. Already, although she was only dimly aware of it, Laura had begun to love another human being.

15

EXACTLY A YEAR later the beautiful Mrs Edward West was coming in at the Place Vendôme entrance of the hotel.

The porter holding open the glass door bowed and smiled.

'What a magnificent morning, madame.'

Cathie returned his greeting with an almost imperceptible movement of her head. She felt suddenly as if she would like to have him shot.—So, it was a beautiful morning! As if she cared what the day was like, as if she needed to be told by him that the sun was shining!

'Madame has been shopping?'—and he moved towards the door of the lift.

Cathie turned abruptly away from him, crossed the hall and started to walk slowly up the stairs.

In the sitting-room of the suite on the second floor, Edward sat at the writing-table. He had heard the key being put into the lock of the outer door; in a second Cathie would have crossed the lobby and come into the sitting-room. He went on with his letter.

'Hullo, darling.' Cathie was standing in the middle of the room, putting her parcels down on the round marble table, taking off her gloves.

As if only just becoming aware of her presence, Edward mumbled a single word and went on writing.

Cathie went over to the fireplace and considered herself in the enormous gilt mirror that hung over it.

The new hat was a success. Perched on her head it was elegant and provocative, it was a Paris hat, compared with which all hats bought in London were dull and workaday. Looking at herself in the glass she was reminded of pictures of ladies in the late eighties. She was reminded of Queen Alexandra. A little straw-coloured hat covered with flowers and the veil which set off the tilt of her nose, which flattered, no, rather drew attention to, the beauty of her neck. The woman in the shop had been right, it had everything that was most elegant.

'Been shopping?' Edward asked, but he still didn't look up.

'Yes,' Cathie said, 'oh yes,' and, 'when do you want to go out to lunch, or shall we have a drink in the bar first?'

Edward said that he was sorry but he had an appointment for lunch; he still didn't look at her.

Cathie shrugged her shoulders; it might or might not be true. 'Then I think I shall order something up here.'

'Do,' Edward said, 'you must be tired.' He turned round. 'Would you like a drink now?'

'Not particularly,' Cathie said; she turned away from the fireplace and sat down on the elaborate Empire sofa. Everything in this suite was very elaborate and the windows gave on to the courtyard which was filled with flowers.

'Then perhaps I ought to be going.' Edward looked at his watch and at the gilt clock which stood on the mantelpiece.

'It's half-past twelve,' Cathie said.

He came across to her, bent down and kissed her on the cheek. 'Well, see you later.'

Wasn't he going to say anything at all? Cathie wondered.

'See you later,' Edward said again, 'and why don't you have a rest this afternoon, you must be tired.'

Suddenly, Cathie could bear it no longer.—Paris in June; this was to have been their second honeymoon, a week of re-furbished and recaptured love, which was to have made up for and put right the disappointments and misunderstandings of the past year.

'I'm sick of you,' Cathie said; 'don't you ever think of anyone but yourself?' She jumped up from the sofa.

Halfway to the door Edward stopped. 'I beg your; pardon?'

'I beg your pardon,' Cathie shouted furiously.—At that moment she felt that she could have borne anything in the world but his cold indifference. 'Don't you know what I've been through during this last year?'

'I thought you were perfectly happy.'

How could he say that, hadn't he any human feelings at all? Did he really not know what she had suffered from the insults which she had received from his friends and relations?—Charles and Georgette, for instance, had completely ignored her—Charles it was true had come to the wedding; but what was the good of that? Had either he or Georgette made any attempt to be friends with Cathie, to treat her as a relation, to draw her into their circle?—no, they had *not*. If Charles and Georgette had behaved decently, everyone else would have followed their example; and Cathie would not have been called on to undergo all the humiliations which she had had to put up with during the last year.

As she stood now facing Edward, she thought of all the people who had *not* called on Mrs Edward West, of all the friends she had *not* made.

'You don't care *what* happens to me,' she shouted at Edward; 'you don't care how unhappy I've been, you only care about yourself.'

'And do you think I've been happy?' Edward asked.

'You,' Cathie said, 'you'—and then she stopped, she had caught sight of herself in the glass; her face was flushed, the little straw hat was askew. She hardly recognised herself.

'Do you think that I've been happy?' Edward shouted, 'living with a bitch like you. You thought you were being very clever when you married me; but you weren't clever enough. *You* made me get rid of Laura and *you've* made me hate you, and I hope you *are* unhappy.'—He suddenly flung open the door and was gone.

Half an hour later Cathie still sat on the Empire sofa. She had taken off her new hat which was now tidily put away in a cupboard in the bedroom. She had taken off her street shoes and was wearing black velvet slippers trimmed with the *frou-frou* of ostrich feathers. She had sponged and redone her face and was now busy resting it, for whatever else was happening in her life, she would never neglect to do that.

Paris in June, the chestnut trees in the Champs-Élysées, the waiters washing the pavements in front of the cafés, women in black shawls carrying the inevitable long loaves of bread. Beautiful women and handsome men, in the bars, in the restaurants, in the shining automobiles.—'The war has changed so much,' but, to the outward eye, it has changed nothing at all. The luxury hotels and beside them the little cafés with the workmen sitting at the tables on the pavement. The bottles of cheap red wine, the expensive night clubs, the women going into the churches to pray, the bands of tourists descending from their charabancs.

And Cathie lay alone in this elaborate and beautiful and hateful sitting-room—with nothing whatsoever to do, but rest her face. And she had quarrelled with Edward.

'Ora pro nobis,' but for what could she pray when she had been granted everything for which she had asked?

Where had it all gone wrong? For now she could no longer pretend to herself that it had *not* gone wrong.—'I only wanted,' Cathie thought, 'what was best for all of us.'

But hadn't it started to go wrong right from the beginning; from that first morning in the London hotel?

'A pity, don't you think,' Edward had said, 'to make that sort of scene.' She could hardly remember now what had happened. They hadn't quarrelled; perhaps it would have been better if they had, for a quarrel can be made up.

'A pity, don't you think, to make that sort of scene'—and he had begun to be unapproachable. That terrible gulf of polite indifference to which any quarrel, however violent, however sordid, is preferable. She had tried not to think about it, she had tried not to think about so much.

Later that day they had gone down to Abbotsmere, the business about the Road Committee had prevented them from coming to Paris. So, they had gone *home*; it was what she had wanted for so long and she remembered that she had been happy. Surely *then* she must have been happy.

She remembered the first few weeks at Abbotsmere; she saw herself standing in the door of the kitchen, looking at the muddle of things on the dresser, at the newspapers spread over the floor, at the clutter of objects in the sink; lastly, she had looked at Nelly, who was wearing a raspberry pink cardigan over a cotton dress and had a blue scrubbing-apron, tied round her waist.

'The soufflé last night'—Cathie's eyes had gone back to the dresser—'was deplorable.'

'There was nothing the matter with it when it left the kitchen,' Nelly said; 'if there had of been I'd have noticed it, and I never had any complaints about my cooking from Mrs West, or from anyone else either if it comes to that. I'm a good cook.'

Cathie had let that go, the reference to Laura was clearly intended to be impertinent, but she could not very well engage in an argument about it.

'And it isn't *only* that,' Cathie said; '*look* at this kitchen!'

Nelly didn't say anything, just stood by the kitchen table, waiting for Cathie to go.

'Well?'

'If you want to know,' Nelly said, 'I've had enough of this.' Without consciously knowing that she did so, she started to untie her apron.

'In that case,' Cathie's smile was triumphant, 'I think you'd better take a week's notice.'

'You,' Nelly said, 'you.' Momentarily words failed her, for there was so much that she wanted to say, but before Cathie was able to stop her she had managed to say a great deal of it.— Cathie, with her nasty sneaking ways, had 'stolen' Mrs West's husband; but the day would come when Mr West would find out he'd made a mistake—and Cathie couldn't give them only a week's notice when they'd partly furnished their own rooms, not that it mattered anyhow, because Nelly wouldn't stay in the house another minute with her. As soon as Arthur came back from work she'd get him to pack up. It would be better for Nelly and all her family to starve in the street than to stay in the same house as Cathie, who made the place a hell on earth for everyone. If Nelly hadn't been soft enough to listen to Arthur, she'd have marched out of the house the day Cathie marched into it.

Cathie repeated that Nelly was to take a week's notice and left the kitchen.

That evening Arthur had demanded an interview with Edward and after it Edward had come out of the library in a very bad temper. He told Cathie that she had no right to treat people as she had treated Arthur and Nelly. 'They've got a child and they've got to have somewhere to live.'

'You said yourself that her cooking was becoming uneatable and, added to that, she was extremely impertinent to me; naturally I gave her notice.'

Edward said that it was a pity Cathie always had to quarrel with everyone, and that it was a pity too that she didn't seem to know how to treat people. The house had always run perfectly smoothly until she came into it.

It hadn't and he was being manifestly unfair; but Cathie had managed to keep her temper; she had excused him to herself on the grounds that he was tired, that he was suffering a reaction from the years of misery he had been through with Laura; better to do that, she had felt, than to admit that there was something terribly wrong.

Cathie looked round the sitting-room and sighed deeply; how pretty it was, how French, above all how elegant. She couldn't understand how she could have allowed herself to lose her temper just now. She wondered again if Edward really *had* had a luncheon appointment; and then her thoughts went back to England. After the trouble with Nelly, there had been trouble with the other servants. Hackett had given notice. He had been at Abbotsmere since Edward was a boy and it was reasonable to suppose that he wouldn't go on working for ever; but somehow Edward had managed to make it appear that his ceasing to do so was Cathie's fault. They had had the whole thing over again, 'the house had always run perfectly smoothly before.' Cathie thought she was so much more intelligent than poor Laura, didn't she? But even poor Laura had not upset his life to this extent, and she at least had had the excuse of being young and inexperienced. Cathie was not inexperienced and she prided herself on being a woman of the world.

Laura, Cathie thought irritably; why, in the end, did they always have to come back to the subject of Laura? And why, of all things, had Laura got to be here in Paris at this particular time? Suddenly Cathie was sure that Edward was having luncheon with Laura. Why hadn't she thought of it before? But how could he be so disloyal; not that there was anything the matter with his having luncheon with Laura, not if one took a modern point of view which Cathie of course did. The disloyalty lay in his not having told her about it, in having deceived her about it. And how dared he, when they had come to Paris to be happy together, leave her alone in the hotel while he had lunch with Laura?

'I might have known it'—and Cathie thought of Laura as she had seen her last night dining at Maxime's.

Edward and Cathie were just finishing their dinner when Laura had come in with a large party—and what right had Laura to be dining in Paris with a large party when she should have been living in the English countryside with a lady companion and breeding dogs; when she should have been fulfilling the rôle which Cathie had assigned to her; that of Edward's discarded wife.

The arrival of Laura's party had caused quite a little commotion amongst the waiters and amongst the other diners. The famous French actor-manager—so well-known in England through the medium of the cinema—and his beautiful actress wife; and there was another manager—almost equally well-known—and his beautiful actress mistress; and there, and there ... almost every member of the party was a celebrity and with them, was Laura. What on earth was she doing here?

'The English lady?' The waiter who was serving Cathie and Edward turned to look over his shoulder at Laura's party. 'That is Mrs West; she is going to be married to Mr Robert Daniel—your famous English composer. She is very beautiful?'

So Laura was known by name in one of the most famous restaurants in the world and the waiters found her beautiful. Cathie, unable to say anything, was looking at Laura.

The waiter, interpreting the silence as encouragement to continue, leant further across the table. 'You know why she is here.'

'No,' Edward said, shaking his head; he too was looking at Laura as if unable to believe in her existence.

The waiter lowered his voice. 'Mr Daniel is to write the music for Monsieur Danton's next production; it is not announced yet; but we know it.' He was proud of his 'secret' information, delighted to be able to pass it on.

'Really,' Edward said; 'very interesting.'

'A cognac, monsieur?'—and the waiter set down the coffee-pot.

Edward turned to Cathie but she shook her head.

'It's incredible,' Cathie said; she was still looking at Laura, unable to take her eyes off her.

'I don't know why you should be so surprised.'

'Because,' Cathie said and stopped. She shrugged her shoulders.

Soon after that they left the restaurant; so far Laura hadn't seen them, but as they passed her table she looked up. Taken unawares she looked startled and for a moment nervous, as she had so often looked in the past when she had been afraid that, for some reason she could not understand, Edward was angry with her. But almost immediately her expression had changed to one of happy recognition, she half-rose in her seat as if she expected them to come and speak to her. When they didn't do so, but only bowed and went on towards the door, she seemed surprised, made a movement as if she would have followed them and then, a little puzzled, sat down again. And it would have been so like Laura, Cathie thought, to have staged a scene of reconciliation in the middle of a crowded restaurant. But why of reconciliation? They had never quarrelled.

And now, of course, Edward was lunching with her. He must have telephoned her when Cathie was out shopping.—Or last night, when he had stayed downstairs after Cathie had gone to bed. It was intolerable; but why after all should she mind?

'And he said he hated me,' Cathie thought bitterly; 'he said he hated me after all I have suffered for his sake.'

'That is Mrs West, she is very beautiful.' The waiter's voice still sounded in Cathie's ears.—'That is Mrs West,' but it was Laura of whom he spoke.

And Laura was going to marry Robert Daniel; for the rest of her life Laura would be surrounded by fame and success. Also, of course, she would be loved, but Cathie was not to know that.

Laura would have everything that she herself had most wanted. 'He'll regret it,' Cathie thought; 'she made an impossible wife for Edward and she'll make an impossible wife for Robert Daniel.' But, even there, there was no real comfort, for she knew in her heart that it wasn't true.

Her mind went back to her own problem. 'I hate him,' Cathie thought, 'I hate him.'—But Edward had said that he hated her. It was unbelievable.—If he hates me he may leave me, but she couldn't really believe that he would do that.—'Dick,' Cathie thought, 'there is always Dick,' but there was nothing now that Mr Hardy could do for her.

She heard the sound of the key in the lock.—'You thought you were being very clever, but you weren't clever enough.'

'I hate him,' Cathie thought again, 'I hate him.'

And then she remembered something else he had said: 'The trouble with you is that you are always true to yourself.'

It was too much, the beautiful mask of her face crumpled and, as the door opened, Cathie turned away from it. She went into the bedroom and, sitting down in front of the looking-glass, she began to make up her mouth.

THE END

FURROWED MIDDLEBROW

Printed in Great Britain
by Amazon

17091003R00120